BREAKING MR. CANE

CANE SERIES #2

SHANORA WILLIAMS

Copyright © 2018 Shanora Williams

All rights reserved. This eBook is licensed for your personal enjoyment only. This eBook is copyright material and must not be copied, reproduced, transferred, distributed, leased, licensed or publicly performed or used in any form without prior written permission of the publisher, as allowed under the terms and conditions under which it was purchased or as strictly permitted by applicable copyright law. Any unauthorized distribution, circulation or use of this text may be a direct infringement of the author's rights, and those responsible may be liable in law accordingly.

Thank you for respecting the work of this author.

Cover Design by Hang Le

Editing By Tamysn Bester of Brazen Ink

Trademarks: This book identifies product names and services known to be trademarks, registered trademarks, or service marks of their respective holders. The author acknowledges the trademarked status in this work of fiction. The publication and use of these trademarks is not authorized, associated with, or sponsored by the trademark owners.

NOTIFICATIONS

To get notified about new release alerts, free books, and exclusive updates, join my newsletter at www.shanorawilliams.com/mailing-list

AUTHOR NOTE

Hey hey!
Just a heads up, this is the second book of the Cane Series and cannot be read as a standalone. To read Wanting Mr. Cane, the first book of the series, you can find it at www.shanorawilliams.com

PART I

A BROKEN HOME

CHAPTER ONE

CANE

PAST

I'm not afraid. I'm not afraid. Fuck him, I'm not afraid!
 Those words chimed in my head, but it didn't stop my heart from pounding in my chest.
 A crackle of thunder rumbled in the sky, a spark of lightning revealing the dark corners of my room. The light in the hallway was on and the floor creaked. I swallowed the bile in my throat.
 I prayed it was Mama coming down the hall, but by the sound of the heavy footsteps and the deep breathing, I knew it wasn't her. I took a step back and hit the wall, wishing I could blend in with it, or even pass through it like a ghost. A ghost meant I would be dead, and in that moment, the last thing I wanted to be was alive.
 The doorknob jiggled. My breathing became shallow.
 I was glad I'd hidden Lorelei. I heard his truck pull up and hid her in the attic. I told her to try and stay up there until I came for

her. She always thought I was brave, but if she could have seen me now, she would have thought otherwise.

I thought about hiding too, or at least running away, but knew he would have torn the house to shreds just to find us. He needed someone to take his anger out on. If it wasn't Mom, it was us.

I hated when he hurt them, so I always made sure to be around. Every time they wound up with a bruise, their lies only fueled my anger. I was so tired of dealing with his shit.

I was fourteen now. I'd developed a little muscle, some height too, but it was nothing in comparison to his. I couldn't wait until the day I was big enough to take him down.

My bedroom door swung open, the doorknob crashing into the wall, and his silhouette was all I could make out.

Broad shoulders.

Thick arms.

Shaggy brown hair.

"The fuck you doin' here in the dark?" he snapped. He was always annoyed about something. Even if I was minding my own business or doing my homework, that annoyed him. My room was about the size of a box, so when he spoke, I could smell the liquor on his breath. I hated when he drank. He was even more hostile than usual.

"I'm getting ready to for bed," I said, keeping my chin up.

"You talkin' back to me, boy?" He took three steps forward. Two more and he would have been right in front of me.

"No sir," I answered.

"Sounds like you are." He turned his head to take a look around my room. "Why the hell isn't this room clean?"

I looked with him. "It is clean. I cleaned it this morning. Mama said it was fine."

"Your mama?" He let out a scratchy, belly-deep laugh. "You really listening to your mama? You know she doesn't know shit! You can't listen to a damn thing that woman says. For one, she's a goddamn liar." I could see his teeth when he spoke, slick and sharp. They reminded me of razors.

"Come here," he ordered. He grabbed my upper arm and squeezed it, and I fought a yelp as he dragged me toward my bed and forced me to sit down. He took the spot beside me, releasing my arm to grip the back of my neck. He squeezed my neck and I tried to hunch my shoulders in hopes that he'd pull his hand away, but he only squeezed harder.

My eyes burned. Tears threatened to spill over, but fuck that. I refused to cry. I was done crying over him.

"Drove by the diner earlier," he continued, "Saw your mama all smiley and happy while serving some man in a suit. I know she has to be nice for those tips and all, but... *shit*. She don't have to be so nice, to the point she has her titties all in his face like a fucking whore." He breathed harder, still clutching my neck.

Relief struck me when he shoved me away and my knees hit the floor with a hard *thunk*.

I rubbed the back of my neck as he stood up to pull the string on my fan and switch the light on. "This room is fucking filthy," he grimaced. "I tell you what. If it ain't clean when I get back in the next ten minutes, you'll have a price to pay. You hear me? And you won't like what I bring with me."

"Yes, sir," I answered quickly. He left the room and I hurried to pick up what little I could find. I really didn't have much. I had a few books and baseball cards on my dresser. I didn't have a TV or that many shoes or shoeboxes. I straightened the rumple in the bed that he'd just created by forcing us to sit, but there wasn't much else for me to do.

Mama always said if she could see the carpet, then my room was clean enough. All I could see was the brown carpet. It was clean to me.

He returned in less than ten minutes. He took a brief look around with flared nostrils then rushed for me. His fist slammed into my stomach, and when I crumpled over with a groan, he kicked me down with a foot to the shoulder.

"You're fuckin' terrible, you know that? Can't even clean a goddamn room! You won't amount to shit! Just a worthless excuse for a fucking son! Drop some goddamn balls already!"

He turned rapidly, shutting the light off and storming out of the room.

When he was gone, I laid on the floor, doing the one thing I had refused to do before.

Cry.

CHAPTER TWO

KELLY

THE MORNING OF CANE'S PARTY.

I thought I had made it perfectly clear when I told that little bitch to stay away from him, but she ran right to his office, seeking even more attention. She was young and naive, yes, but I didn't give a fuck.

She'd crossed the wrong person, and since he didn't want to stay away, it was up to me to leave him no choice but to stay away from the entire Jennings family.

I'd sent Mindy a text, hinting at things about her husband. I asked her things like what they were up to for the day, to which she replied that she was helping her daughter pack up, while Derek was going to go out to run errands to prepare for their car ride to her college.

I didn't want to do this, I really didn't, but the USB in my hand was searing hot. I lifted it out of my palm and twirled it in my hand, parked across from the Jennings' home. Derek's truck was parked there, and the minutes slowly ticked by before I saw him leaving the house.

There was something about Derek that fascinated me. Maybe it was because of his size, and how masculine and buff he was compared to Cane's lean, smooth build. He was, at best, a very intimidating man—one even *I* wouldn't want to piss off. I knew how he felt about his daughter—knew all about the great lengths he would go just to protect her—so this had to be done to settle it all.

He pulled out of the driveway, drove out of the neighborhood, and I followed him. One thing I noticed about Derek was that he had a bad habit of keeping his windows rolled down at home. I hoped he did the same when going out.

His first stop was at a home supply warehouse. I waited a beat, driving around the parking lot as to not seem too obvious, and watched him walk to the entrance of the store. When he was gone, I drove back to where his truck was and parked two spots over.

His windows were slightly cracked.

Perfect.

In a flash, I unclipped my seatbelt, grabbed the sticky note I'd written on just moments before arriving at the Jennings house that morning, placed it on top of the USB flash drive, and pushed out of the car, hustling toward his truck.

There was just enough space above the window for me to push the USB through. Mindy had mentioned he had to stop by the police station to sign off on some paperwork at his desk. I'd hoped he would make it a priority to see what was on the flash drive. I walked to the driver's side, slid it through the crack, and it landed on the seat perfectly.

With a smirk, I walked off, and made it my mission to leave another copy of the flash drive on the Jennings' front porch.

It was only a matter of time before her parents would watch it, because on the note were words only a fool would ignore.

If you want to protect your daughter, watch this immediately and take action.
Stop him before it's too late.

CHAPTER THREE

KANDY

There was a point in my life when I used to think my Nana Alexandra was psychic.

She once told me that my future would be unique. She never explained how, just said I would probably end up with a very unusual, thrilling life. If she hadn't passed away when I was ten, I would have asked her just how that very night.

When it came down to it, I figured she was right. Perhaps she meant I would be different in the sense that I didn't like ordinary things. I didn't really care for boys my age, or *Barbie* dolls when I was little, or even pop stars and boy bands.

The bar had been set after meeting Cane at the age of nine, and after having him to myself for more than a day, I doubted I would ever go back to younger guys after getting a taste of someone so patient and experienced.

For all I know, she could have meant I would be unique in a *bad* way, and by saying I would have a "thrilling life" she meant I was fucked.

I couldn't see the light at the end of this tunnel. I couldn't figure a way out of this one.

My mother stood between the frames of my door and stared at me in utter disbelief. Her eyes were red and wet and her face was blotchy. "Is it true?" she demanded with a thick voice.

I looked down at the white box again. Inside of it was a black USB flash drive. I didn't know what it was or what was on it. I didn't even know what she was talking about…but I had a very bad feeling it had something to do with Cane. Why else would she have been so distraught? So heartbroken? The only bad things I'd done were with him.

"Is what true?" I put my focus on her again, but my vision was blurry now. "What are you talking about?

She charged into my room and snatched the flash drive out of the box. She then turned for my laptop and jammed it into the port a little too roughly. In seconds, a video came up, and my heart plummeted.

It revealed the corner of Cane's office, where the arm of the sofa was. I could only see our head and shoulders. Cane's face hovered over mine and my moans were loud as our bodies shifted up and back down. He was on top of me, shoulders and upper back working fluidly to form a steady thrust.

I shot up to a stand when Mom slammed a finger down on the space bar to stop the video.

"Where did you get that!" I demanded. "Did Cane send that to you?" *No, he wouldn't.* Why would he do something like that? He wasn't that kind of person!

"Kandy? I—I don't even know what to say to you! I can't believe this! What the hell is that I just saw on that tape?"

"Where did you get it?" I barked back.

"That doesn't matter right now! You were having sex with Cane! *Cane!* Are you out of your goddamn mind!"

I blinked hard, fighting the wave of emotion. Normally, Mom never backed down. She was persistent and could be harsh and pushy, but when she noticed I was on the verge of tears, something stopped her from blasting me. It was a first, which made the situation all the more excruciating.

She shook her head and then pinched the bridge of her nose, sealing her eyes shut.

"Mom, I— " I had no words. None at all. This wasn't supposed to happen. She wasn't supposed to find out. "Who gave that to you?" Maybe no one had given it to her. Maybe she had been on to us all along. Did she suspect this and have someone spy on us? Or did Kelly tell her something?

Her head shook again and several more tears spilled beneath her sealed eyelids.

"Mom! Tell me how you got it!"

"I don't know who it was from, Kandy! There was a note with it that said to protect you and to stop *him*. It was left on the doorstep, but there wasn't a name!" She waved her hands in the air dismissively. "Does that even matter? I am *livid* right now, Kandy! Can't you see that? I don't even know what to do! He had no right to put his hands on you that way!"

"How didn't he?" I demanded. "That tape doesn't show everything. I asked him to do it!"

"It doesn't matter that you asked!" she shouted back. "Even if you were to ask him for a gun to kill someone or God forbid, yourself, I expect him to say no because we trusted Cane! We trusted him to take care of you! God, and there were so many times when you two were alone together," she sobbed. "I should have known. Christ! I had this nagging thought in the back of my head, but I figured there was no way in hell he could be so stupid! That *you* could be so stupid! I can't even imagine how it started! Did he come onto you? Did he *rape* you?"

"What?" I screeched. "No! He didn't rape me! I told Cane what I wanted. I wanted him and he wanted me too! It was mutual! How is that so hard to believe?"

"Did he tell you to say that? He's a smart man and knows

you're young and easy to manipulate. I should have known a man like him wasn't as perfect as he seemed. We can take this to court if we need to! Just give me your permission to press charges and I'll do it immediately!"

Oh my God. This was unbelievable!

"I am not taking Cane to court! He did nothing wrong! I love Cane, Mom!"

She breathed unevenly and clenched her fists, like she was fighting the words she really wanted to say. She was trying to be strong, but she'd quickly let her guard down, her eyes filled to the brim with tears. "But...why, Kandy? Why him? Why *Cane*?"

I looked away. I hated seeing her cry. My eyes stung and I sat down on the bed, staring out of my window instead. "I don't know," I whispered. "My heart chose him."

"Your heart? Oh, my goodness—sweetie!" She walked my way and sat beside me. She didn't care that my hands were tucked between my thighs. She snatched one up and held it tight, which brought my attention back to hers. "Look, I get your attraction to him. Cane is a good-looking man and I see that, trust me. He's wealthy and nice, and sometimes his friendliness can feel like it's coming off as something more...but that's just how he is, Kandy. Your heart is still young and you're so gullible, honey—"

"I'm not that young—"

"Please, just listen to me!" she demanded, voice firm. "I am trying to understand you here, but...I don't get it. I guess I always thought you saw Cane as family, like we did, not as something more."

I dropped my head when hot tears spilled over my lips. "I know you think I'm young and don't know much about anything but, Mom, I really do love him. I do," I sobbed harder. "Trust me, I've tried to stop caring about him plenty of times, I swear, but it's so hard! I—I think about him every single day. I feel good around him. I'm happy when I'm with him." I couldn't fight the tears anymore. In that moment, I broke down, and

Mom shushed me, reeling me in and holding me tightly in her arms.

"I know, baby. I know." She released a breath. "But you shouldn't want him. You just shouldn't. Even if we didn't know him, he wouldn't be the right person for you."

Mom was torn. I could hear the hurt in her voice and I felt awful, but Mom was just a friend of a friend to Cane. She wasn't in Dad's position. At the thought of Dad, my heartbeat stuttered.

"Wait—does Dad know?" I whispered.

She shook her head. "No. I don't think so. I got the flash drive first and he hasn't been home all day."

"Are you going to tell him?"

She let out a thick, weary exhale and I felt her chin move as she shook her head. "I hate keeping secrets from your father, Kandy. He's my husband and my best friend. I tell him everything." She lowered a hand to tip my chin, forcing our eyes to meet. "But you are my only child and I love you. I want you to be able to tell me that you're going through stuff like this. I want you to trust me."

"Okay, but please don't tell him," I begged. Dad was the last person I wanted to know.

She hugged me again. "I won't, baby." She kissed the top of my head. "I won't." She huffed. "If I could see Cane right now, though, I'd rip him a new one. Touching my daughter like that. I just...I can't believe that video, Kandy. Thank God it didn't reveal everything, but even so, I will never be able to get the image out of my head."

I cringed then. One, because Mom saw me in an intimate, vulnerable moment and would probably see me that way for a very long time. She wouldn't look at me the same, and that scared me.

There was only one person who was out to ruin me, and it was Kelly. Telling my parents meant that Cane would have no choice but to never see us again. The bonds would be broken, trust shattered. She'd win, but luckily, Mom wasn't going to tell Dad. There was still a chance to spare this...Cane just couldn't come over anymore. It didn't mean he had to be out of my life completely.

I couldn't believe she'd done this, though. She had cameras in his office? Was she spying on him? She was fucking psychotic. Hell, was it even Kelly? Did Cane have other enemies?

Just as I was about to go to the bathroom and clear my face, Mom's phone rang.

"Hello," she answered softly, but then her voice got louder as she said, "WAIT—WHAT!"

I frowned as she focused on me. "What's going on?" I asked, facing her.

"No—do not book him in! I will be there in fifteen minutes!" Mom rushed out of the room without a look back. I ran after her, hustling down the stairs and watching her snatch up her keys and purse.

"What's happening?" I asked as she yanked the door open.

"Your father was just arrested for an assault."

"What?" I gasped. "An assault? On who?"

"Cane."

CHAPTER FOUR

KANDY

I was lucky Mom let me come with her, but I was on edge the entire ride. She was usually the chatterbox, the one to avoid any awkward silences, but that night she hardly spoke, and she drove faster than I'd ever seen her go before.

She sped through stoplights, avoided stop signs, and didn't even bother using her turn signal, like she always told me to do during the rare moments she'd let me drive.

I couldn't really wrap my head around what had happened. Dad had assaulted Cane but how? Why? It couldn't be because of me...*could it?* I clutched the strap of my seatbelt, praying I wasn't the reason why this was happening.

When it all added up, it was the only thing that made sense. Mom said she'd found the flash drive, but Dad had been gone all day. Kelly could have gotten to him while he was away. She had his number too. She knew where he worked. She knew a lot of things about us because we trusted her.

My heart dropped to my stomach. I felt sick all over again, and Mom's reckless driving wasn't making it any better.

We finally made it to the police station, and once parked, Mom snatched up her purse and pushed the door open. She hustled up the steps in her ballerina flats and tan pea coat. I followed her lead.

The police station was just like I remembered it, with the same smell of coffee, stale donuts, and the stench of cigarettes. Dad had brought me here once, when I was eleven. I kept asking him about his job for one of my class assignments. We had to write a small story about one of our parents' workplace. I was more interested in Dad's than my Mom's.

Dad brought me in for about an hour and after seeing so many people coming in with silver bracelets around their wrists, being dragged through the halls, and some of them cursing at the cops, strung out or drunk, I didn't want to go back. Not that I wasn't warned. Daddy said it was no place for a little girl, but did I listen? No, I never listened. I was stubborn, and that's exactly why we were there.

Mom rushed up to the desk and asked a redheaded officer for my Dad's location. While she spoke, I looked around to see if I could find him. It took me a minute—the office was pretty big—but past a few desks and windows that separated the room, I could see the top of his head.

The redheaded woman walked off, shortly returning with a heavy set man wearing a dingy white shirt and gray slacks. He seemed familiar, but I couldn't place him.

"Mrs. Jennings," the man said, clearing his throat. "I'm afraid we can't allow you back to see Derek at this time."

"What?" she snapped. "Why not?"

"Because you have personal ties with the detainee." The man cleared his throat again. "You're his wife and we have questions to ask him. We need him to answer them honestly and without any distractions."

"Oh, you have to be fucking kidding me! No!" Mom took a step forward, and she immediately went from Nice Mrs. Jennings to Mrs. Bitchy Lawyer Jennings. "I am an attorney. I know the law, and he doesn't get to speak to *anyone* until someone who can represent him is in the room with him. Why else would he have had them call me?"

The detective sighed and glanced back in the direction Dad was in. His eyes then shifted over to mine. "Fine, but the girl can't come back with you."

"Her name is Kandy," Mom corrected him, voice harsh. "Maybe if you weren't always blitzed at the fundraising events, you would remember it, Detective Young." She turned to me as the man agitatedly shook his head and turned away. "Here." She held her keys out. "This will probably take all night. We have a long morning ahead of us to get you to school, so go home and get some rest. Okay?"

I frowned. "What about Dad? Won't you guys need a ride?"

She gave me a blank look. She couldn't answer any of the questions. Instead, she said, "I'll call an *Uber*, or I'll call you when we're done and see if you're still awake. Go, Kandy. Now." Then she turned and marched away, walking between the desks and through a few open doors to get to her husband.

I walked down the hallway to see them a little more clearly. Mom entered the room with her chin up, but when I focused on her eyes, I could tell she wanted to cry, especially when Dad looked up into them and his immediately glistened.

"Where's Kandy?" I watched his mouth form the words. I wanted to yell that I was right here. I wanted him to *see* me, but at the same time, I was terrified to have his eyes on me, only for him to see nothing but disgust and disappointment. I wouldn't be his little girl anymore. He wouldn't take pride in me...

I don't know what Mom said to him in response, but it didn't matter. The detective had cut their conversation short.

I left before the tears could blind me. I didn't drive off right away. Instead, I sat behind the wheel and buried my face in my hands.

This couldn't be happening. This couldn't be my life. What had I done?

I didn't mean for Dad to get in trouble, or for him to ever find out. *And Cane...Oh, God, Cane.* Where was he? Was he hurt? Did he press charges?

I needed answers, so I cleared my face with the back of my arm, swiping a little too roughly, and then left the police station.

A little less than twenty-five minutes later, I had pulled up to Cane's house. All of the outdoor and indoor lights were on. The place looked regal and made of gold, but something felt off.

I stepped out of the car, clutching the keys as I headed for the front door. The air was too still, considering the night was still young. It was way too quiet. On my way to the door, I saw blood on the cement steps. I stalled for a moment. It wasn't much, but it sparkled beneath the bright, gold lights. Fresh, too.

"Your father was just arrested for an assault." The words rang loud and true. What in the hell happened? It was far from cold that night, but I still shivered at the sight of the blood.

I finally made it to the door that was halfway open. I pushed it open and heard things moving around. Then I heard a female's voice. A familiar one.

The voice got nearer as I stepped into the foyer, and when she walked out of the den and into the hallway, she lowered her phone and shook her head. I had never seen her before. Porcelain skin and almond-shaped eyes. Raven hair that made her appear paler and revealed flushed, rosy cheeks.

As if she'd sensed a presence, she picked up her head and frowned when she found me. "I'm sorry, who are you?" Up close, I recalled where I'd heard the voice. It was on Cane's phone the second day at the lake house.

"Are you Cora?" I asked.

She blinked rapidly. "Do I know you?"

"I um... I don't know. Probably not. I'm a friend of Cane's."

"Oh." She held her phone close, looking me over. That probably sounded stupid. Cane didn't have many friends, and she probably knew that and was wary now.

"Is he around?"

She held her arms out and rotated her upper body with them while looking around. "No, unfortunately." She focused on me. "I'm cleaning up as much as I can and then going to the hospital to make sure he's okay."

"The *hospital?*" I frowned then. "Wait...he was hurt that bad?"

"He had blood on his face and he'll probably end up a black eye. He blacked out when his head hit the ground. I called the police and he was picked up a short while ago." She seemed pained, like the thought of her boss being hurt crippled her heart just as much as it did mine.

"Why didn't you go with him?"

"Because Miss Hugo rode with him. Said she wanted to be alone with him."

"Miss Hugo? You mean *Kelly?*"

She nodded. "His girlfriend, yes."

His *girlfriend?* That. Bitch. "Wow...um...okay. Thank you for letting me know. I—I have to go."

I turned and gripped the doorknob, but Cora called after me before I could walk out. "Are you Mr. Jennings' daughter?"

I peered over my shoulder, afraid she'd call the cops on me too, but I wasn't going to lie. I was done lying. Done hiding. "I am."

"Oh." She gave a very faint smile. "You look just like him." I sensed there was more to it. Did Cora know more? Did she know why all of this had happened, or at least my father's motives?

I dropped my head, turning halfway. "Is Cane going to be okay?"

When I looked up, her features were solemn. Her lips pressed together before she answered, "With how badly his head hit the concrete, I'm honestly not sure. We're hoping it's just a concussion and nothing more."

That broke my heart, crumbled it right to pieces.

"I'm sorry this happened," I murmured.

Cora waved a dismissive hand before her phone rang. She excused herself before answering it. I left the house and got into Mom's car again. I wanted to go to the hospital, but with Kelly there, it wouldn't have been pretty. Hell, I had no clue which hospital he was even at, but I should have asked Cora. I'm sure she'd have known.

Cane was unconscious. How could it have gotten so bad? Cane was Dad's best friend. How could Dad be so reckless that he'd hurt him so much? He still cared, I was sure, and I had no doubt that Dad was regretting his actions. He showed up at his home to hurt him. I couldn't wrap my head around it.

That whole night left me utterly exhausted. I went home and up to my room, like Mom told me to do, curling up beneath my blankets.

I don't know what came over me, but I had to do something. All I could do to reach out was send Cane a text. I knew he wouldn't respond, but I wanted him to know I was at least thinking about him while he was hurt.

Ten minutes after my text was sent, my phone vibrated.

A text.

Cane: I told you to leave him alone. Don't make this any worse than it already is.

My throat had never felt dryer. My mind had never been so boggled.

I wanted to destroy Kelly, but how? How could I destroy a woman the world assumed was his girlfriend, without giving myself away? I wasn't the kind of girl to rush into a hospital just to pick a fight. It just wasn't me.

The realization of what had happened that night slapped me right in the face, punched me hard in the gut.

I was going to be over a hundred miles away in less than twenty-four hours. I would be in school, and probably wouldn't come back home for months.

Things would change. The atmosphere would be heavy.

Kelly had won. Everything she'd said would happen, happened. My perfect life with the perfect family, was no more. She'd destroyed us, just like she said she would.

There was no going forward with Cane.

Not anymore.

CHAPTER FIVE

KANDY

Dad had finally been released from jail, but couldn't leave the city due to pending charges. I couldn't believe Cane was thinking about suing him. When Mom told me over the phone, I was almost tempted to drive to the hospital and demand him to drop the charge, but I couldn't. I needed to be home for Dad.

When my parents arrived, I rushed to hug Dad before he could even get through the threshold. He hugged me back, but it wasn't tight or strong like his usual hugs. His arms were slack around me, like he was afraid to touch me—afraid of who I was—but I ignored that thought and looked up at him.

"Are you okay?" I asked as Mom trailed in behind him, giving him a sideways glance. It was a dumb question. Dad looked rough. Rougher than I'd ever seen him before, honestly.

"I'm fine," he mumbled, then looked at Mom, who gave him a stern look. Had they talked about this moment? Did she tell him not to make things weird? "Just need a shower." That was all he said before walking past me, shoulders hunched as he went upstairs. My gaze fell to the floor, the rims of my eyes raw and hot. He couldn't even look at me.

"Give him time," Mom murmured, rubbing my shoulder, making her way upstairs too.

I had all my things packed and in the car by the time my parents came back downstairs. With Dad not being able to drive, we could fit everything in the trunk and backseats of the rental car. Mom had decided she would take a flight back to Georgia from Indiana since Dad was no longer going. I was sitting on the trunk of the car when they came outside.

"We really need to get on the road," Mom announced. "Before it gets dark."

"You're still stopping at a hotel tonight, right?" Dad asked. "I don't want you driving for long without much rest."

"Yeah. I will. If I get too tired, I'll have Kandy drive. Don't worry, honey."

"Good." Dad sniffed, still avoiding my eyes. He had no idea how much he was breaking my heart by doing it. What hurt most was that I couldn't even blame him. What do you say to your daughter after finding out those things? After seeing her in such a vulnerable position—witnessing her in the act? The fact that Mom was acting like things were okay and that nothing had happened wasn't making the situation any better. I could tell she was forcing a happy moment, but it was impossible. There was tension between all of us—a tension so thick I felt suffocated.

"Well, I guess you guys should get going." Dad took a step back.

I hopped off the trunk. "Are you going to be okay here alone?"

"I'll be fine," he answered, and he finally looked at me. And his eyes. *God, his eyes.* I will never forget how they looked. They were so sad. I'd never seen him like this before. Ever. I couldn't believe I'd hurt him so much. Me. His daughter.

"Dad, I'm—"

He held up a hand, shaking his head. "Don't, Kandy. Just get in the car and leave all of that behind. You hear me?"

I swallowed hard, immediately blinded by tears. In that moment, I didn't care that the lines had been blurred or that he saw me in a new light. I still needed him, much more than he thought I did, so I rushed into his arms, slamming my face into his chest. I held him tight, and relief struck me when he eventually folded his arms around me and held me tighter than ever before. He kissed the top of my head several times.

"I'm sorry," he whispered. It's all he could give at the moment, but he had nothing to be sorry for. I was the one who was sorry. I wanted to take it all back. Why did my heart have to be so desperate?

"It's okay," I murmured. After several seconds, he let me go and Mom and I got into the car.

This wasn't the way I wanted to be sent off. Before everything went haywire, I pictured Mom and Dad in the car with me, Dad driving on the way to my school while she sat in the passenger seat, both of them with chipper moods while I sat anxiously in the back. I had even pictured Cane standing in this very driveway, seeing me off for the final time, giving me quiet, heated stares and whispering in my ear that I would always be his.

I wanted everything to be perfect and full of life and happiness and peace. Instead, it was dull and depressing, and though it was sunny, everything around me was cloudy and gray. Saying "see you later" to my Dad felt wrong, and not being able to say anything at all to Cane before I left broke me to pieces.

Before I knew it, I was riding with Mom. Just the two of us.

"It will be okay," she cooed as I silently sobbed in the passenger seat. "It's life, Kandy. These obstacles are thrown at us, but we get through it. We're family. You'll learn soon enough. Life isn't easy or simple or even practical. It can get really messed up sometimes, and the only thing you can do is take it day-by-day." She rubbed my arm. "Cheer up, baby. Give it a few months. Things will be back to normal before you know it."

But would they really? Because without Cane, there wouldn't be a 'normal'. He'd become apart of our unit. We were a happy quartet, but in the blink of an eye, were cut down to a collapsing triangle.

Nana Alexandra was right. My life was unusual. I only prayed my abnormal life would make me resilient one day.

CHAPTER SIX

CANE

The first thing I heard was white noise. Like water or the ocean. *Destin.*

The white noise transitioned to beeping. Then the beeping led to soft murmurs.

My heavy eyelids peeled apart, the lights above nearly blinding me. I groaned and tried moving, but the pain on the back of my head stopped me. "Shit," I mumbled. My mouth was dry and tacky. My lips felt numb.

"Oh my gosh," a voice gasped, and a hand wrapped around my upper arm. "Quinton, babe? Are you okay?"

I peered up, meeting glistening green eyes. I'd hoped they would be maple brown, like Kandy's, or even gray, like Lora's. I looked past her to a tall man with graying hair at the temples. A stethoscope was draped around the back of his neck, a clipboard tucked beneath his arm.

"What the hell is going on?" I rasped.

"Mr. Cane, I'm Doctor Welsh. How are you feeling?" he asked.

"Head hurts," I grumbled.

"As it should. You took a pretty hard fall."

I frowned then. "Fall?"

The doctor looked from me to Kelly, who was still holding my arm. "Uh—y-yes," he stammered, picking up the clipboard to read over it. "You were rushed into the ER last night. The back of your head was split and you suffered a minor concussion." He focused on me again. "Do you remember falling, Mr. Cane?"

I drew in a breath, trying to remember. I couldn't, for the life of me, recall the fall. "I don't remember," I responded, and he scribbled something down on his clipboard.

"Derek hit you, Quinton," Kelly said, and I put my attention on her. "Your guests said he pointed a gun at you and then he punched you, which made you fall backwards and hit your head on the concrete. They said he was drunk, hostile, and mad at you about something."

I dropped my head and squeezed my eyes shut. That's when it hit me—the memories of last night. It rushed back to me like a wave, nearly drowning me. I sucked in a sharp breath as the worst of them all came to me.

His words.

His voice that was laced with so much anger.

"Fuck you, Cane."

Those were the last words I heard. After that, I couldn't remember anything. "Shit." I shoved the crisp, white sheet off my legs and started to twist around to get my legs off the bed, but Doctor Welsh rushed toward me, while Kelly held my arm tighter. His hand pressed down on my shoulder to keep me seated.

"Quinton, what are you trying to do?" Kelly demanded.

"I need to call Derek."

"Sir, I can hand you your phone, but you should rest until further notice. Any sudden moves or actions could hurt you in the long run." The doctor's eyes were serious.

I shook my head, and even that hurt to do. Derek did this to me? Derek? And shit! Where was Kandy? How the fuck did he find out about us? Did she tell him? That wouldn't have been like her. I needed to know.

"Give me my phone," I snapped, and Kelly hopped up, going for my things on top of the counter. She brought it back to me, but even while pressing the buttons, the screen remained black. "You have to be fucking kidding me!"

"Mr. Cane, I understand your frustrations, but please try to relax. We can have your phone charged and get you anything you need. Are you hungry? Thirsty? Let us accommodate you and get you healed up. You'll have plenty of time to make calls when you're well-rested and healthy." Doctor Welsh took a step back. "I'll call the nurse, tell her to bring you some water and food after she checks your vitals."

"Thank you," Kelly responded, because I sure as fuck wasn't in the mood to thank anyone. When he was gone, she turned to face me with a pleading expression.

"I need to call Derek. Do you have a charger with you?" I asked.

"I do, but Quinton, you should seriously reconsider this. He hurt you! He could have ruined your life—your career! The cops came and told me to ask you if you wanted to press charges on him. I told them that you might want to when you're conscious."

"What!" I barked. "Kelly, why the fuck would you tell them that? It was a mistake—"

"Was it, Quinton? Seriously, I could see from the trip in Destin that Derek is unstable, and if you want me to, I can use that to vouch for you. He's unfit to be a cop, let alone your best friend. All he did was take advantage of you—"

"Okay, you need to shut the hell up right now 'cause you're really starting to piss me off." I snatched my arm out of her hand, rubbing my temples. "I would never press charges against him, best friend or not. He should know that! Now there might be a possibility that he thinks I will!"

"He left you unconscious for a whole day! He's not safe to be around!"

"Do you even know why he hit me? Huh?" I snarled.

She blinked rapidly, straightening her back. Her face then became solemn, her eyes narrowing. "I do."

"You do?" My tone was flat, stale. "So if you know what it was about, then why in the hell are you here right now, Kelly?"

She pressed her lips and then, after several tense seconds, sat back in her chair, placing her hands on her lap. "Listen, Quinton. I am trying to do you a favor here. If you stay away from Derek, you'll stay away from Kandy. I know that's the only reason you want to make things right with him. You want to get close to her again. Maybe it was a mistake on Derek's part. Maybe he did react out of anger. I mean, finding out that your best friend is *fucking* your daughter is a tough pill to swallow but…that's the card he was dealt and he handled it the wrong way. Now he has to deal with the consequences…and so do you."

My brows stitched together and I pushed up on my hands to sit up higher. "You think the shit you have on me is going to keep you around, Kelly? Really?"

She smirked. "I've been in this room with you for nearly twenty-four hours, Quinton. I worried about you—worried about your career and our future. Are you seriously going to tarnish yourself and everything you've built over an eighteen-year-old girl after everything I *know* about you?"

"You don't know shit," I growled.

"I know the letter that I found in your home office from your father wasn't to be taken lightly. Imagine if the world found out you built Tempt by doing the wrong things. What do you think they'll say about you? How will you bounce back from that?"

I flared my nostrils. I wanted to grab her by the throat and choke her. "You're a fucking bitch."

She leaned forward, smiling as she ran a finger over the top of my hand. "I'm a fucking bitch who loves you. Accept that, and there won't be any problems."

"Blackmailing me is the problem, and if you think for a second that I'm going to let you continue to use that shit against me, you better think again. I'll rat myself out before I ever let you think you own me." I leaned closer to her, so close I could feel her breathing. "You think you know me, Kelly, but you don't know a goddamn thing. You don't know shit about me or what I've done to get to where I am now, and as soon as I find a way to get rid of your worthless, desperate ass, I'll make sure you *always* remember who the fuck I am and to never cross me again."

Her throat bobbed, green eyes swirling with darkness and excitement, like my threat thrilled her. She was fucking insane.

She was lucky the nurse came in to check my vitals—lucky that I couldn't cause a scene in that hospital, or better yet, toss her ass out of the room. I'd never wanted to hurt a woman as much as I wanted to hurt Kelly. It wasn't in me to hurt a female…but she was asking for it. She was trying to ruin my life, all for her own selfish needs.

She was the reason all of this had happened and she was going to fucking pay for the damage she'd caused.

CHAPTER SEVEN

KELLY

PAST

When I first met Quinton, I knew I had to have him.
I had just left group therapy and headed to the cafeteria for a cup of coffee, when I bumped into him.
The first thing I noticed were his eyes. For a man who seemed edgy and mysterious, his eyes were clear and bright with yellow flecks shimmering in the corners of his irises. The next thing I noticed were his hands, and how big they were when they wrapped around my upper arms to steady me.
Then I noticed the way he smelled. Manly and clean and delectable, a trace of nicotine that only increased my desire. Though it was an unhealthy habit, there was something about seeing a man with a cigarette that turned me on completely. A man who defied good morality was truly delicious.
"Shit, I'm sorry," he apologized. My heartbeat sped up several notches at the sound of his deep, silky voice, and his apology suddenly meant nothing. I didn't care that he was sorry for

bumping into me, or the fact that my coffee had spilled all over my skirt and Gucci shoes. All I cared about was having him. Making him mine.

"It's okay," I murmured, placing my cup down on the nearest table and picking up a few napkins to wipe myself off. "This blouse wasn't really a favorite of mine anyway." There was a familiar chant inside my head as I cleaned myself up—something that begged me to rope him in, get to know more about him. Unfortunately, I wasn't quick enough to make it happen the first time.

He helped me wipe off my shoes and cleaned up the floor with the napkins from the table nearby, apologizing again for the mess. A buzzer chimed, luring him away from me. I watched him go after he apologized once more, and made a mental note to return the next day.

So I did...because I had to.

I finished talking to my therapist and went to the cafeteria again, hoping I'd bump into the handsome stranger again. I didn't see him that day. Or the day after, even though I didn't have therapy.

But the third day after our run-in, I saw him. He was sitting in the cafeteria, across from a woman with thick brown hair that swam to the middle of her back. Her skin was pale, her cheeks hollow, dark circles beneath her eyes. She fidgeted as he spoke to her, and in his eyes I saw the pleas. The desperation. I was too entranced to enter the cafeteria. Too busy staring at him. He was so damn handsome. It was clear he was wealthy. Anyone who had family in Polly Heights had to have money. He was perfect, honestly, and would have made a great fit for me.

The woman repeatedly shook her head, telling him no. He was persistent with whatever he was asking of her though, but she was just as stubborn, from what I could see.

"I told you no, Q! No—goddamn it! I just want to get the hell out of here!" The woman hollered. I could hear her through the door. "I need to get out!"

My eyes widened, and I covered my lips, watching as the handsome man stood up and walked to her side of the table. I couldn't help going into the cafeteria then. His back was facing me now. I wanted to know what he was telling her. I was desperate to find out, so I sat at the empty table beside theirs to listen.

"Mama, you have to get better, don't you understand that? I'm so sick of this shit," he snapped.

"Quinton...please," she begged. "Please, stop putting me through this. I—I've been here for a week and I feel like I'm losing myself—like I'm dying. Don't you want to make your mother happy?"

"Yes, I want to make you happy, which is why you're here. When you're out and clean, you'll be happy, I promise, Mama. You'll get that bakery you wanted. You'll get to travel with me and do fun things. You'll be living your life again in a better way. For me and Lora."

"I don't care about any of that right now," she moaned. "I just want one line. A sniff—anything, please! It's all I want—I won't ask for anything ever again."

"No, Ma!" His tone was harsh. Though I didn't know anything about him, I could tell he was frustrated and fed up. "I put you in here because I fucking know you, and I know you want to get better. Stop letting the drugs beat you!"

"I don't care!" she wailed. "I don't care! Just let me out!"

"You agreed to do this, Ma. You promised me! It's just withdrawals! They'll pass soon!"

She blinked up at him but couldn't rid herself of the tears. Everyone was watching them, but he didn't give a damn. He cared about her that much, to the point that no one else's opinions mattered but hers and his. That was awe-worthy.

The man's phone rang and he sighed, pulling it out of his back pocket. He ignored the call, placing his phone on the table, before grabbing her hand.

I couldn't hear much of what he had to say next. The volume of his voice had lowered, but I continued watching him, and all I could remember was how warm and safe his hands were when he touched. How good he smelled. I'd dreamt about his smell.

"Just get me out of here, Q. Please," his mother begged. "Please!" Her voice pulled me out of my daydreaming haze. I hadn't been paying attention before, but the security guards that were standing at the door were closer now. The man, Q, shook his head, eyes glistening, as he pinched the bridge of his nose and gave one simple nod to the security guard.

But his mother fought. She looked like a fighter, just like me. She elbowed and kicked and swung her arms, and her son yelled for her to stop it and cooperate, but she wasn't having it.

They had to settle her down somehow, otherwise they were never going to get her out of there. Before I knew it, a nurse rushed toward them and a needled pierced his mother's arm. The man breathed raggedly, the rims of his eyes red and glistening. "Take it easy on her!" he shouted at the nurse.

"Stand back, sir," the guard ordered.

"No, fuck that. I pay this place to take care of her, so ease up!"

The guard glared at the man before putting his focus on the nurse who'd given his mother the shot. The nurse nodded, and the guard eased up on his vice grip.

"Take her back to her room," the nurse commanded. "Sir, you can visit on another day, when she's feeling better."

The man let out a heavy breath as his mother stared into his eyes. "I'm doing this for you, Mama," he said, still watching her. "You promised me. Don't let this ruin you."

The man picked up his phone after her limp body was carried through the doors that led to the clients' rooms. "Be careful with her!" he shouted.

When the doors closed, he hurried out of the cafeteria and I rushed to a stand, following behind him. I didn't know what the hell possessed me to do it. Perhaps I knew I couldn't let him go again. I needed more. Craved more. I followed him out of the clinic and watched as he made his way toward a black Chrysler. Maybe I was stupid to think he hadn't seen me. Or maybe I wanted him to know I'd seen him—seen *everything*. Either way, before he could reach his car, I'd come face-to-face with him.

"Can I help you?" he snapped, and I stopped walking as he rushed away from his car and toward me. "You saw what happened and got a good show. Good for you! Now why the fuck are you following me?"

I blinked rapidly. "I...just wanted to see if you were okay."

"I'm fine, but I'll be better if you'd stop fucking watching me."

He started to turn, but I shouted after him. He frowned, peering over his shoulder.

"I'm sorry about your mother," I added. "I also had to deal with something similar." As if that statement eased him, he turned to face me again, slowly this time. "You have a family member in there? Is that why you're always here?"

In that moment, I could have told the truth, but I didn't. I refused, because I didn't want him to see me like how he saw his mother. As someone who needed help. Someone weak and desperate and...lonely. I could confess the truth later, once he got to know me.

So I replied, "Yes."

His shoulders relaxed. "Oh...shit. I apologize. I didn't realize—"

"No. Stop. It's okay." I shrugged and he dropped a hand in his pocket. "Look, this is going to sound crazy—I mean, I know we don't know each other at all, but maybe you'd like to talk about it? It's hard finding people to talk to when it comes to situations like this. Maybe we can grab some coffee—that is, if you have the time. Maybe this time I won't spill it all over myself." I laughed and he put on a small smile.

He then flipped his wrist, checking his watch. With a heavy sigh, he picked his head up and looked toward the clinic. It was a big place, very hard to miss. It reminded me of the white house with how grand and white it was. Too bad the inside didn't uphold the same elegance.

"I have an hour. Coffee sounds good."

To that, I smiled, and when he offered to give me a ride, I smiled even harder.

"Sorry for snapping at you." He rubbed the back of his neck before starting the car up. "I didn't catch your name…"

"Oh, I'm Kelly," I filled in for him. "And your name?"

"Uh…Quinton. Quinton Cane."

I nodded with a small smile, and he pulled away from the clinic. I was beaming inside.

I had him. I was close to him. He was in my clutches and that pleased me in more ways than one.

Little did he know that I belonged to Polly Heights Rehabilitation Clinic, too, just like his mother. Little did he know that I'd been checked in for drug overuse, and was still in therapy to control my personal disorders.

Little did he know that he was going to be stuck with me *forever*.

CHAPTER EIGHT

CANE

I hated that I couldn't be around to see Kandy off. Instead, I was in the hospital recovering, ready to break the hell out already. *Just a few more hours*, I reminded myself, but it was getting harder to settle with the idea of that with Kelly on my back.

I had to find a way to get rid of her without being too crazy about it. She'd found the letter my father had sent to me from prison. The words weren't delightful either. They were a threat.

Though I hated him and he hated me, he knew a lot of things about me—things that I'd wanted to keep buried for the sake of my new life, my business, and my family, but he would use my mistakes just to piss me off and ruin me.

I knew that my past would bite me in the ass one day...I just didn't think it would be so soon. My father had eight more years to go in prison so anything he had to say, even now, would have been meaningless. His word as a jailbird wasn't worth shit...but anything *Kelly* said could have tarnished me completely.

I never thought I would be able to hate someone as much as I did my father, but I hated her. I always felt something was off about her, but assumed it was my paranoia and lack of trust in everyone kicking in.

My gut was right about her. With all her beauty and patience, there was no choice but for her to have a major flaw or two. Meeting her at the clinic, but not knowing why she was really there? Never seeing her there again after she'd run into me? It was like she'd planned all of it—staged it somehow, but why on earth would she go out of her way to do such a thing?

Later that night, I dreamt about my sister. It was funny how that worked. I remember telling Lora that our bond was like the one of twins. If she were in trouble, I would know it. I'd feel it deep down in my soul—a tingle so deep in my palms it drove me mad—and sure enough, she'd call text or call me a few hours later about her problem.

The same went for me—whenever I was in deep shit or just overwhelmed with stress, I'd get a random call from her. Always on time. Always to pull me out of my funk and away from reality for a while.

But in my dream, something was wrong. Someone was chasing her through a dark alley. She ran into a building and hid for a while, but he grabbed her. She was screaming. I could see it all but couldn't do a damn thing to stop it. It's like I was a fly on the wall, helpless, only a small buzz to a loud storm.

I gasped, springing up a little too quickly on the bed. The rush made the back of my head throb, and my breaths came out labored.

I looked around the hospital room, so glad Kelly was nowhere in sight. None of her things were here either. *Thank God.*

I stared down at my lap, listening to the many footsteps going back and forth outside my door.

I sat back again, trying to relax, but I couldn't help remembering Lorelei always begging to die, and the thought of the memories made my heart ache. That's probably why I had that terrible nightmare.

She hated her life—was so fucking miserable, and it killed me because there wasn't much I could do about it to help her. At sixteen, I was still worthless. I played sports and attended debate clubs after school, just to have an excuse not to come home until my father was too tired to deal with us. I would sign Lora up for anything that would keep her after school with me. Cheerleading, yearbook committee, even reading programs. I did what I had to do to make sure my sister was always nearby and safe.

Don't get me wrong, she wasn't suicidal. No, she was too afraid to ever commit such a heinous sin and had too much pride to bother. She just wanted to die. She wanted to be struck by lightening or hit by a car. She wanted death to claim her so much that she hooked up with drug dealers and coke-heads, just to wind up in trouble with them, probably praying she'd get shot at or murdered by some lunatic by chance.

All it'd ever gotten her was a warning from a cop or a simple slap on the wrist because my mother was the type of woman to do *anything* to get out of a sticky situation. Yeah, the whole town knew who Nyla Cane was. They knew all about the seductive, beautiful woman with the brown hair and pretty face, with two kids and a shitty husband, so we never really got in trouble.

Lora would relax for a while, whenever the slap on the wrist happened, but then she'd find her next fucked-up drug dealer. While Lora wanted to ruin her life because of the shit she was going through, I sought to better mine. I wanted to do great things. I wanted to get my family away from the bad side of town and especially away from my abusive father...but I knew I couldn't do it clean. I couldn't get out unless I committed crimes too...

I did what I had to do, and Kelly knew all about it. She preyed on me from the very beginning and I was too dumb to see it.

If I'd known any better, I would have shoved my middle finger in her face the moment I saw her at Polly Heights.

I was an idiot who trusted a manipulative, psychotic bitch and now I had to figure out how to dig myself out of this deep, unforgiving hole with only my bare hands.

I hoped Lora would call. I would have called her, but she'd changed her number. After what we last went through, she swore she never wanted to speak to me again, but I kept my number the same, just in case.

I'd hoped she'd let me hear her voice again. I hadn't heard it in two years. I missed my sister to death and hoped that, despite her stubbornness, she'd feel our spiritual connection and know that I needed her.

CHAPTER NINE

KANDY

I had the last drive on the way to Indiana while Mom napped. Ten and a half hours didn't seem so bad until we were actually on the road. We had only made four stops, and made sure to keep our drinking and eating to a minimum.

The closer we got to the school, the more on edge I became. I tried to see this as a new chapter—a chance for me to start over and make new friends and try new things, but it was kind of hard to see it that way with Cane constantly running through my mind.

When we were finally there, I parked and let out a lengthy breath, staring ahead at the building. I'd seen it once before.

All of the buildings looked the same to be honest. Gothic architecture that seemed a bit daunting at first, but after staring at it for a while, the look grew on me. It was unique. I loved them— the vintage bricks and intricate structure.

Not only that, but compared to Georgia, Indiana was different. For one, it was much livelier here. It could have been the trees, and how the tips of them were splashed with color, proving fall was well on it's way, or maybe it was the freshly cut grass that I could smell through the open sunroof. Everything here was earthy and real, unlike where our suburban home was located.

I spotted several students, all female, walking to the building I would be residing in with their parent or parents. They all carried luggage or big items like comforters and sheets and some even had softball gear. Most of them had smiles on their faces, and I instantly envied their joy. I wanted to walk into this building happy too. Instead, I longed to go back home and make things right again.

"Well," Mom sighed, unclipping her seatbelt. "You ready, sweetie?"

"Yeah." I let out a breath, unclipping mine too. "Better now than never." We both pushed out of the car and before we grabbed my things, we checked in with a redheaded girl with a clipboard standing in the lobby. Her name was Henley and she was one of the resident assistant's for our building. She had frizzy hair and freckles, but was super petite and adorable.

"We're so happy to have you here, Kandy!" Henley chimed. "Believe it or not, I've heard so many great things about from the other softball players!" Henley followed Mom and me back to the car to help us unpack. One thing I learned during the first two minutes of meeting Henley: she loved to give compliments and loved to talk even more.

"Lots of them admire you," she went on. "Especially the other freshman! As a matter of fact, you're sharing a dorm with the girl who was just talking about your pitching record. She's super excited to meet you, but I won't tell you her name—it's best if roommates meet each other and form their own introductions first, you know?"

"Sure," I said with a soft smile. "Makes sense."

"That's a really good thing to do," Mom noted. "It'll give you someone to hang out with, hopefully. You know, I remember when I was in college. It was a while ago, but I had a roommate who *loved* to party."

"Seriously?" Henley squealed—literally *squealed*. She had a high-pitched voice and normally I would have found voices like hers annoying, but it wasn't at all. She had a welcoming, comforting tone to hers—a genuine one that made you feel like a friend. I realized now why she'd become an RA.

"Yep. She was such a fun girl. Really sweet too," Mom responded. "We hit it off as soon as we met each other, became inseparable, but then we graduated and life got in the way. She got married right after graduation and moved to New Mexico with her husband. We still keep in touch here and there."

"Wow, that is so cool," Henley sighed. "Well, at least we know that your mom won't mind you getting down and partying every once in a while, Kandy!" Henley nudged my arm with her elbow and a small wink.

"I guess not," I laughed.

We collected the smaller items first, and then took the elevator up two floors. It wasn't a long walk down the hallway before Henley beat us to the door to open it. It was vacant, but one of the beds was already made up, swathed in a pink and purple polka-dotted comforter, as well as decorative pillows.

I was glad whomever my roommate was had taken the bed by the wall. I loved being by the window. The room was pretty spacious for a dorm. There was even a two-seater sofa between the beds, pressed against the north wall. I'd seen one of the example rooms a few months ago, but it was slightly smaller than this.

"Wow, this is really nice!" Mom exclaimed.

She wasn't kidding. Though the walls were ivory and the beds combined were half the size of my bed back at home, it was a quaint, comfortable size. The floors were covered in clean blue carpet and it actually looked new. Whoever my roommate was, she had a nice setup on her end. Even her laptop had a purple and pink case. I had a feeling we were going to get along just great. I mean, she loved purple. That sealed the deal.

It took us three more trips up and down the elevator before we could start unpacking. Henley left us to it, and went to help the other student athletes check in and unpack, and when she was gone, all Mom could talk about was how she loved the dorm and hoped I would love it here too. She also talked about how sweet Henley was and was glad I'd made a friend already. I wouldn't have called Henley a friend just yet, welcoming us was her duty, but she was nice.

With every step closer to finishing, my heart began to race. I realized I wouldn't see Mom or Dad again, probably until Thanksgiving. For four whole months, I would be away from my family…and that frightened me in more ways than one. I had never been away from them for more than a week, and even with that timespan, I always missed them.

We wrapped up on fixing my bed. It looked dull in comparison to my roommate's. My comforter was white and teal. My pillows all white. She even had fuzzy purple pillows. It truly put mine to shame.

When we finished, Mom and I decided to grab some lunch at a pizzeria on campus.

After devouring the slices, our stroll back to the dorm was leisurely. We knew our time was limited. Even though Mom was staying the night in a hotel and would only be a short drive away, this was going to be our last walk together for a while. Honestly, our last of *anything* for a while.

"I have a question, Kandy, and I want you to be completely honest with me." Mom's face had turned serious, her pace slowing.

I avoided drawing my brows together. "What is it?" I already knew what she was going to bring up though. Cane. We hadn't spoken much of him in the car. While she drove, I slept and vice versa.

"How long was it going on? What you and Cane were doing?"

I snatched my eyes away. "Mom, I really don't want to talk about that right now."

"I know, I know, but, I can't help wondering, sweetie. Was it before you turned eighteen?"

"No," I answered, head shaking. "Nothing happened until I turned eighteen."

I noticed the relief glitter in her eyes. "Well...I guess that's good. I mean—not good, but...ugh. Who am I kidding? None of this is okay." She looked ahead again. "I really thought he was one of the good ones. A good friend."

"He is good, Mom. And he is a good friend, too. Friends aren't perfect."

"He had sex with my eighteen-year-old daughter." Her tone was harsh. When she noticed the frown steal my features, she softened up. "I just...I'm at a loss for words, I suppose."

"I understand."

"I just keep thinking about all the times he was around," she murmured. "There was one time, a few weeks after he and Kelly split, when I saw him staring at you. You were talking to your father, so I thought he was just admiring the way you two interacted because he'd never had a father figure...but the more I think about it, the more I realize he was probably looking at you because he wanted you."

I dropped my head, pressing my lips flat.

"Did you protect yourself at least?"

"What do you mean? I'm still on my birth control."

"Yeah, but with a condom too?" she asked sternly, eyes boring into mine. "He's older. You don't know who he's been with or what he does in private, Kandy."

"Oh my God, Mom! Please! Stop acting like I'm on trial here! I'm not one of your plaintiffs in a courtroom."

She breathed in through her nose and stopped walking, sealing her eyes to collect herself. "I just need to know," she said, looking at me again.

"You want the honest answer? No."

Her throat bobbed. She looked everywhere else but at me. "Do you need to take a pregnancy test?"

"No, Mom. I'm fine. I promise." I grabbed her hand. "Can we please stop this? I'm so sorry for hurting you and Dad. I didn't think…" I sighed, looking down at my feet.

"Didn't think you'd get caught?"

"Yeah," I whispered.

I couldn't bring myself to look at her anymore, but I could feel her scanning me like she could hear every thought running through my head.

She started walking again, huffing lightly as she tossed her hair over her shoulder. I matched her stride. "Thank you for being honest with me." We were quiet again. I could hear other students talking and calling for each other, wheels running over gravel in the parking lot close by. "Let's stop talking about that for now, okay? You're in a new state with new things surrounding you. You've got a fresh start. You ready to be out in the real world alone?"

I shrugged. "I guess so. Kind of nerve-wrecking though." I paused. "I'll miss you guys."

"Yeah," she breathed. "We'll miss you too, baby."

We were quiet a beat, going toward my building again. "Mom…look, I really hope I haven't ruined things back at home—I mean, I just hope Dad will be okay and can go back to work soon. I want things to go back to normal…for all of us."

She stopped walking again, which made me stop too. She then grabbed my hand, leading the way to a bench only several steps away. We sat down and she turned so her knees were touching mine and my hands were in hers.

She rubbed the back of my hand with the pad of her thumb, a trembling smile sweeping over her lips.

"Mom—"

"It's easy for us to forget that you are growing up, Kandy," Mom sniffled and I clamped my mouth shut. A tear slid down her cheek, but she pulled her glistening eyes up to look at me. "Especially your dad. He still wants you to be the five-year-old girl who ran to him about every little problem. Sometimes, I wish you were that girl too, but I have to remember that you are growing and that certain things in your life will be just *yours* and we aren't allowed to interfere or disrespect that. Your privacy is important. What you do on your own time, is yours. We all have our escapes —our *thrills*." She lifted a hand to swipe at her face. "Once your father realizes that you are independent, and capable of making your own choices, things will go back to normal. We all do dumb things and he knows it. He will be okay, though. As soon as I get back, I will be applying for jobs—hell, I may even start up my own firm. I've always wanted to, and it'll be great working from home."

"That would be really good for you, Mom."

"It will. I already have previous clients who are happy to give me the chance. They know how dedicated I am to my job."

"So…that means you won't take the job that Cane set up for you?"

She let out a ragged breath, pushing her gaze to the side and shaking her head. "I'm not going to lie, it's a great job. It pays really well and I have a shoe-in so I'd have it in the bag, plus the company has clients with really deep pockets. They're willing to pay for hard work. I would love to have it. Even if I took it, I'm almost certain I would never see Cane because of how busy he is and the fact that his attorney goes to meet him…but I can't do that to your father. Not right now. He wouldn't be happy with that decision, whether I see Cane around or not. I don't want to cause any tension."

"Yeah, I understand," I murmured.

She put her focus on me again. "You'll be here for a while, sweetie. I want you to focus on that, okay? Focus on yourself.

Have fun. Make new friends. Live your life and forget about what happened. By the time we see you again, I'm sure things will be better." She cupped my cheek. "You've worked hard to get here, baby. Don't let a little setback keep you from doing great things, all right? We're the Jennings. We don't let anything weigh us down for long."

I struggled to smile, but put one on to satisfy her. "Okay," I whispered.

"Okay." She wiped her face again. "Good." She wiped off her lap, even though nothing was there, and stood up with my hands still in hers. "Let's finish getting you settled in and then I'll be heading to the hotel. I could really use a shower and a nap. You sure you ate enough?"

"I'll be good 'til morning, but if I do get hungry, I'll ask Henley what time the restaurants around campus close."

There wasn't much else for us to do when we got back to the room. Mom really wanted to meet my roommate, but she was nowhere to be found. I was eager to meet her too, only to see if we would get along.

I didn't want a roommate like Frankie's. Hers was a total bitch and a snitch, and since Frankie loved to have fun, I knew she was going to have a miserable first year. Thinking of Frankie made me leave a mental note to call her tomorrow and fill her in on my first day.

We couldn't wait all night to meet one person, so eventually I was walking Mom to the parking lot.

"I'm going to get out of here, but call me if you need anything," she said, opening the car door. "I'll be back in the morning before I take the rental car to the airport. I'd really like to meet your roommate before I go."

"Okay, Mom. Text me when you get checked in."

She nodded and pressed her lips into a smile. "Make sure you call your dad, let him know you're settled in."

"Okay." My heart ached a little from the mention of Dad.

I had a feeling she wanted to say more, but she didn't want to ruin this moment—the first day jitters, anticipation, and excitement and all that. She constantly talked about how I needed to experience every single feeling and learn from it. She refused to take away from that with trivial matters.

"Love you, sweetie," she sighed while hugging me. She released me and climbed behind the wheel, started the car up, and tossed me a wave goodbye.

Watching her leave was...strange. I wanted to cry, but I also felt this zing of liberation rush through me.

She was right before. This was my chance to start over and find myself. This was my chance to become unstoppable and to live my life, and I was going to do just that—right after giving my father a call.

CHAPTER TEN

KANDY

When I made it back to my room, I took my cellphone off the charger and called Dad. My heart drummed harder and faster with every ring.

I'd never been this nervous to call my Dad. Ever. My life had really, really shifted.

"Hello?" His voice was gruff.

"Hi, Dad."

"Hey, Kandy." I don't know if it was just me, but he sounded relieved, like he was glad to hear from me. Did he think I wouldn't call him? "How's the dorm life treating you so far?"

I laughed. "Good, I guess. My RA is really nice and helpful and the pizza here is extra cheesy with not too much sauce."

"Oh, man. Pizza? Be careful or you might get caught up in the freshman fifteen!"

I smiled. "I doubt it. We'll be training and conditioning. I'll have no choice but to burn it all off, but thanks for the heads up."

He chuckled lowly. We were quiet a moment. The silence was

deafening. I hated it. "Your mom left already?"

"Yeah. She's on her way to the hotel now. She was trying to stick around to meet my roommate, but I'm sure she's exhausted after the drive. I haven't met my roommate yet either."

"No? Is she around?"

"I don't know. Her bed is all made up but I haven't seen her since we started moving stuff in."

"Oh. Well, I'm sure she'll show up soon." He cleared his throat. He only did that when he had something important to say, but was finding the right time to squeeze it into the conversation.

"What is it, Dad?"

"What do you mean?" he asked, as if he were truly clueless, but I knew something was up.

"You only do that throat-clearing thing when you have something to say. What is it?"

I hated asking. To be honest, I didn't want to know what he had to say. I was afraid he would blast me, tell me he'd never be able to accept what had happened and move on from it.

But that wasn't it at all. "Um...Cane didn't go through with the assault charges. He also told my boss what really happened...that I got angry because of what he'd done with you. I'll be back to work next week."

"Oh...uh...wow. That's good!" I couldn't believe it. "That was nice of him." Really nice of him, in fact.

"I guess."

"*You guess?* Dad, if he hadn't dropped the charges and told them the truth, you might've lost your job."

"I know that, Kandy. I'm glad he did it, but I'm not going to go around thanking the man for something he shouldn't have done in the first place."

I bit back all words. His anger was creeping in again. Not only that, but he was still hurt about this. Deep down, I knew Dad wanted to thank Cane, but his anger was fiercer than any sympathy he could give.

"I—I know. I'm sorry," I murmured.

He let out a long, weary exhale. "Don't be sorry. I'm not angry with you, Kandy. I'm angry about the situation, you know? I mean...I just. I don't know. Maybe I'm mad at myself for not seeing it before having it shoved in my face like that. Now that I think about it, there were signs and I ignored them all. He was always...*different* with you. Always very careful and attentive to your needs."

I didn't know what to say to that, and was glad he kept talking to spare me from filling in.

"As a kid, I understood his protectiveness over you. You grew on him, stuck to him like a little leech, and it was impossible to say no to you. But last year...I noticed there were changes. I noticed it but thought it was just my paranoia and cop instincts kicking in. I should have listened to what my gut was telling me. He was such a good guy that I thought, 'No, not Cane. He wouldn't do that to me. He's my best friend. I'd take a bullet for him and I'm sure he'd do the same for me.'" He sighed. "There's a reason I don't have many friends. I don't trust a lot of people."

"Cane didn't come onto me, Dad," I said. "I just want you to know that. He never did anything to me that I didn't want."

"Kandy—"

"No, Dad, listen. I'm serious. I know you want to place all the blame on him but I knew what I was doing with him. He didn't force it or make me do anything I didn't want to do. As a matter of fact, he told me no repeatedly from the start but...I didn't like it, and like you just said, it was always impossible for him to say no to me. Eventually, he caved and gave me what I wanted."

He grumbled something, but I couldn't comprehend it. "I just don't get it," he muttered. "Why him? Why the only real friend I had?"

I stared down at the zigzags on the blue carpet then plucked at a string on my comforter. "I...I don't know. I really don't." A tear escaped me as I thought of all the people I could have chosen to do something with instead of Cane. How all of this could have been prevented if I hadn't been so selfish and needy several week sago. "Ever since I met him, I've liked him. A lot. I've always wanted him...and I'm sorry it was him, Dad. I tried to ignore the way I felt so many times but...I couldn't fight it. I really love him."

He scoffed. "*Love* him? Really, Kandy? Listen to yourself! What did he tell you that has you so damn brainwashed?!"

"He didn't tell me anything and I'm not brainwashed! I don't know why you and Mom think that! I'm old enough to know better and old enough to understand." I huffed. "Doesn't matter. I'm sure I'll never see him again anyway."

"Damn right you won't. You're in school and you're starting over. You're better off there, you hear me?"

"Yes," I whispered.

"Good." He was quiet a beat. "This changes nothing between us and I want you to know that." His voice was softer, so sincere that my heart ached and my throat thickened. "You're still my baby girl and I love you to death. There is nothing you can do that will *ever* change that."

Another tear came rushing down, hot and swift. "I love you too."

"Okay." He grunted. "Stay safe and keep in touch. Get some rest too. I'm going to call your mother, check on her."

"Okay."

We said good night and I stared down at my phone screen. I had this sudden urge to cry—to just break down right then and there, sob into my pillow, and collect myself later...but I didn't get the chance and truly, I was glad.

The door swung open and a husky girl with broad shoulders, thick arms and legs, and a slightly round mid-section walked through the door.

Her dirty-blond hair was tied up in a ponytail, her skin tan and sun kissed, and her eyes as blue as sapphires. She wore softball gear, her socks stained with grass and red dirt. She was almost intimidating in size. She had to be nearly four feet taller than me, and she had a strong build.

"Oh—shit!" She clutched the heart of her shirt when she spotted me. "Jesus, you scared me! I didn't think anyone would be in here when I got back!"

I stood up, fidgeting with my phone. "Sorry—yeah, I got here about four hours ago." I pointed at her bat and glove when she dropped the gear on the floor. "You were practicing?"

"Oh—yeah! I wanted to try out the new field, see if it felt as good as the rumors said." She smirked, snatching the hairband out of her hair, her curly strands swimming around her heart-shaped face. "We weren't supposed to, but oh well. Was totally worth it. No rocks or pebbles. Nice red dirt. The perfect playing field." She stepped to her side of the room, pressing a palm to the nightstand and pulling off her cleats.

So, she was my roommate. I had to admit, she wasn't who I was expecting after seeing all the purple and pink.

"Shit—I'm sorry. I'm Morgan. Morgan Page. Best outfielder you'll ever fucking meet."

I smiled as she extended an arm and offered her hand. She had a potty mouth too, just like Frankie. I loved it. "I'm Kandy," I said, grabbing her hand to shake it. "Kandy Jennings."

"Oh my gosh—wait. WHAT?" She dropped her arm, her eyes so wide I thought they'd pop out of her head. "Okay, I am legit having a fan-girl moment! I have been *dying* to meet you! If I'd known you were going to be my roommate I would have showered first! Henley didn't tell me anything about you being my roommate! Gah—you look much different from when I saw you two years ago!"

"You saw me two years ago?" I laughed. "Where?"

"Okay, so funny story. I'm from North Carolina. I played for Providence High School in Charlotte. You may not remember this, but during playoffs our junior year, we played each other in South Carolina!"

"Oh wow—I do remember playing Providence! You guys were really good!"

"Yeah—I totally remember because you gave one of our best batters these really tough pitches. She couldn't hit *any* of them—well I mean the ones she did hit sucked and didn't get far. Everyone was so shocked. The crowd was cheering your name—*Kandy! Kandy! Kandy!* It was fucking awesome, not gonna lie. Don't get me wrong, I was pissed that we lost, but I also give credit where it is due and you, ma'am, are one of the best pitchers I've ever had the pleasure of meeting! I can't believe I'm sharing a room with you!"

I giggled. "Well, it's nice to formally meet you. Sorry we whipped your butts that year."

She broke out in a hoarse laugh. "Well, we're on the same team now, so it's all good. Just so you know, you won't get any trouble from me. We're in the same boat. We're the only freshmen on the team, can you believe that?"

"Yeah, Coach Carmen was telling me that in an email. It's going to be weird. Have you met any of the other girls yet?"

"I've met Gina, she's a sophomore and really cool. I saw a few of the seniors and Gina tried to introduce me to them but they pretended like they were too busy." She shrugged and rolled her eyes. "It's whatever. I don't have time for these fake bitches. There's a girl here, Sophie. She's a pitcher too, but you know she got injured over the summer and can't play too well. I saw her and she frowned at Gina and me. I think she's pissed because she knows someone good is here to replace her."

"Oh, wow. I've heard about Sophie." Lots of things about Sophie Banks, actually. She'd taken the Notre Dame team to sectionals twice with her quick arm. Not only that, but she'd entered a beauty pageant for her county last summer and won. She was all Coach Carmen could talk about.

"Well, I'll tell you now, you're ten times better than she is. Only reason she's still on the team is because Coach Carmen wants her to finish her scholarship. She's also an ass-kisser, which Carmen loves. I have no doubt that Coach Carmen is a pussy-muncher through and through. She loves to have her ass kissed and to be adored by her players." Morgan threw her hands in the air carelessly. "Whatever floats your boat, you know, but I'm not an ass-kisser. I'm just here to play and hopefully lose a few pounds with conditioning."

"Yep," I sighed. "It's a new start. Just want to learn and play and have fun doing it."

"Eh, I don't know about the learning part," she teased. "Really though, I'm super laid back. As long as you don't touch or eat my shit, we're cool."

"Cool," I laughed.

"Wanna catch dinner? Maybe Gina will be out and I can introduce you guys. Have her show us around a little?"

"Sure. That sounds good."

"Okay, cool. Let me hit the shower then I'll be ready to go."

She left the room with her shower caddy in seconds. I sat on the sofa and smiled.

My roommate was awesome, and my call with Dad didn't end with lashing out and bad words. I was having a surprisingly good day, despite the guilt that lingered, and I should have been grateful for that, but the longer I sat there alone, the more I realized something was missing.

I wanted to hear Cane's voice—tell him how things were going. I wanted to fill him in on every single detail but this was my reality now.

This was life. It was unfair and sometimes cruel. Life could throw a bucket of ice water in your face and you'd have no choice but to dry yourself off, warm back up, and keep it moving.

As I sat in my new room and took a look round, that's what I promised myself I would do.

Keep moving. Find myself. Forget about the past.

Even if forgetting meant hurting every day.

CHAPTER ELEVEN

CANE

As soon as I was told I could check out from the hospital, I called a driver and had him pick me up first thing.

Of course, Kelly was still around. I was so fucking sick of her and she had no idea just what kind of shit I could pull out of my sleeve. She thought she had me backed into a corner but she was sadly mistaken.

My driver, Neo, pulled up to the hospital in no time. When he opened the door for me, Kelly asked, "Do you want me to meet you at your place?"

I grimaced over my shoulder. "Why the fuck would I want that?" I growled.

"I'll be over later," she declared, ignoring my remark.

"Don't bother. I have a few stops to make first, then I'm going by the office. I won't be home." I got into the car and Neo shut the door. He got behind the wheel, but of course Kelly knocked on my window. I let out an agitated sigh, cracking it slightly.

"Call me when you're home. We have a lot to talk about, Cane."

Her eyes were narrowed but serious, her lips pursing after her sentence.

I glared at her through the crack, while a smile spread across her lips like she had no fucking care in the world. "Don't you have some work to do somewhere? Or did you lie about that too?"

She smirked. "I took a week off to take care of you, Quinton." She stood up straight. "I'll see you tonight."

I rolled the window up and looked away, telling Neo to go. I needed to distance myself from her immediately, before I did something I regretted.

"Where to, sir?" Neo inquired.

"I'll text you the address."

When I sent it to him, I rested the back of my head on the headrest, which gave me a clear reminder that maybe I shouldn't have been going to the place I had in mind. I had to make things right, though, even if it felt like it was too soon.

As soon as Neo pulled into the driveway of Derek's home, I felt my stomach clench. I'd forgotten what it was like to be nervous about an outcome. I was so confident with my job and my life lately, that feeling anxious had never fazed me.

Maybe this was why all of this had happened. It'd knocked me down a notch, shortened my ego. Right now, I was in a sticky bind, not only with my best friend, but with my company too. It was on the line, thanks to Kelly and her bullshit.

I'd lost a big deal and Zheng refused to speak to me again after witnessing the horrors of that night. If I couldn't make my work life better, I at least had to try with my personal life.

With a heavy sigh, I pushed the door open and stepped out. I faced the familiar house, taking it in for a moment, before lowering my gaze and focusing on the black pick-up truck in the driveway. He was home.

After knocking, I waited. And waited. I could hear the TV playing, definitely some kind of sport with all the whistles and yelling happening. "Come on, D," I called. "I know you're in there. Open up please."

Several more seconds ticked by before the lock clinked. The door drew open slowly, and there he stood, a tight frown on his face and his lips pinched tight. "What the hell are you doing here?"

I straightened my back, holding his eyes. I couldn't back down —refused to back down. Unlike my father, I was a man. A man who faced his problems instead of running away from them. "I'm here to apologize, D. In person."

"Don't you think it's a little too late for that?" He folded his arms over his chest, bushy brows drawing together.

"It is. I know it was wrong, and I apologize. I swear I didn't force her into anything. I know that's what you're thinking. I should have told you that things were getting blurry for me with Kandy. I didn't want to ruin our friendship or have you thinking I wanted to hurt her or your family."

His nostrils flared.

"I didn't hurt her. I didn't force myself onto her. I did what she *wanted* me to do, D. I fucked up, yeah. I know. If I could go back and change things, I would. I would have made her stop and actually *think* about our consequences. I'm truly, truly sorry, man."

His jaw ticked as he took a step forward. He looked me over twice, before peering over my shoulder at the black car that waited for me. "Why did you drop the charges?"

"Because it was a mistake. They never should have been drawn up in the first place."

"Really?" he scoffed. "A mistake? You think me beating your ass and giving you what you deserved for *fucking my daughter* was a mistake?" he snarled through his teeth.

My brows narrowed. "I did deserve it, which is why you didn't deserve for me to press charges. I never put the charges on you. It was Kelly who told the police I would be considering it. Kelly is the reason you even found out."

He dropped his arms and shook his head, turning quickly to

get in the house and pick something up from the table in the hallway. He came back with a white flash drive, holding it in my face, "So you're telling me that Kelly used a flash drive with *your* company's name on it and recorded *you* in the act with *my* daughter? Why would she do some shit like that, Cane?"

"Because she's a psychotic bitch and she knows too much. She's dangling shit over my head. She found out, told me to stay away…but I didn't listen. She thinks this is the only way to keep me away from Kandy. By destroying our friendship. If there's no Derek, there are no Jennings' at all. "

A deep growl formed in his throat. "Well, she's damn right about that." He shoved a fist into my chest, which forced me to take two slight stumbles backward. "I'm going to burn this shit, and then I'll burn the copy my wife has. As for you, I don't give a fuck about your apology. I don't give a fuck that you dropped the charges out of whatever *pity* you had to help me or try and salvage this friendship. There is no friendship anymore. That's dead. And if you ever come around my family or me again, what you get next will be much worse than a fucking concussion."

With that, he shoved my chest one more time until I had no choice but to step off the porch, then he turned around and slammed the door in my face.

I stood there a moment, staring at the door, realizing I would probably never see it again. I couldn't lie and say I didn't see that coming. I knew Derek. He would never forgive me for this, but at least I tried.

This was it.

There was no coming back from this.

There was no denying the truth.

I no longer had a best friend, and that was the reality I faced during my walk of shame to the car.

I got home, took a hot shower, and tried to work, but it was impossible to concentrate. Frustrated, I slammed my laptop shut and went downstairs to the kitchen. I poured myself some scotch, and after the first sip, my phone rang in the pocket of my sweats.

Pulling it out, I checked the screen. It was from a number I didn't know.

I frowned, ignoring the call. Several seconds and one sip of scotch later, it rang again. I ignored it.

It rang one more time and I cursed beneath my breath, frowning at the screen. I received a lot of crazy calls from random motherfuckers who found my number. Normally, I would ignore them, but that night I was pissed and hostile, and wanted to shout at someone—*anyone*. Maybe I should have invited Kelly over. Cursing her out would have been a fucking relief.

I answered when the number showed up on the screen for the fifth time. "Who the hell is this and why do you keep calling me?" I demanded.

"Well, shit, bro—is that any way for *CEO* to answer the phone?"

My back straightened, my frown rapidly disappearing. I couldn't believe the voice I was hearing. This couldn't be real. This had to be a joke.

"Lora?" I breathed, gripping the phone as if it would be snatched out of my hands by some criminal with a gun to my head.

"Hey, big bro. You missed me?"

"What the hell? Where are you? What made you call?"

"Whoa, whoa, whoa—slow your roll, Q! Look, before I answer any of your questions, I need to know where you live. I'm at the Atlanta airport and would like to hug my big bro before I get around to the serious shit."

"Shit—you're at the airport? Uh—okay. Stay there. I'll have a car sent to you right now."

"Oh my gosh—look at you! You always have to use your big bucks and big moves to make a statement, don't you?" She laughed, that same infectious laugh that warmed my spirit and made me feel at home. "I'm using some stranger's phone, but text me your address really quick and I'll call up an *Uber*. No big deal. Bye loser."

She hung up before I could speak again. I stared at the phone for a split second before sending my address. I couldn't hesitate for long. I didn't need her having second thoughts about being here.

Why was she here anyway? I knew we had a bond and a connection that was familiar…but did it really run *that* deep?

She showed up when I needed her most.

I hoped. I prayed. I *begged*.

I couldn't believe it had worked.

CHAPTER TWELVE

KANDY

"*She's* the new pitcher?" The tone of disgust coming from my own teammate was like a slap right in the face.

As soon as we'd walked into the diner, Morgan and Gina, another lovely teammate of mine, groaned at the same time, and when I looked where their eyes were focused, two girls were coming our way, both wearing basketball shorts and Notre Dame T-shirts.

The girl who'd given me the rude tone was Jay and it was clear she wasn't a huge fan of the freshman pitcher.

"Have a little class, Jay, seriously." Gina folded her arms over her chest. She was a sweet girl—strawberry blonde hair, freckles, green eyes, really toned legs and arms, and a sweet southern accent.

"I don't know if I'm the main pitcher yet," I responded with a slight frown.

"Well, of course you are. The senior pitcher is hurt and will still be out when the season starts. You're the only other pitcher we have…for *now* anyway." She smirked then sipped from the straw of her cup. The girl beside her giggled at the snide remark.

I didn't know who she was, but her skin was a smooth sable, her eyes a rich dark-brown, and her hair in coils so tight I was sure it was a bitch to comb through it. Trust me, I knew all about the kinky hair. My hair coiled a lot too, to the point that if I didn't comb it after a shower, I'd regret it when it dried.

"I guess you're another one of those, huh?" Morgan asked Jay.

Jay frowned at her. "Another one of what?"

"One of Sophie's ass-kissers. You know what? It's cool—I get it. I mean we can't all be as talented as Kandy or even Sophie, and I bet it's super fucking scary to know you can easily be replaced by a *freshman*. Wait, aren't you an outfielder, too?" Morgan seemed truly curious, but I knew her motive was to get under Jay's skin. Jay looked around the diner nervously, focusing on the girl with coiled hair before looking between us.

"Yeah, so what?" Jay grimaced.

"Oh—just wondering." Morgan took a step forward. "Because I'm coming for you. You might wanna watch out." She winked and flashed a smile in Jay's face. "Come on, ladies. Let's get something to eat. I'm starving."

I walked past the girls, fighting a smile as they looked at each other and scoffed, watching us walk away.

"You are a badass," I laughed.

"I told you I don't have time for these bitches. I dealt with the snobby bullshit in high school, but I'm not dealing with it in college. If we don't put our feet down now, they'll never respect us."

"That's true," Gina agreed. "Some of the girls on the team can be really snobby."

"You know, you'd think since we're a team, that we'd all get along. I mean, at the end of the day, we're going to see each other all the fucking time," Morgan went on as we slid into one of the booths. "We all got here by working our asses off and staying dedicated. I just don't understand girls like them, or how they make it onto the softball team at all with their prissy, arrogant personalities."

"Eh, well, I couldn't care less. I'm good at ignoring the snobby bitches." I shrugged as I picked up one of the table tent menus. "I only had one real friend in high school and she was all I needed. We kept to ourselves and got by just fine. I had some really cool teammates, but most of them were kind of like Jay. Only they'd smile in my face *and* talk shit behind my back. Wasn't cool, so I hardly hung out with them. I think most of them despised me because my best friend dated most of their boyfriend's before them."

"Man, your bestie sounds like she likes to get down," Morgan tittered, and Gina laughed with her, throwing her hands in the air as if she had no right to say anything. "Your old teammates can talk all the shit they want, but I bet none of them are where you are right now, at one of the best colleges in the country, playing for one of the best softball college teams around. Screw those bitches."

I chuckled while Gina said, "Amen," in her adorable, southern accent.

I ordered a garden salad and fruit bowl. Morgan chowed down on a cheeseburger and a milkshake, and Gina went with a chicken sandwich and slice of apple pie. My salad wasn't as great as the pizza I had the day before. No wonder so many students turned toward cheeseburgers and pizza. The salad was literally thrown together and looked as if it'd been sitting out for days. I ate my fruit bowl instead.

Being around Morgan and Gina was a breath of fresh air, that was for sure. They were understanding and good listeners, which I loved. It was nice to have genuine people at my side. It took away some of my nerves, plus Gina was a big help with where to go and how to get around campus. She loved answering our questions.

Later that night, it was hard to fall asleep. The night before, it was easy because I'd had a long trip and I crashed. But this night, it felt impossible.

Morgan was like a rock, I learned. It took her no time to get comfortable and drift into a deep snore. Lucky for her, my father was a heavy snorer and I could hear his snoring from my room three doors down so I was used to the noise.

I tossed and turned. Grunted and groaned. I gave up eventually and laid flat on my back, staring out of the window at the milky moon. While I stared at it, my eyes became tight and wet, my throat thick with emotion. I picked up my phone and sighed.

Cane was only a phone call away. He'd reminded me of it every time I saw him. But it wasn't like that anymore. I couldn't call him without risking everything. There was a chance Kelly was around and as badly as I wanted to know what she had on him to make him so wary, I wanted more for him to be safe.

Helpless, I cried silently, half of my face buried in the pillows that smelled like home, until finally, I'd fallen asleep.

CHAPTER THIRTEEN

CANE

The hardest thing about my entire situation was whether or not to call Kandy. I wanted to know how her first two days had gone, hear the nerves and excitement in her voice as she filled me in on everything.

I remembered my first day of college and how nervous yet thrilled I was to start a new life—a new adventure. I was sure she felt the same way.

I wanted to hold her hand along the way, tell her that there wasn't anything to worry about and that she'd get through the next four years just fine—that I was always going to be here for her, no matter how screwed up all of this was. I wanted to hear her sweet, sultry voice, hear her tell me that she still wanted me. Still cared for me, despite being backed into a corner.

It was useless, though.

I stared down at the phone on my counter, glaring down at her number on my screen, my palms pressed on the edge of it. Would it have been selfish of me to call her, ruin her first few days? Was she even thinking about me, or was she trying to move past it and live a better life? If so, who was I to set her back?

I had my time and I'd ruined it. I told her I would ruin her, but in the end, I was the one who was crushed.

Headlights rolled across the wall in the hallway. Someone was here. I picked up my phone and marched to the door quickly, pulling it open and spotting a white Impala parked in the driveway.

"Thanks, man!" I heard the familiar voice shout, and then she was coming toward me.

She, as in my sister. My baby sister.

She looked different. Way different. Her hair that was once brown and straight the last time I saw her, was now wavy and dyed a pastel blue. The sleeves of tattoos on her arms I could make out in a busy crowd, but I couldn't recall the lip piercing.

It was funny. When people who didn't know us, saw us together with our tattoos on display, they automatically knew we were related, or assumed we were a couple if they didn't look at our faces long enough.

Lora and I looked very much alike. We had the same gray-green eyes that we got from our mother, though hers were more gray than green, and similar lip structure. The only difference was our noses. While Lora's was rounder and smaller, like Mom's, mine was narrower and wider, like my father's.

"Oh. My. Fucking. Gosh!" she squealed, looking all around. "Look at this house! The pictures you sent me a while back didn't do it any justice!"

I slid my phone into my back pocket, smiling. "I've told you repeatedly to come and see it for yourself. Repeatedly, butthead."

She gave a playful scowl. "Oh, cut it out, monkeyface! I'm serious—this is really nice!" She stepped in front of me with a bold grin. "You did good brother—getting all of this without my help." She dropped her suitcase down and wasted no time throwing her arms around me. I wrapped my arms around her, hugging her tight.

"Don't ever go that long without talking to me again," she muttered over my shoulder.

I pulled back, and that's when her eyes became wider. "Oh my gosh—what the hell happened to your eye?"

"An accident, it's nothing. Lora, I called, texted, and emailed you constantly, but you have that shithead so far up your ass that he probably blocked my fucking number. How can you tell me not to go that long when I tried to get in touch with you so many times?"

She hissed and winced, like she was just now remembering the fallout we had. "Just be glad you didn't change your number. Oh, and about that shithead...yeah, we aren't together anymore."

That caused my brows to draw together. She pushed past me and I picked up her suitcase to bring it inside. When I set it down and shut the door, I trailed after her.

"What do you mean you're not together anymore? I mean, trust me, I'm fucking relieved, but what happened?"

She gazed around, like she was truly in awe, like she hadn't even heard my question.

"Lora," I called.

"What, Cane? It's no big deal, seriously. Just wasn't working out like it should have."

"No big deal?" I took a few steps forward as she opened the fridge and snatched out a can of Mountain Dew.

Seeing the can made me stop talking almost immediately. Kandy had brought the sodas over and left them here.

"What? You wanted this? It was the last one," Lora said, eyes wide.

"No. Keep it. It's fine." I straightened my back and tried brushing off the memories of Kandy, but the smile she always gave me when she took her first sip of soda, claiming the first sip was always the best, played like a movie in my head.

I pulled myself out of it though, focusing instead on Lora as she cracked the can open and took a few swift chugs. "You two were about to get married, right?" I asked, keeping my voice level.

"Yeah, well the wedding is off now. The fucker got caught and was arrested for possession of cocaine. He's a fucking idiot. They searched the car, found coke under the hood." She sighed, and even though she tried to remain defiant, I could also see the glisten in her eyes, like her heart was broken. "He's doing serious time, Cane," she said, staring me in the eyes. "He told me they're talking fifteen to sixteen years max if he pleads guilty."

"Shit." I walked around the counter, pressing my back against the edge of it and focusing on the wall across from me. "Is that why you're here? You want me to send a lawyer to get him a shorter sentence?"

"What?" she spat, narrowing her eyes up at me. "No! What the fuck? Why would I fly all the way here when I could have just called and asked you that, you fucking idiot!"

"I'm just asking, Lora!" I threw my hands in the air. "No need to be so upset. Shit happens and I'm here to help...though not always for Aaron."

She placed her soda on the countertop behind her, then rested her lower back on the edge like I did. "Doesn't matter if you send one or not, he's out of luck. Aaron has had too many slip ups. He's gotten rusty. When you dropped out, he got worse at it, Cane. He had no guidance or anyone to tell him if something was stupid. That's why he was so pissed. He didn't know what to do and had too much pride to ask for your help. And you remember when he did ask you for a favor? You turned him down."

"Because I had to, Lora. I didn't have a choice. You know how bad that would have made me look with Aaron as an employee of my company? He had a bad background. He was arrested too many times and the background checks are heavy. Not to mention, Aaron was trying to get one of our highest paying positions. I couldn't have it. That would have left me sunk and I've worked too hard to build Tempt to lose it over his terrible reputation."

She rolled her eyes, but didn't respond to it because she knew I was right. Aaron was smart, but only street smart. He had no manners whatsoever, but I couldn't blame him with the way he was raised. He had a similar past to mine when it came to his parents, only his father wasn't physically abusive. Only mentally.

He would have been a major liability and because of that, I refused to let him be an employee. I did tell him he could be a driver for Lora and myself if I needed one, but he told me to fuck off. That was two years ago and Lora had resented me for it ever since. She said that it wouldn't only be helping him, but her as well. And that's when I gave her the ultimatum: if she left him, I would give her a great job that paid well, but Lora had too much of a free spirit. She didn't want to work. All she wanted to do was chase thrills and shop and sleep. To put it simply, she was a lazy twenty-eight year old.

Because I wouldn't hire her fiancé for a *real* job, she stopped talking to me. Stopped calling and refused to answer my calls or texts—said they'd make it on their own without me. Eventually, it got so bad that I flew out there, only for her to tell me to my face that she never wanted to speak to me again unless I was dying or unless I gave Aaron a real job with Tempt. In the building and all. Neither happened, obviously.

I looked up, and Lora's eyes were focused on the plastic bracelet around my wrist. "Why do you have a hospital band on? Is something wrong?" Her eyes were serious now and she searched my face and looked me all over, like she was looking for signs of sickness or disease.

"Oh. I don't know," I sighed. "I don't wanna talk about that shit right now."

"Well, make it quick! What is it? Are you sick? Is it AIDS? You have fucked a lot of random bitches, like that dumb one Juni, who would sleep with anyone—"

"No. No." I shook my head. "It's...a long story."

"Well—" she threw her hands in the air, "—I have nothing but time, Brother. What the hell happened to you? You look like a bulldozer hit you."

My lips pressed together as I glared at the band. Why hadn't I cut this shit off already? Was it because I wanted to be reminded of how badly I'd fucked things up?

I met her eyes. "You remember my friend Derek?"

"Yeah, D? The cop who helped Mama?"

"Yeah, him."

"What about him?"

"He...found something out about me and didn't like it. Punched me so hard I hit the ground and got a mild concussion."

"What? Are you serious right now?" she gasped. "Is that why you have the black eye?"

I nodded, then shrugged.

"Well, what the hell could you have done to make him do that? He seemed like such a nice guy and he looked after you a lot!"

I debated whether or not to tell her, but then I thought about Kelly, and how I was certain she would show up and pour it all on the table, leaving me to look like a fucking fool. "I slept with his daughter."

She frowned so hard her brows stitched together. "You did *what?*"

I looked away—anywhere but at her. "Q—" she gasped. "How old is his daughter?"

"She turns nineteen in September."

"You slept with an *eighteen-year-old girl?* Oh my fucking gosh, you really can't keep your dick in your pants, can you?"

"It's not what you think, all right? I...cared about that girl. I didn't come onto her and I didn't force her into anything. It just fucking happened and don't ask me how. It's hard to explain it all. It still blows my mind when I think about it sometimes, but it happened. Can't deny it."

Lora looked me over twice, her head going into a slight tilt. She pressed her lips and did the thing that used to annoy me most. Just stared—stared like she could read me like a book and knew my deepest, darkest secrets. Truthfully, she was one of the few who knew the most about me.

"You *love* her." It was a statement, not a question.

Knowing they would have been a dead giveaway, I snatched my eyes away.

"Wow, Q. I... I mean...*wow*."

"What?" I mumbled, finally meeting her gaze.

"Nothing...it's just...I've never seen this kind of love on you. It's...*weird*." She lowered her line of vision, focusing on the bracelet again. "How did her dad find out?"

"By a conniving bitch, who still happens to be in the picture."

"What?" she scoffed. "Why would you still have her in the picture?"

"She knows too much about me—about us, Lora. She's threatening my company, but I'm working on a way out of it."

"Fuck, Q. We stop talking for, like, two years and your life goes to shit. I guess you can't live without me, huh?" She was teasing, but her smile didn't touch her eyes. There was no spark in them, no humor. They were dull, and in the depths of those cloudy irises, I could tell she was crying for help. She wasn't just here to tell me what had happened to Aaron. Like she said, she could have called for that.

Lora rubbed her arm, staring at the floor again.

"If you're not here for Aaron, then what's going on with you? Must be serious for you to call *and* show up at my place around the same time."

Her eyes flashed up to mine and I swear her face had paled.

She ran a hand up and down the back of her arm, over the tattoo she'd gotten to cover one of her worst scars caused by a cigarette burn.

"I—I talked to Mom the other day," she said, avoiding my eyes. "She sounded a lot better." She took a lengthy pause. "She also mentioned that she'd gotten a letter in the mail."

"From who?"

Lora's eyes swooped up to mine, and in them I saw panic and worry swirling like never before. "From Buck," she answered, and my fists immediately clenched. "Mom has been writing him, Q. She initiated it. She was dumb enough to believe his lies and to think he was getting better, so she sent him my address because he wanted to 'check on me', and then I get this." She pulled out a piece of folded paper from the pocket of her jean jacket, handing it to me.

I opened it up rapidly, and while reading every word, fury burned at my fingertips.

Hey, bitch. I don't have much to say to you. Your mother told me all about how you're still with some fucked up drug dealer, and since I can't seem to get your worthless brother to take me seriously or get him to respond to my letters, I thought you could deliver a little message to him for me.

Do me a favor and tell your piece-of-shit brother that I'm coming for him and my million-dollar company. Tell him to be ready, because I ain't backing down without a fight.

Your favorite man, Buck

I picked my head up, staring at her, lips parted. "This is real?" I rasped.

She nodded. It was all she could do.

"Fuck," I muttered.

"That's not the only thing," she murmured, focusing on the

paper I had clutched in hand. "Mama told me that since the jail he's in is overcrowded and he's been out of trouble in there, he's getting released in four to five months."

"What?" I barked. "Are you fucking kidding me? I'm in the same fucking state as she is and she couldn't tell me that shit?"

"You know why she didn't tell you, Cane. She knows how you would have reacted, especially with her writing to him!"

"That's bullshit! He needs to be in there for fucking life after what he did to us! To *her*! How could she fall for his shit?"

"I know," she mumbled. "And I really came because Aaron isn't around, which means his people aren't around to look out for me. I have no one to watch my back there. I—I couldn't fucking sleep. I was so worried Buck would come looking for me first or I—I don't know. I'm freaking the fuck out, Q, and right now you're all I've got."

I sighed, pinching the bridge of my nose. "Fuck. I know, I know. You did the right thing by coming here."

Her shoulders relaxed and I pushed off the counter to place a hand on her shoulder. "Take your stuff upstairs to one of the guest rooms. We're going to visit Mama tomorrow. She has some serious explaining to do."

"But what about Tempt? You read the letter right? He's coming after it. You've worked hard on it, Cane, but if Buck comes out and starts telling people it was his—"

"He can say whatever the hell he wants, Lora. I have lawyers. Heavy hitters too. He won't be able to come near us."

She pressed her lips, like she was highly doubtful. See, that was the thing about Lora. She always doubted me until I proved myself. I don't know why she was that way. Everything she'd asked for, I'd done, other than give her ex-fiancé a job at my company.

When she needed a car, I bought it. When she was tired of seeing Mom laying face flat in her own puke, I was the one who took Mama to rehab and paid them twice, while getting her to agree to stay.

I guess doubt was what kept her on her toes. Doubt was what made Lora, *Lora*. Like miracles, she didn't believe in them unless she could see one happen for herself, and sadly a miracle had never happened for my little sister.

CHAPTER FOURTEEN

KANDY

I'd caved. Like, truly, honestly caved.
 I couldn't even go three measly days without giving in.
 Don't get me wrong, I had a great third day. My new friends gave me a tour around campus and let me come to the mall with them for smoothies. Morgan and Gina were great girls with big hearts and I loved that...but something was still missing.
 Morgan and Gina decided to hit the field again after our smoothie run. They were rebels that way. They'd told me that the fields were still under maintenance and that they weren't supposed to be on them, but of course they didn't give a damn. I warned them not to get caught, especially by the snobby teammates who would snitch in a heartbeat.
 I had yet to see Coach Carmen or Coach Tally, then again their offices were way across campus and meetings weren't starting until next week. For all I knew, they probably weren't even here yet. If they were, I was certain they'd have come to greet us at the least.

I sat on top of my bed and pulled out my laptop, lifting the lid and going to the search engine. I searched for Tempt, something I'd promised myself I wouldn't do, and a few articles popped up, all of them with split candid photos of Cane and a heavyset Asian man. All of the red and yellow made it clear the articles were important and yielded warnings. I clicked the first one:

Tempts very own Quinton Cane blows big deal with big-time Tokyo investor, Mao Zheng.

The article went on to report how Cane's party led to a disaster. A few anonymous guests reported that a man had shown up at Cane's house with a temper and threatened and assaulted Cane, and when Zheng was asked how he felt about the night, he told the media that he would never invest in a man who dealt with ruthless people like the one who'd assaulted Cane at the party. It also went on to say that the man who'd threatened Cane was toting a gun and had even pointed it at Cane, and that they seemed *familiar* with one another.

Wait…*a gun?* I couldn't believe what I was reading. Mom didn't say anything about a gun. The man with the gun was Dad, but… why would he do that to Cane? Bring a gun *and* point it at him too? Was he really going to kill him that night? What the hell was Dad thinking?

My first instinct was to call Dad and blast him. Literally yell at him for being so reckless, no matter how bad the situation was. He handled it improperly and jeopardized Cane's business. Because of this, so many others probably felt the same as Zheng and were thinking of backing out of contracts too. He'd truly put Cane's company on the line, and all because of his horrible temper.

I advised myself against it, though, and climbed off the bed with my cellphone. I wanted to call and ask Dad what all had happened that night and what all was said. Yes, I knew Dad had assaulted Cane, but I didn't know a *gun* had been brought into the mix. I had reason to believe Mom didn't tell me that detail for a reason.

No wonder Cane hadn't called me. He was probably too wrapped up in the scandal and getting his company out of the flames to bother.

I hated that thought and needed to know he was okay, so without mentally preparing myself for what I did next, I went to my call log, found his name, and called him.

CHAPTER FIFTEEN

KANDY

It took everything in me not to hang up after the first ring.

I didn't even know what I would say to him after what he'd gone through. What do you say when your own father threatens a man you slept with, with a gun? How do you help him overlook that and accept you, without that horrible memory coming into play?

The phone rang several times and defeat washed through me when I got his voicemail. I hung up before the beep, a sigh pushing through my lips. Of course he wasn't going to answer. He was probably knee deep in work shit, trying to dig himself out of a hole.

I was the reason all of this had happened. If only I'd kept my hands to myself, he would be fine now. I closed my laptop, slid it back in the case, and then grabbed the room key, locking it up before walking down the hallway.

I needed fresh air, and the weather was pleasant, so I took a trail that wasn't too far off campus. On the trail, green and yellow leaves were scattered on the ground. The trees were covered in moss and snaked with green vines. This was way different to Georgia. Everything was fresh and real here. I had my phone clutched in hand, praying he would call back during the walk.

When I'd reached a bench on the path, my phone vibrated and I jumped, like it'd shocked me. I checked the screen and my heart immediately stated racing when I saw his name.

Suddenly, I felt like it would have been dumb of me to answer. Why put myself through this? Why bother, when it would only lead to nowhere? He was over ten hours away—miles apart with nothing to really pull us together again. Surely, nothing would come of this.

Despite the back and forth matters in my head, I lifted the phone and answered. I took a seat on the bench, worried my knees would buckle from the sound of his voice. My pulse thundered in my ears, my heart jumping to my throat.

"Hello?" I answered.

A sigh. "Kandy." He breathed out, and even from miles away, I could sense the relief washing through him. "How've you been?"

I looked down. "Good, I guess. And you?"

"Could be better."

I smiled a little. Vague, but I could understand where he was coming from.

"How was the move in? College life treating you well so far?"

"I've made two friends already, so I think so. They're on the softball team. We agree on a lot of things. One of them is my roommate."

"Oh, well that's good, right?"

"Yeah, she's a pretty cool person."

We were quiet a moment, and as I sat there with a bouncing knee, I let all of my worries sink in.

"I'm happy you called," he'd finally said, and my worries hit the back burner.

"I'm happy you called back. I didn't think you would."

"Why wouldn't I?"

"I don't know. After what happened, I—I assumed you would stay away. Never look back..."

He let out a tattered breath. "You know damn well I can't stay away from you. I made a promise to you. Do you remember?"

"What promise?"

"That I wouldn't avoid or ignore you. You said that things would change, but to not let it be for the worse. You remember that?"

Oh, yeah. That's right. I asked him to promise me at the lake house. I was surprised he'd remembered. "I remember," I said softly.

"I'm trying to fulfill at least one of my promises."

"I'm glad," I murmured, and I really was, though I knew he was hurting. He'd promised my dad a great deal of things. He'd betrayed him, and I knew that alone was eating him alive.

"Sir, here is the paperwork you were asking for," I heard someone say in the background. I knew that voice. It was Cora. He was at work.

"Thanks," he mumbled.

"You're working late," I noted.

"Yeah. A lot to catch up on."

We were quiet a beat. I could hear paper rustling and a scratching noise, like he was signing off on them. "You know, I met Cora that night...when my dad confronted you?" I told him.

"You know about that, huh?" he asked with an uneasy laugh. He was trying to keep the conversation light but that was going to be damn near impossible. This conversation felt thick and heavy and not at all like us. He went on. "How did you meet her?"

"I drove to your house to check on you. She's the one who told me you were in the hospital."

"Really?" He seemed surprised. So surprised that I no longer heard the paper rustling or the scratching of a pen. "Hmm. She hasn't said anything to me about it."

"She also told me that your girlfriend, *Kelly*, wanted to ride alone with you on the way there."

Cane gave a bitter laugh. "Kelly is a bitch. Fuck her. "

"I sent you a text that night too," I went on, before he could rant. "She responded and told me to leave you alone."

"She did what?" he snapped.

I closed my eyes and swallowed the bile building up in my throat. "She told me not to make things worse than they already were."

"Are you fucking kidding me? I swear, I am so fucking sick of her!"

"How?" I asked, opening my eyes. "I'd really like to know how? What does she have on you that is so big that you can't just kick her out of your life already? I know about your mom and how she was in rehab, but you can't control your mom's actions, Cane. People will understand!"

"It's not that simple," he ground out, teeth probably clenched as he spoke. "I...*fuck*, Kandy. I've got shit on me. Shit that she knows about. And there is so much happening here and all of it is coming at me at once, and then that bitch wants to throw this shit in my face."

"Throw *what* in your face?" I demanded.

Silence poured through the line. "I want to tell you, Kandy, but I can't talk about it on the phone." He breathed hard. "Listen...I have to go. I have a teleconference in ten minutes. I saw your call and wanted to return it while I had a little free time."

Well, thanks for that, I wanted to say. This conversation went nowhere. I knew I shouldn't have answered the phone.

"Sure, yeah," I muttered. "I understand."

"Don't do that please," he pleaded. "I want to talk more, but my plate is full right now, Kandy. I swear."

I bit my bottom lip, fighting emotion.

"Call me if you need anything. You know I'm here."

"I will," I said, but deep down, it felt like a lie. Would I call him again? And for what? Just to talk about Kelly? The past? How much my dad has probably fucked up his life, all because of me? On the phone with him, it felt like the passion had faded and I hated it. I hated it so much.

Tears burned the rims of my eyes, but I bit them back.

"Talk to you later," he said softly.

"Later." My voice broke, but I hung up before he could say anything else. I shut my eyes, ignoring the fire behind my eyelids, breathing in and out repeatedly until I felt stable enough to open my eyes.

I had two choices. I could either sit on the bench and pathetically cry into my own hands, or go and find Morgan and Gina and pretend the call I had with Cane never happened.

My feet moved before my heart could decide for me.

CHAPTER SIXTEEN

CANE

Here I was again.

Back at Polly Heights Rehabilitation Center.

I hated this place. I'd lost count of how many times I'd come here to visit my mother. Last year, after several attempts of begging and bribing her with better things for her future, she'd checked in twice. This year, only once, but she'd been inside for a while now. Five months to be exact. In one month, she would be out, and I prayed she wouldn't resort to the old shit. Change is hard to come by, but my mother could do it. She wasn't the strongest, but she was resilient.

Lora and I were seated at one of the cafeteria tables, the blue chair beneath me too damn hard to get comfortable in. Lora flipped through a magazine, legs crossed, chomping on a wad of gum. The gum chewing was a nervous habit. She was pretending to be okay with being there, but I knew she was nervous to see Mama again after so much time apart. She hadn't seen her in over two years.

"How the hell is anyone supposed to get comfortable waiting in here," Lora grumbled, slapping the magazine shut. "The coffee is fucking cold and they're out of cinnamon rolls." She pulled her gum out of her mouth, stamping it down on the magazine with the pad of her thumb.

I sighed and flipped my wrist to check the time. "She should be coming out any minute now."

Several minutes later, the double doors buzzed and they automatically opened. Several of the patients scurried into the visitation room, some of them a little too jumpy and some of them seeming too sluggish to function, most likely from the meds.

They met up at the tables with their loving visitors, some smiling, some frustrated, others looking as if they had no clue what was going on. Several more trickled in, and that's when I saw Mama.

I'm sure my eyes were as wide as saucers. "Shit."

"Shit is right," Lora breathed.

Mama walked into the room without so much as a fidget or a scratch, staring right at us with a bold, white smile—a smile I hadn't seen her wear in years. I saw this smile often when she was sober—back when her life was content and peaceful without Buck in it.

The sight of it made my stomach flip, the memories of the good old days hitting me hard. I remembered when it was only the three of us in a two-bedroom apartment. Mama would make pancakes and cut up some fresh fruit every Sunday before she went in to work, and Lora and me would hang out at the pool, or at Killian's unauthorized tattoo parlor in his garage down the street.

She was sober for three years straight back then. Not a drop of liquor, not a sniff of coke, not a shot of heroin. There was no Buck, only us. Though she'd worked several jobs, she still smiled and had fun. She lived her life. She took care of us…then he came back and ruined everything. He was always coming and going.

The longest he'd stayed away was those three years. I never understood why he returned.

"Oh my goodness," Mama cooed when she met up to the other side of the table, her eyes fixed on Lora.

Lora and I stood. Putting on a coy smile, Lora said, "Hi, Mama."

"Nah-uh. Don't do that." Mama hurried around the table, her arms spread wide. "Get over here, baby. Come hug me!"

Lora pushed her chair back with the backs of her legs, walking straight into Mama's arms. They hugged for a long time, making up for the two-year absence. "Look at you," Mama sighed. "Still so beautiful. And I love this hair color on you! My baby girl!" she cooed, pressing her cheek to Lora's. "I've missed you so much!" She kissed Lora on the forehead and Lora laughed.

"Mama!" she said, fighting laughter. "Chill! It wasn't even that long!"

"It was two years, Lora. Too long for you to be away from me. I at least hope the guy who stole you away from us treated you good."

Lora sighed and shrugged, and she was lucky Mama let it go. I could tell Lora wasn't in the mood to talk about Aaron.

Mama's eyes pinned me next and she came in for a hug. I held her tight, and was glad her hair smelled like the honey and vanilla shampoo she'd asked me to send during the last visit. She was keeping herself up, like she'd promised last time. Her hair was brushed and she even had makeup on. Only mascara, but it was a start.

"You look good, Ma," I told her. "I'm glad to see you like this."

"Well, you know, I try," she teased with a grin. "One of the girls here, Carrie, takes real good care of me. She found out about my birthday when you last visited and bought me some of my favorite makeup the next day. She wasn't supposed to, but she painted my nails and even did a little makeover on me. She just transferred from another clinic. Such a nice girl."

"Good. I'm glad they're treating you well."

We all sat, Mom taking the seat beside Lora while I took the one across from them.

"So, how's everything been?" Lora asked, a hand under her chin, unable to fight her smile.

"Oh, so good, baby. I know I always say this, but I think this is it. Really, really it. No more fooling around. I'm ready to live my life and make a fresh start with my kids."

Lora pursed her lips, giving her a suspicious look. "You aren't just saying that because Buck is getting out soon, are you?"

Mama's eyes widened. "What? No! I really want to do this for myself." She looked from Lora to me, like she was really trying to prove a point, but even I had my doubts. I kept my lips shut, though.

"Well, in case you even try to consider it, I want you to read this. Maybe it'll make you think twice before caving this time." Lora pulled out the folded letter that was now crumpled around the edges, sliding it toward her on top of the table.

Mama glanced sideways at Lora, eyes burning with curiosity, before picking it up and reading it. Her eyes moved quick, and with each line read, they filled with a familiar horror.

Her throat bobbed as she folded the sheet of paper and placed it down on the table again. "I thought he was getting better too."

"He's never going to get better," I muttered, and she peered up at me, eyes glistening. "Ma, he's a worthless piece of shit. He doesn't care about us. He never has. You read the letter. He's trying to come for Tempt when he's out."

She dropped her head.

"I won't let him mess with my company," I went on. "I have worked too hard to let him ruin things. The only way he won't be able to get close is if you keep your distance. Lay low, ignore his letters, and forget he ever existed."

"He's your father, Quinton," Mama pleaded. "That's a lot easier said than done."

BREAKING MR. CANE

"No. That's where you're wrong. He is not a father. A real father wouldn't be out to hurt his children or tarnish their career. A father wouldn't have beaten his own son to a pulp at the age of ten because he forgot to bring home a carton of milk." The thought of it made me clench my fist on top of the wooden table, but I didn't stop. She needed to hear this. I'd hidden a lot of things from my mother for the sake of her sanity and happiness, but enough was enough. I would do whatever I needed to do, say whatever needed to be said, in order for her to stay away from that conniving prick. "A real father, wouldn't have tried to come onto his own *daughter* while you weren't around."

Through the corner of my eye, I saw Lora flinch. "Q," she warned.

"No, Lora, she needs to hear this shit. She always runs back to him, no matter what he's done or how badly he beats her. It has to fucking stop."

"Lora," Mama gasped, a trembling hand covering her lips. "Is that true?"

Lora shook her head and bit her bottom lip, fighting the tears.

"Why didn't you tell me? Why wait so many years later?" Mom demanded.

"Because you wouldn't have believed me, Mama!" Lora barked. A few people looked our way, but prying eyes weren't going to stop my sister from finally confessing the truth. During the ride here, Lora and I both agreed that we would let Mama know about it, no matter how bad it got. Lora tried to hide it from her, but it was time. Mama loved Lora to death, and even we knew that Buck coming onto her would have been crossing the line for Mama. "You were always too high or drunk to ever do anything about it anyway, Ma!"

Mama flinched and as she stared into her eyes, Lora's softened to match. Sighing, Lora lowered her gaze to the magazine instead.

"He never got farther than groping and grabbing," she went on. "Q was there to stop it every time—he refused to leave me there alone for long with Buck around—but you know how Buck was. When Q interfered, he got frustrated and took his anger out on him, pissed that he couldn't touch me and get away with it like he wanted."

I looked down.

"Lora," Mom whimpered, reaching for her hand. "I promise I'm not like that anymore and I will not let it happen again. I want to do better, not only for myself, but for my kids too. I love you both so, so much and I know I haven't been the best mother but..." Her voice shook, thick with emotion. "But I want to try to be the best I can be now."

"Then prove it," Lora snapped, pulling her hand away. "When you get out of here, prove to us that you've left all of that shit behind, including Buck. Don't call him, don't write him anymore stupid fucking letters—hell, don't even *think* about him. He's no good for you. He's never been any good for you or any of us and you know it."

Mom bobbed her head eagerly. "I can do that. I promise. Just—just give me a chance to start fresh so I can be there for you both. Something stable is normally required for when I check out of the clinic."

"Yes, and you'll have that and more," I assured her. "But we mean this, Mama." I reached across the table, grabbing her hand and squeezing it. "You can't talk to him anymore. No more letters. When you get out, I'll move you two to a safe location where he'll never find you. You'll have a nice place with a big kitchen you can bake in and a big, comfortable bed to sleep in. You'll get whatever you want...just promise to actually *try* for us. Just this once. Okay?"

She shut her eyes for a brief moment and nodded. "I can do that," she murmured, eyes peeling open to focus on me. "I will do better. I promise."

"Good."

"What will you do about the company?" she asked. "I'm sure he knows where the building is. He can walk right in there."

"Yeah, I know he knows. That's why I'll amp up the security and have his face plastered all over the place so everyone knows not to trust him or let him in. He won't set foot into my building or anywhere near my house without my knowledge. I'll contact my attorney and have a restraining order filed for all three of us as well. We all know he won't give a damn about the order or causing a scene so if I see him anywhere, I'll handle him myself. He doesn't scare me." My jaw clenched. "Not anymore."

They both nodded, and when Mama smiled and Lora took her hand and squeezed it too, I had hope we would be on the same accord again.

Together, we could be unstoppable. We could do anything. But first, we had to set ourselves free.

Free of the past. Free of the drugs. Free of everything that held us back.

We had to do what was right for our family to thrive, and that was making sure Buck never fucked with us again.

CHAPTER SEVENTEEN

KANDY

Three days sluggishly went by and not a text or call from Cane. Not that I was expecting him to call me again anytime soon, and it wasn't like the phone didn't work both ways, but, I was hopeful, proceeding with giving him the benefit of the doubt.

He's busy, I reminded myself.

Somehow, in my fucked up head, I thought that taking a walk on the trail would be my good luck charm. Maybe he'd call me while I was walking it, interrupt me with a shock like last time.

I walked the trail, much longer this time than last.

Not one call.

Not one text.

Seriously, what was I hoping for?

Before I knew it, the trail had ended and I was greeted with a different part of the school campus. The grass was manicured and smelled sweet. Brick pavements and cement sidewalks led to every which way, tall buildings built so high I had to pick my head up to take it all in, even from my lengthy distance away.

The bass of music caught my attention and I turned my head to find the noise. There was a parking lot less than a yard away. Several cars were there, as well as a group of young people. Some of the guys were shirtless, the girls in belly shirts, really short shorts, or both. Some of them had blankets spread out on the grass nearby, bathing in the sun.

Being nosy, I walked a little closer to get a better view. They mostly looked like upperclassmen. Normally, I would have walked the opposite direction of a crowd like theirs, but there was something about this one that intrigued me.

From my distance, I assumed they were athletes, by their toned builds and easygoing demeanors, but they weren't boisterous or obnoxious. They appeared to be having fun, but were subtle about it. The music wasn't so loud that they couldn't hold a conversation. Though most of them were half-naked, everyone appeared comfortable with the next person. Now that I could really hear it, the music wasn't even party music. It was more like soulful lounge music.

"Hey! You gonna join the group or are you just gonna to stand here and watch?" A deep voice spilled over my shoulder and I gasped, spinning around to face him. A boy, tall and broad and chiseled, gave me one of the whitest, straightest smiles I'd ever seen as I clutched my chest. He threw his hands up in the air almost immediately, saying, "Whoa—sorry! I didn't mean to scare you!"

"Uh—no, no. It's okay." I waved my hands. "Just wasn't expecting your voice."

"My voice?" He smiled, and when he did, the middle of his cheek sank, creating a deep dimple on his smooth umber skin.

"Yeah, sorry. That was dumb to say," I laughed. "I just—I meant that I wasn't expecting anyone to say anything to me at all."

"Head in the clouds, I presume?" His easy smile transformed to a smirk.

"You could say that." Honestly, he had no idea. It wasn't that my head was in the clouds. It was more like my mind was back at home, reminiscing about things that would never happen again.

I looked toward the party, watching as they all sipped from brown cups with green labels on them. "That doesn't seem like the typical college party."

"Oh, it's not. It's not a party at all, actually." He took a step closer, and even with the several inches between us, I could feel his body heat. "It's a mindfulness and peace gathering. Ever heard of that?"

"Um...no, not at all," I replied with a giggle, but he didn't laugh with me, which made me feel stupid. "Shit, that was rude. I'm sorry."

He finally laughed, and it was gruff and deep, creating a stir inside me that I wasn't so sure I liked. "Nah, don't be. You'd be surprised by the funny looks I get when I tell people about it." He tucked the tips of his fingers into the front pocket of his jeans. "Its called MPA, which means Mindful Peaceful Athletes. This group started about two years ago. A bunch of the athletes were having the same issues and felt overwhelmed and stressed with juggling academics and sports in their schedules, plus all the traveling and what not. So a chick named Frida Gonzalez, who was a kick-ass volleyball player here, decided to create this new wave. Every Wednesday night, after practice, all of the student athletes who felt overwhelmed or were seeking an escape, would meet in this parking lot, have a sip of this amazing herbal tea her mom would send—because her mom is totally into all that herbal wellness stuff—and we'd do homework on the grass some nights, help each other out if we had the same assignments, or just meditate. Only requirement is bringing your own blanket. Grass gets a little itchy."

"Wow, that sounds really nice."

"Yeah. When I first came, I wasn't all that into it, but my roommate dragged me to it, told me I would really benefit from it. Didn't turn out so bad. I actually enjoy coming now and I have

BREAKING MR. CANE

benefited. It's little escape for all of us. We work so hard, but being there almost takes away the stress."

"So they're drinking tea in those cups? Not alcohol?"

"Yep, tea," he laughed. "Frida gave a few of the MPA coaches the ingredients. They make the recipe overnight and bring it. It supposedly reduces stress, removes tension from the muscles, and calms the mind. And it doesn't taste too bad either." He turned to look at me, his whiskey eyes sparkling from the sun. "You an athlete?"

"Yeah. I play softball. Only here for a one-year ride, though."

"Hey—and that's perfectly okay! Notre Dame is tough to get into as it is. I'm Brody, by the way. Brody Hawks. Junior, and Linebacker for the big ND!" He extended an arm.

"I'm Kandy. Kandy Jennings. Pitcher for the *big ND*," I laughed and he laughed with me while we shook hands. At least he wasn't making this awkward.

"Well, it's nice to meet you, Kandy Jennings. Takes some getting used to with all the rules they have here, but I think you'll love it." His smile was warm and made me feel at ease. "You should join the meeting. It's not an official one, just a little get-together, but it'll be a good way to meet new people."

"Oh, I don't know. I don't want to interrupt. It seems like you guys already have the party going and everything."

"Stop. Come on. Seriously, there is plenty of tea and cups to go around. It's always nice to have more people." He started to walk toward the party, glancing over his shoulder once with bright eyes and a pleading smile—a smile that was impossible to say no to.

Though my shoes felt like they'd been pumped with lead, I followed him toward the parking lot. The music became louder, and I don't know if it was a sign from above, or just the right timing, but when a song by Khalid came on, I figured this was where I needed to be. Surrounded by a group of people with great taste in music.

"Hey, guys!" Brody called with his hands cupped around his

mouth. He had climbed onto the bed of one of the pick up trucks. Everyone looked up at him, but a few of them locked their eyes on me, probably realizing they'd never seen me before. "I think I have a new recruit!" He turned around to lower the volume of the music, then he faced me, extending an arm and offering a hand. I placed mine in his, my heart clamoring, mind rattling. *This is so fucking crazy.*

"This is Kandy Jennings. She's a new student athlete here. A pitcher for our softball team and she's super interested in MPA!"

Everyone cheered and hooted and hollered and I couldn't help myself. I blushed, but made sure to wave to let them know that this group had indeed intrigued me.

Brody wrapped an arm around my shoulder and pulled me into him. The contact had thrown me for a loop and as badly as I wanted to push away, I didn't. For one, he smelled nice. Really, really nice. And two, he was kind and had welcomed me in with open arms. It would have been absolutely rude of me to shove him off.

His smell was different than Cane's. Where Cane's was manly and crisp, Brody's was earthy and ripe, like he'd just hit his peak of becoming a man. He had the kind of musk that could drive a woman crazy—a scent only an athletic guy could pull off and make sexy.

"Welcome, Kandy!" One of the girls up front yelled.

"See—told you it'd be cool." Brody finally pulled his arm away, and the lost weight made me feel too vulnerable.

Right now, he was my MPA guide. I didn't want to be left alone in this pool of athletes, though they all seemed pretty nice. I was fresh meat, easy to rope in and demolish. Brody hopped off the truck and I sat first before climbing off.

A girl met up with us. Her hair was blond and bouncy and her smile was wide. "Hey, I'm Lidia, one of the coaches. It's really nice to have you, Kandy." She handed me one of the brown cups. "The tea is really good, but if you wanna add a little honey, I have some in my car. Just let me know."

"Thank you." I smiled at her then sipped the tea. Brody's eyes expanded when I swung mine over to him, like he was waiting for me to tell him how it was.

"Well?" he mused.

"You were right. It is pretty good."

"See! Good! I think she's good on the honey, Lidia. Thanks," Brody said.

"Cool!" Lidia walked off and returned to the group of people standing by a red pick-up truck. I noticed she was standing with a girl who had a pink cast on her arm. I knew exactly who she was without having to take a guess. I'd seen many pictures of her when I searched for Notre Dame softball.

Sophie Banks. She looked at me with a light scowl, like she knew who I was too. The volume of the music was turned back up again and I looked away, toward the speaker.

Some of the athletes started dancing. Since school hadn't started yet and some of them were probably only getting into conditioning, there wasn't much to talk about academically, other than majors and classes. Dancing and head-bobbing felt like the right thing to do.

"So how is the meditating performed?" I asked Brody, who had been lightly bobbing his head to a song by Miguel.

"Oh! Okay, so we choose a partner or two, take a few blankets to the grass over there, and we ask a few of the questions from the prompts the coaches type up. Sometimes we ask things like, 'was your day okay?' and then follow up with 'how could it have been better?' if someone has had a bad or negative day. At first it's weird asking the questions and answering them, but you get used to it. Plus the questions they tell us to ask always lead to genuine conversations. We switch partners every meeting, that way we can get to know someone new. Honestly though, most of us stick with the people we connect to the most. It's easier that way, when the person actually knows what you're going through and can comment on it. It feels great to get certain things off your chest."

"Wow. This group seems very relaxing—like a breath of fresh air."

"Oh, it is. Trust me. And it changes you. Believe it or not, I used to be this big, dumb jock who thought football was life."

I cocked my brow and smirked, giving him a *yeah, right* look.

"What?" he laughed, hands in the air. "Okay, I might still be a bit of a jock who still thinks football is life, but I'm a jock who is much more aware of my surroundings. If someone is having a bad day, I can tell and I try to reach out to let them know there's always a helping hand." He paused for a moment, watching as I sipped my tea. "Like you…I noticed your slumped shoulders, your sad eyes—the hints the MPA coaches tell us to look out for in another athlete or student."

I tried not to frown when he said that. "What do you mean by that?" I asked a little too softly.

"I could tell something was wrong. For one, you were walking alone and when I first spotted you, your head was hung low. You looked upset and kind of anxious."

I wanted to smile and wave it off, but I couldn't. There was a reason for that—a reason I refused to share with a guy I'd just met. "It was nothing, really. I'm just adjusting to this new life of mine. I'm miles away from my family. It's scary, but refreshing all the same."

"Where are you from?" he inquired.

"Decatur, Georgia. What about you?"

"Katy, Texas."

"Oh, wow. Long way!"

"Yep." He took a step backward. "I understand what you mean about it being scary and refreshing, especially when you have a family that loves you a lot."

"Yeah. Exactly that."

The song changed and one of the coaches announced that we'd

be wrapping up and meeting again next week. They collected all of the plastic cups from us, several of the athletes chugging theirs down before adding to the stack. A couple students left the scene, Sophie Banks included, and since they were leaving, I decided to walk off too.

"Which building are you in?" Brody asked, catching up to me.

"Oh, umm, Providence Hall."

"How's your roommate?"

"She's really cool. She plays softball as well. Outfielder."

"Damn. You are a lucky one. Joining MPA on the first few days *and* having a cool roommate. No one's ever that lucky as a freshman. Maybe I need to stick by your side, hope some of that lucky dust rubs off on me for the season."

I fought a grin. He was flirting, that much was clear. He'd been flirting since the first question he asked over my shoulder. The funny thing was he *didn't* suck at it, like most guys did. Brody Hawks was a smooth talker and very charming.

"Do you do this to all the freshmen girls you meet?" I asked, slowing my pace.

"Do what?" His brows dipped, like he was truly curious.

"Flirt with them? Make them feel cool and secure? Because that would be a good way to bag a girl, especially a freshman. See a new girl wandering around, assume she's a freshman, and then try to add her to your collection."

His head tipped back as he broke out in a laugh, and his throat was long and smooth and...attractive. How the hell could a throat be so attractive? Why was I so damn attracted to this guy?

"I mean, I apologize for the flirting, but it's not every day I see a freshman that looks like *you*."

I blushed. God, I hated blushing. I wished my hair was down so I could hide my face behind some of it. He noticed and his smile continued.

"That's probably another one of the lines you use on the new girls on campus. Hey, we're easy targets! I get it, man."

"Would you stop?" He fought a grin, head shaking. "It's really not like that, I swear. I mean, do I find you attractive? Yes. You got me there. But that isn't the only reason I came to speak. You looked like you needed a friend...or maybe just an escape from what was going on inside your own head. I remember how tough it was when I first got here. I missed my family like crazy. I wanted to make new friends, find things to do that actually interested me. I'm just here as a helping hand."

"Well, I appreciate that, Brody. It was really sweet of you."

"Of course, but since you think I'm trying to make a score on you, maybe I should ask before we keep walking. Would you like me to walk you back to your side of campus?"

I giggled. "No, I should be okay from here, but thanks for the offer."

"Cool. No pressure." He threw his hands in the air again with a charming smile, a guilt-free gesture. "Maybe I'll see you around campus then, and hopefully next week at the next MPA meet?"

"Hopefully!" I called as he started walking backwards.

He winked and put on that bold white smile of his again. "Later, Kandy Jennings."

I tossed him a wave and he turned almost instantly, meeting up with a group of guys who'd decided to toss a football back and forth on the lawn.

I turned just as quickly, walking as casually as possible, but deep inside my heart was racing. I couldn't believe my body's reaction to him.

For a split second, I didn't think much of Cane or what had happened back at home. He had truly, without much effort, put my mind at ease. He made me live in the *now*...and that astounded me.

Brody was sweet and confident and smooth and so damn handsome. I couldn't deny that. He was a beautiful guy with a great body and a nice smile. But as handsome and nice as he was, he wasn't Cane.

I checked my phone once more as I entered my building. There was a text from Frankie. Nothing from Cane.

Maybe meeting Brody was a sign. I wasn't in Georgia anymore. I was in Indiana, living the college life. It was expected of me to find boys attractive and to want to hang out with them. After all, Cane said I would meet someone eventually and move on from him. Perhaps it was time.

Brody seemed like he could provide an escape. His personality gave promises of a future full of fun and laughter and easy-going moments. I just hoped I'd actually see him enough to make it happen.

I knew from the start that Cane wasn't meant for me, which meant I had to let him go. I had to start living my life for myself, not pining over a man I would probably never see again. Plus, he did say after we shared our weekend in North Carolina, that what we had would be over.

Maybe he'd promised himself that and was finally living up to his word. Sure, he would check in here and there, but it would never be the same, and that was okay, because I told him it was fine. I told him I wouldn't ask anything else of him, and I meant that. He gave me what I wanted and risked so much for me.

It was done.

Fate always won, and if it was meant to be, we would be. We wouldn't be hundreds of miles apart, wondering what the other was doing. We would be together, trying to figure out how to make this work.

I had to take what was right in front of me and make the best of it.

I could do that.

I could try.

PART II

MENDING THE WOUNDS

CHAPTER EIGHTEEN

KANDY

TWO MONTHS LATER...

There's a saying that when you're in the process of self-healing and letting go, you will lose many things from the past, but in the end, you will find yourself.

Well, it's not a saying—more like one of the many inspirational posters my roommate has taped on the walls. I look at it every day and it's a clear reminder to live my life, and I swear I have tried, but it's so much easier said than done.

I hadn't found myself. To be honest, I don't think I was trying to. I was tied to the past, wishing to relish in it—relive the moments in the lake house or in his car, or even the innocent dinners with innocent chocolate and notebooks and pens.

To be fair, I had learned a lot about myself, like how much I loved to jog and burn off steam or stress from homework or exams. I learned that I loved nature, and that my college had the best trails when I needed to get some air. I also found out that I hated the cold. It didn't get as cold in Georgia as it did at Notre

Dame. I missed the weather back home and couldn't wait to go back to it.

Another thing I realized was that my coach hated me. Well, Morgan thought I was just tripping out, but I really felt like she didn't like me, or maybe I just wasn't good enough. She didn't encourage or push me to succeed. She constantly compared me to Sophie. She'd even made a remark once that we would never get to finals with how lousy I was throwing.

She had a good heart, but she could be a bitch. I'd ranted to my parents about it a great deal. Mom wanted to call the coach and give her some "kind" words, but Dad was against it, told me to ignore it and to keep practicing until I was *"so good she'll have no choice but to shut her damn mouth."* His words exactly.

Even though Mom called every other day, she would have to force Dad to talk to me. I'm sure he thought I didn't notice, but I did every single time. She would say things like, "Oh, hey, here's your father" or "your father wants to speak to you." But if he really wanted to speak to me, he would have called me himself.

I won't say he didn't try, because he did. He would text me stupid, mildly funny memes and I would put the cry-laughing emoticon, but there was minimal conversation. To say things had been knocked off balance would have been putting it lightly.

Still, I couldn't believe how quickly time was passing by.

The days went in a blur, and I gave most credit to conditioning, practice, and hanging out with new friends.

Two months.

That's how long it'd been since I started college. Since I last saw Cane. Moving on wasn't easy—hell, I still hadn't. The thought of him infiltrated every single part of my mind and even seeped into my life. My friends knew I was hiding something, but I refused to tell them, especially Brody.

God, Brody.

He knew something was up, but he was patient and kind and never pushed too much on the subject. He always told me to tell him when I was ready to talk about it...but Cane was a topic I refused to discuss with anyone. It didn't stop me from checking the company's website, Twitter, and Instagram accounts for updates.

    His company wasn't doing too well. Stocks had gone down, and there was even a rumor saying that Cane was looking to sell Tempt. I didn't believe that. Though his company was in bad shape right now because of his lost investment in Tokyo, I knew Cane would pull himself out of it and would never give up so easily as to sell what he'd worked so hard to build.

    Just like me, he was ambitious and driven and when he wanted something to happen, he made it happen, despite the doubts and criticism. It just sucked that all of this was happening because of me. Dad had created chaos in Cane's life, leaving many investors unsure whether they should continue working with him or not.

    I wanted to call. Check in. But he'd never called or text me again after that one call when I got here.

    I figured it was for a reason.

The one thing I'd learned the hard way was that winters were *brutal* in Indiana. I had practically frozen my tits off walking across campus to get to my dorm.

    I'd had my last class and was so damn glad when I made it inside my building where the warmth enveloped me, causing a fierce shiver to rush through me. When I got off the elevator and started toward my room, I noticed someone standing in front of the door.

    His arms were folded over his chest, his upper back and the bottom of his right foot pressed to the wall, like he'd been waiting there for a while.

    I smiled when Brody tipped his chin, revealing a set of dimples that I would probably never get tired of seeing. He pushed off the wall when I got closer, a casual smile still gracing his lips.

"My lady," he teased in a horrible medieval voice. The day we met, he'd told me he would see me around, but I didn't think I'd see him in my Renaissance Studies class the very first day. I didn't expect someone like him to sign up for a class of that nature, so it was both exciting and strange to see him sitting in one of the chairs, fiddling with a pen on the desk.

Apparently, he loved the Renaissance and Medieval era and was also a big *Game of Thrones* and *Spartacus* fan...just like me. With our MPA meet ups and Renaissance class, we had no choice but to bump into each other more than once a day.

"You have to stop with that terrible accent," I laughed.

He chuckled, and then continued with his medieval voice. "What is it? Do you not like my voice, my lady?"

I sputtered a laugh, pushing the door open and dropping my tote bag in the empty chair. Morgan wasn't around. Probably still in class. "You're a mess."

"You going to MPA tonight?" he asked walking into the room and shrugging out of his coat.

"Yeah, but I need a nap first. Woke up early to go for a jog with Morgan at the gym. Classes have me beat. It's still at the basketball gym, right?" I asked, shrugging out of my jacket too.

"Yep, basketball gym. Six on the dot." He walked toward one of the inspirational posters on the wall. Morgan had lots of posters taped to the walls, but the one he was looking at was one of my favorites. *"Live your life and don't be a dick,"* Brody read out loud. "That one's new," he mused, wiggling his brows.

"Yeah. It's one of my favorite ones." I sat on the edge of the bed. "How do you keep getting past Henley anyway? She really doesn't like guys coming into our building."

"Oh, I didn't. She caught me. With my dashing smile and big brown eyes, I got a pass. She told me I couldn't stay past curfew, and that I only get a pass because she likes you."

"Well, lucky for you!"

He was quiet a moment as I opened my laptop and wiped the keyboard with the pads of my fingers. I glanced up when he started coming my way. He sat on the edge of my bed with me, smiling again.

"What?" I asked nervously, tucking my hair behind my ear. His eyes dropped to my lips and I immediately snatched my gaze away, focusing on the screen of my laptop instead.

"I knew you were gonna do that. Why do you always do that?" he questioned, and I peered up.

"Do what?"

"Look away when I look at your mouth."

I shrugged, pretending it was no big deal. "I don't know. Nervous habit I guess." I huffed a laugh.

"After two months of hanging out, I still make you that nervous? To the point you're afraid to let me kiss you?"

"Well, it's not like we hang out every single hour of the day," I teased.

"We could, if someone didn't always have an excuse to not meet up." He pressed back on the palms of his hands and his chest looked buffer beneath the white T-shirt. The shirt hugged his torso, not doing a damn thing to hide his impeccable chest, abs, and biceps. His head turned, eyes pinned on me. "I would like to kiss you one day, you know?"

I bit a smile but said nothing.

"If I stole one from you right now, would that upset you?"

I drew my lips in and smashed them together. Because I said nothing, he probably assumed it was safe to go in for the kill. He leaned forward and placed a kiss on top of my shoulder. His lips were soft. Smooth. He also smelled really nice. Tilting his chin, he brought his face closer to mine. So close I could feel him breathing.

Just as he was about to guide his lips to touch mine, I dropped my head, running my thumbnail over my cuticle and focusing more on that.

He dropped his head too, letting out a low, throaty chuckle. Pushing away, he stood from the bed and blew a sigh. "Man," he laughed dryly, but it hardly held any humor. "So many mixed signals." I looked up and could tell his frustrations were getting to him. I understood, trust me, I did, but...I wasn't ready for it yet.

Two months of hanging out often, some mild flirting, and teasing, and not one kiss from me. Not one move. Only hugs and long, heated stares. I had to hand it to him, he had more patience in his left pinky than I did in my entire body. I don't know why he still wanted to hang out with me after so many failed attempts of trying to kiss me. Maybe he liked the chase.

"I'm sorry," I murmured. "I'm just...it's a long story. I don't like talking about it."

He looked at me, slightly confused, slightly intrigued as he sat again. "Did something bad happen before me to make you so hesitant?"

"Something bad like what?"

"Like...*bad-bad*. Things that can happen to girls that they can't fight off, you know?"

"What?" I gasped, closing the lid of my laptop. "You mean like *rape*? No—God, no!"

"Okay—phew! Sorry if that offended you! You're just really shut off, Kandy. I feel like you're into me, but afraid to take it up a notch for some reason and I figured that could probably be a reason why, but I didn't want to ask and end up scaring you off. I'm not rushing you or anything, but I'm curious why you are so guarded. It's clear to me that something is holding you back."

I lifted a hand in the air and dropped it like it was dead weight, unsure what to tell him.

"You know you don't have to be scared to talk to me. I'm pretty good at keeping things quiet, you know?"

"I know...but it's a lot. Talking about it will only take me back to it and I'm trying to get past it."

"No, no. I get that. You don't have to. No pressure." He dropped his gaze to my lap and then rose to a stand. "There's going to be a party at our house tonight after the MPA meeting. I know you aren't big on parties but it's my birthday, so I'd really like you to come."

"What?" I slid off the bed. "Oh my gosh! I knew it was your birthday but didn't know there would be a party! Why didn't you tell me sooner? I could have gotten you a gift or something from the gift shop!"

He waved it off. "It's no big deal. Just another year older," he laughed. "The guys tried to make it a surprise thing, but one of them got drunk the other night and started blabbing about it. Not so much a surprise anymore." He took a step forward, grabbing my hand and reeling me toward him. My chest was pressed to his, and his mouth was close to mine again as he asked, "You won't let me party alone, will you?"

My teeth sank into my bottom lip. "I'm not a big party girl, but since it's your birthday, I'll show for you. And also because I feel bad that I don't have a gift for you."

He smirked. "Having you there is the only gift I need."

"Then I'll be there."

"Good." Releasing me, he stepped away and gripped the doorknob, twisting it and opening the door.

"Tell your friends they're welcome to party too. It'll be fun. You'll see." He winked and walked out the room. When he was no longer in sight, I sat on the bed again, huffing.

I wasn't trying to lead Brody on. It wasn't my intentions. He would ask to hang out or study and I'd say yes. He was fun to hang with, and his presence took my mind off reality, but he felt things for me that I didn't feel for him. He liked me a lot, I could tell, but I didn't like him enough. Not enough to move on.

I don't know. I guess after being with Cane, I didn't want to share my lips with anyone else. Deep in my heart, I still belonged to him. I didn't want to move on, no matter how much I kept telling myself to try. I had this part of me that was hopeful and burned bright with yearning. It was a part of me that knew one day I'd see Cane again. That maybe one day, we would be together, happy and blissfully content.

It was wishful thinking. We'd met in the wrong lifetime. Our paths had crossed, but we weren't destined to be.

At the end of the day, I was better off with someone like Brody. Someone who wasn't so...*complicated*.

CHAPTER NINETEEN

CANE

If the world didn't know who I was, and I could still get away with the things I used to do, Kelly would have been taken care of a long time ago. Unfortunately, she talked me up too much—made it seem like we were this happy couple when really I hated everything about her.

I'd had enough. My sister had had enough.

At first, I had her shut out. I told security not to let her through or anywhere near my home. It lasted for about a month, then she started making threats—said she'd go to my sponsors and other important partners of mine to tell them that I'd built my company on lies and dirty money. It would only be a matter of time before an investigation happened, and even though I'd covered most of my tracks, there was still an open line that had yet to be taken care of, and if authorities discovered it, my life and career would be over.

She was hanging what she knew about me over my head, trying to treat me like some dog that would be lost without her, but that was where she was wrong. I wasn't a dog and I had no fucking owner. I was a fucking wolf, an *alpha* in fact, and you could only cry wolf so many times before the wolf finally took action and demolished you and everything you cared about.

There was a knock on the door as I ate lunch with Lora. Lora got up from her chair to get it, but came right back with a fierce scowl.

When she and Lora first met, it didn't go well. Kelly was annoyed by the fact that there was another woman in the house. When I told her Lora was my sister, she got annoyed that I hadn't informed her my sister was in town. Like it was any of her fucking business.

Lora had one conversation with Kelly and had settled it. In Lora's words, she *"didn't like her uppity bullshit."* What made things worse was that I told her how Kelly was trying to use what she knew about my mother, Buck, and my past as bait. That made her truly despise everything about her.

Kelly stepped into the kitchen, her hair pulled up into a ponytail and her lips stained with a pink gloss. "Hi, Cane," she said, coming to my side to rub my shoulder. My jaw clenched as I placed my fork down.

"What have I told you about showing up at my house without telling me first?"

She smiled down at me, but it was tight. She picked her head up to look at Lora who was finishing off her salad and completely disregarding her presence. "Your sister has no manners. I hope you know that," she muttered.

Lora scoffed, but kept chewing, staring down at her meal. I knew if she'd looked up and saw the look of disgust on Kelly's face, she would have flipped and punched her right in the face. She was holding off for my sake. She didn't want to make things worse than they already were.

I picked up my plate, purposely bumping her out of the way to put it in the sink. "What do you want?" I turned to face her.

"It's been two weeks since I last saw you, Quinton. You just got back in town. How was the meeting in Chicago?" She took the seat I was just in and Lora finally picked her head up to glare at Kelly. She finished the bite of salad in her mouth and then snatched up her plate, walking past me to get to the sink and then heading out of the kitchen.

"Annoying bitch," Lora muttered under her breath on the way out.

Kelly frowned at her back, then pushed out of her chair. "Okay, you need to get her under control right now, Quinton! She has no respect whatsoever!"

I cocked my head, folding my arms. "Unfortunately, my sister says and does whatever the hell she wants. And unlike Kandy, she's not so easy to fool or manipulate with your fake bullshit and girly shopping trips."

She took a step toward me, narrowing her eyes. "How dare you say her name around me," she hissed.

I shrugged, picking up my keys from the counter. "I have to run to the office. Things to do. Deals to close." I walked by her, but didn't get far. She caught my wrist and yanked on it. I glared down at her, challenging her heated glared.

"Tread carefully, Cane," she warned, her voice eerily calm. "I would hate to see you drowning in this cold, cold world."

"Trust me, the one who should be afraid of drowning is you, Kelly." I turned to face her, squaring my shoulders, my upper lip peeling back. "You know things about me, but I've been you studying too. And trust me when I tell you, I know things about you that I would love to blast to the media. Imagine what your clients would think if they found out what I know about you?"

Her eyes narrowed. "What are you talking about? What could you have possibly found out?"

"I found out you were a *patient* at Polly Heights, not a visitor."

She blinked rapidly, swaying on her heels a little. "Who told you that?" she demanded in a whisper.

"You spied on me, fucked a few things up. It was only fair that I did the same."

"So what?" she snapped. "It doesn't change the fact that I can let the world know who you really are. If I go down, I won't be going alone. I'll drag you right down with me, Quinton, I swear to God."

I tightened my grip around my keys, smirking as I took a step back. She was afraid. Good. That was the plan. "I suggest you *tread carefully*, sweetheart. I mean, I would hate for your clients and your friends to find out a lovely, perfect woman like yourself had to be checked in for something terrible. Imagine how many people would drop you? Pity you. Yeah, you'd hate that, wouldn't you?" I grinned as she breathed unevenly through her nostrils. "But, for now, let's make things simple. We'll hold the secrets we know about one another and start by giving each other some space." I grimaced, pointing a finger in her face. "Don't show up at my house anymore. Don't fuck with my sister or Derek and Mindy. Don't even mention Kandy's fucking name. You have something to say, you fucking text or call me. You may not get an answer, but at least you get to do something."

She glared for a short moment, then a faint smile snaked over her lips. "You won't get rid of me. I will ruin everything you have ever loved before you even get the chance to do that."

I sighed, making my way out of the kitchen. "See your way out," I told her, and walked out of the house.

When I got in the car, I sent Lora a text and told her to keep a close eye on Kelly while she was still there. She would snoop—it was what she did best, after all. But Lora didn't bite her tongue. Not much. If Kelly looked like she was up to no good she would call her out on it. The one thing Kelly hated most was being embarrassed.

I had plans to get Kelly out of my life. I didn't know how to go about it exactly without tainting my reputation, but I was going to make something happen.

It'd been two months of this ridiculousness. It had to stop. She was fucking with my livelihood. Right now, I had her on a short leash.

I'd hired a private investigator to look into her. I knew she was hiding something, and when he told me that she'd been checked into Polly Heights, it'd truly surprised me. All this time I thought she was a visitor when really, she was a patient.

When I put two and two together, though, it made sense. She was there almost every single day. I saw her often, but never thought much of it. She bumped into me, we grabbed coffee, got to know one another, and I never saw her show up at Polly Heights again after that. I don't know how I could have been so stupid.

I should have known there was something up with her. A sane person wouldn't have just stopped showing up for a relative, no matter how busy they were. She was a liar, a manipulative bitch, and I was going to get down to the bottom of who she was and burn her to the ground. Even if the flames were to catch onto me too, I would be prepared.

After all, what was the point of life without playing with a little fire?

CHAPTER TWENTY

KANDY

If I thought the high school parties I attended were wild, they weren't anything in comparison to college parties.

There were kegs in every corner of the two-story house, bottles of all kinds of liquor on the tables, and empty cups scattered on the floor. The music pulsed so hard I could feel it through my shoes.

We'd gotten to the party thirty minutes late because I couldn't decide which outfit to wear. Gina insisted that I wear something hot and drool-worthy, mainly because she didn't want to be the only one wearing a risqué outfit. I'd dressed in one of the shortest black dresses I could find, with fishnet tights and a pair of chunky-heeled maroon Doc Martens. I was slowly but surely regretting the decision of my attire with every tug and pull to cover my ass.

The room was dark, but I looked around anyway, searching for Brody. I didn't see him anywhere. All of the partiers were practically wasted. Several of them flitted about with plastic cups in hand, others with beer bottles. There was a section in the living room for dancing, and it was packed with bodies. Strobe lights flickered and bounced off the walls, highlighting a few of the partygoers. The room was hot in comparison to the chill outside, so hot that my dress was starting to stick to me in certain places.

"Let's have some shots, loosen you gals up a little!" Gina shouted over the music.

Morgan and I nodded and Gina led the way to the kitchen. One countertop was set up with bottles of liquor. There was a cooler by the patio door, where a tall guy dug through the ice to pull out a Corona.

Gina got right to work, whipping cups out and picking up bottles like she'd done this routine plenty of times. She had a bottle of *Jose Cuervo* in hand and poured what she considered a shot into the cups, then smiled as she turned, handing one to each of us.

"Here's to a fun night!" she yelled over the music.

"Hell yes!" Morgan yelled, raising her cup in the air to bump Gina's.

I smiled, raising my cup too. "And to many more!"

We chugged our shots back and I winced as the burn rushed down my throat. Doing shots was going to take some getting used to. I'd done them with Frankie and I literally hated them. I'd rather have a mixed drink than a pure shot any day.

Just as I'd placed my cup down on the marble counter, a hand touched my waist and I peered over my shoulder, meeting familiar whiskey eyes.

"Hey! You made it!" Brody exclaimed.

I twisted around in his arms, smiling up at him. "I told you I would come!"

"Yeah! I guess I'm just surprised," he said. "I thought I was going to get a text with some kind of excuse about studying or needing sleep." He laughed, pulling his hand from my waist. I could smell the liquor on his breath.

BREAKING MR. CANE

"Nah, I wouldn't do that. But man, how much have you had to drink already?" I scrunched my face and waved my hand like a fan, fighting a laugh.

"He's one shot away from being shit-faced," Leo said from behind him. Leo was one of Brody's roommates and his best friend. They were both on the football team and members of MPA. I'd met Leo during a meeting and had even meditated with him several times. He was a cool guy, but not the most attentive. Gina had the biggest crush on him for some reason. She'd even joined MPA just to get the chance to meditate with him. It hadn't happened yet.

I glanced at Gina who was tucking her straightened hair behind her ears and avoiding his eyes as much as possible, trying to play it cool. Morgan had walked off to grab a beer out of the cooler.

"Yo, stop lying!" Brody exclaimed. "I am not *that* drunk. I can handle a few more. Besides," Brody stuck his chest out, "it's my birthday. I'll get drunk if I want to."

Gina and I broke out in a fit of laughter.

"Hey, aren't you in MPA too?" Leo asked, fixing his eyes on Gina.

"Oh—uh, yeah. I am! Just joined last month!" She bit a smile, and her eyes sparkled like she was so happy he'd even realized.

"Cool! Yeah, MPA is awesome! Some good stuff." Leo pointed a thumb back, taking a step toward her. "Can I get you something to drink?"

Gina, nearly speechless, only nodded at first.

"Speak, Gina," I teased, giving her the side-eye.

"Oh, duh," she giggled. "Yep, a drink would be really nice."

Leo smiled and placed a hand on the small of her back, ushering her toward the cooler, where Morgan was standing, chatting with someone.

That left Brody and me alone. I didn't realize we were so close until I looked at him again. My back was pressed on the edge of the counter and his groin was almost pushing into mine. If I weren't mistaken, he was kind of hard. His head was hanging low, his eyes fixed on my lips. *Yet again.*

"So, you having fun?" I asked, hoping to distract him.

"Yeah, I am. Even more fun now that you're here."

I only smiled, straightening my back.

"You've never seen my room, have you?" he inquired.

"Nope." I popped my lips. "Never even been to this place before."

"I know, I know. It's just...the guys are fucking messy. I don't want to bring you around it." Brody finally pulled away, sliding the tips of his fingers into his front pockets. "Would you like to check it out? My room?"

I drew my lips in and looked down. "What's in there for us to see?"

"It's a little more quiet," he answered, leaning closer. "There's something I'd actually like to talk to you about too."

I knew what he was trying to do. He wanted us to be alone. As badly as I wanted to keep my guard up, I would have hated to say no on his birthday. The whole point of my attendance was to hang with him, after all.

"Sure. Why not?" I finally said, and his eyes lit up, like it was the greatest news he'd had all day.

"Cool." He grabbed my hand and smiled, leading the way through the crowd. His hand was big and locked around mine. He made sure our grips never slipped, despite the sweatiness of our palms.

He'd made it to the stairs, taking them up casually, glancing over his shoulder to check on me. We passed a few couples making out, groping, and sighing. I looked over the guardrails and saw someone looking up.

Blonde hair. Big green eyes. It was Sophie, and with her was Jay. I looked away when they rolled their eyes.

With my hand still clasped in his, Brody met the top of the

staircase and continued down the hallway until we stopped in front of the last door on the left with a STOP sign pinned to the door. He finally let go of my hand to open it.

The room was typical for a football player's dorm. Two twin-sized beds were across from each other, football trophies and rings and books stacked on the shelf above the computer. A small window was above one of the beds and I assumed it was Brody's because of the *Game of Thrones* poster of the *Night King* pinned above it.

"This is what you had to show me?" I joked, walking into the room. "It's pretty bland if you ask me."

He shut the door behind him, shrugging a bit when I glanced his way. "Meh. It's a chill spot when you need to escape the bullshit." He rocked on his feet a bit. "So...can I be honest here for a second?"

I glanced at him. "Sure."

"I'm not digging the party. I mean, don't get me wrong. I'm grateful that they planned anything for me at all but... I don't know. Too many people—more than usual. The guys went all out."

"Well, that's a good thing! It's your birthday and they invited more people. That means they cared enough to step out of their way and let more people know about your awesomeness."

He smiled, but it didn't meet his eyes. I felt them on me as I turned to fiddle with the trophies on the shelf.

"Can I ask a serious question?" His voice was lower. Calmer. I looked over my shoulder and found his eyes. They were soft, mellow.

"Of course."

"What's up with you and me? Like, where do we stand, Kandy? I'm tired of being in the dark about us. My friends always ask me and I never know what to tell them and it's getting pretty embarrassing." He huffed a laugh.

I blinked rapidly. Um...okay. *Wow.* This was not the question I was expecting. Pretty deep. "I...I don't know, Brody. I guess I thought we were friends?"

"Friends that hang out more than three times a week, even with practices and conditioning? I don't think so." He took a few steps toward me, cupping my waist with one hand and using the other to tip my chin. "I really like you, Kandy. I do, and maybe it's the drinks making me say all of this, but I want you to be mine. I'm tired of letting the time we share go to waste. I want to kiss you, and hold you, and do so much more with you."

Shit. *No. No no no no.* I mean, *SWOON!* But no.

"Brody, I—" I started to push away, but he held me tighter.

"I know something happened in your life that makes you not trust me—or any guy for that matter—but I promise you I'm not like other guys."

"I know you aren't," I murmured. "Trust me, I know. You're the sweetest guy I know."

"So why won't you give us a chance? Why do you still keep your guard up around me? Am I doing something wrong?"

My heart was beating faster with every word he poured out, my pulse rushing to my ears. I dropped my eyes and tried focusing on anything other than him. I didn't know what to tell him. As badly as I wanted him to let this go, I knew he wouldn't. Brody was persistent that way.

I refused to tell him about Cane, about my past, about my parents and how ashamed of me they probably were. I didn't want him to know about the Kandy Jennings before college, the one who had, and still did, crave a man she knew she couldn't have.

I didn't want him to know that I wasn't ready to move on, so I did the one thing I knew would shut him up.

I kissed him.

CHAPTER TWENTY-ONE

KANDY

The kiss felt wrong and weird and...*dull*.

These lips weren't the same lips that ravished and devoured me months ago. These lips were hungry, yes, but they were also careful and diligent.

Brody moaned, wrapping his arm around my waist and picking me up like I was the weight of a feather. Twisting us around, he laid my back flat on his bed and thrust his hardening cock between my thighs.

I tried my hardest to get lost in the moment. *Just try. Maybe this will give you the extra boost to get over Cane*, I thought to myself. I wanted Brody to take over every single one of my senses. I wanted to *want* him just as much as he wanted me...but I couldn't.

When his tongue plunged through my lips, I didn't feel the heat roll through my belly and zap me in the core. When one of his hands skimmed down my waist and the other palmed one of my breasts, I didn't whimper or sigh with utter satisfaction. I was just...there. Stuck in a moment that did nothing for me.

But Brody didn't care. He kept kissing me, quenching his thirst after two long months of waiting. He thrust hard between my legs, groaning when he broke the kiss to suck on my bottom lip. I sighed to give him satisfaction. It was his birthday. This was a gift from me to him, I suppose. We kissed until our lips were raw and his cock was straining in his jeans and digging into me.

"Damn," he groaned, pushing up a bit to look down. "I'm so hard right now."

"You are." I forced a laugh.

He peered up, running the tip of his tongue over his plump bottom lip. "Should we—I mean...do you want that to happen yet?"

I swallowed and could taste the liquor from his tongue, as well as the tequila I'd downed not even ten minutes ago. Now was when I needed to be honest. It couldn't go that far with him. I shook my head. "Maybe not tonight," I whispered.

He nodded way too quickly, like he already knew I was going to turn him down. "Yeah. I understand." With a grunt, he pushed up on his palm until he was standing. I sat up too, and couldn't ignore the hard ridge in his pants. He dragged a palm over his face and groaned. "I'm sorry," he apologized. "I shouldn't have come onto you like that. I mean—I wasn't trying to rush things and I hope I didn't make you uncomfortable—"

"Brody, stop. Please." I grabbed his hand and tugged on it, forcing him to sit beside me. "It's fine, I promise. You didn't force anything."

"You sure?"

"Positive."

He nodded, lowering his gaze. We were quiet for a while, the bass of the music filling the void.

"He must have been one hell of a guy," he said. "For you to fully deny me like that."

My heart dropped. "W-what? What are you talking about?"

"I think I figured it out," he went on. "Why you're so hesitant. It's not because of something bad happening to you. You just aren't ready to move on from whoever had you before you got here. Hell, for all I know, you're still keeping in touch with him."

He picked his head up and our eyes bolted. I had no words. None. He looked at me with so much empathy and sorrow, like I was some poor, lost soul who would never be fixed.

I panicked.

I couldn't handle it.

The kiss shouldn't have happened and staying there on that bed with him would have led to him asking about my past, about Cane, and he was the last person I wanted to talk about.

"I—I have to go." I pushed off the bed and rushed for the door.

"Wait—Kandy! What's wrong?"

"I just... I need to go. I need some air." I could feel my bottom lip ready to quiver. *Don't cry here. Don't cry in front of him.*

I opened the door and rushed out to the hallway, while he stood in his room, confused and unsure what to do. "Happy birthday, Brody," I said, then took off, rushing down the stairs.

I made way for the kitchen and found Morgan and Gina still there. Gina was still flirting with Leo in a corner and Morgan was sipping on a beer while scrolling through her phone by the patio door. I didn't want to interrupt Gina. I knew she'd longed to hang out with Leo for months, so I went for Morgan.

"Can we go?" I asked, grabbing her arm.

"Really?" Her eyes expanded. "We just got here. What happened?"

"I'm just...not feeling too well. Kind of getting a headache."

She didn't feed into my lie. "Shit, did something happen with Brody? I knew that fucker was too good to be true! You need me to go up there and kick his ass?"

"No Morgan, he didn't do anything wrong, I swear. I just...I really, really need to get out of here. I need fresh air. Please," I begged, holding her eyes. She must've realized I was serious because she gave a hard nod and grabbed my hand, leading the way out the patio door.

"Kandy!" I heard Brody call. I looked back and he was trying to get through the thick crowd that'd gathered in the kitchen. I didn't stop. "Wait—Kandy!" he called again.

We trekked through the backyard, on top of icy grass and plastic cups, until we reached a gate. Once we hit the sidewalk, we walked pretty fast to get back to our building. Well, maybe I was the only one walking fast. Morgan was struggling to keep up with me.

"What the hell happened, Kandy?" Morgan asked, trying to match my pace. "If he did something, then let me know and I can help. We can let someone of authority know."

"He didn't do anything wrong, Morgan! It was me! I fucked it up!" I stopped walking, twisting around to face her. Her eyes were wide and probably more confused than Brody's were minutes ago.

"What do you mean you fucked it up? What was there to fuck up?"

I shut my eyes and shook my head. Drawing in two deep breaths, I opened them again to focus on my roommate. "Can I tell you something and you promise not to judge me?"

"I would never judge you. You know that," she insisted, taking a step closer.

I blinked hard, fighting the emotion, a tremble trying to claim my lip again. It didn't help that it was thirty-fucking-degrees outside. "Brody wants to be more than friends…but I can't do that with him. I can't give him more."

"Why not?"

"Because I can't move past the last guy I was with."

"An ex-boyfriend?" she inquired.

"Well, that's the thing. He was never really my boyfriend. Just…someone I messed around with. But it got serious the more time we spent together. Then something bad happened." I shut my eyes, reliving that terrible night all over again. Remembering how

Mom cried so hard when she had the flash drive. Seeing the blood on the ground. How Dad couldn't even look at me the next day.

"Something bad like what?"

I opened my eyes. "The guy was my dad's best friend…and my dad found out about us. It ruined everything."

"Holy shit," she gasped, eyes widening.

"I haven't heard from him in a few months. When my dad found out, it was the night before I had to come here. I didn't get the chance to see him because he was in the hospital."

"Shit, Kandy."

"I know. It's so fucked up and we promised to move on and get past what we were doing, but it was so hard. Harder than I imagined it would be. I think about him every single fucking day. I even called him the third day I was here. He called back, we talked a little…but there was no depth to the conversation. It was almost like he was already moving on." I wiped at my face when a single hot tear slid down. "I haven't heard from him since."

"Wow…I'm so sorry, Kandy." She shook her head. "I mean, I knew there was something up because you never talked to us about relationships or your ex-boyfriends, but I didn't realize it was like that."

"It's fine," I sighed.

"So…Brody doesn't know about the last guy? That he was your dad's best friend?"

"He knows there's someone I can't get over, but not that the guy was my dad's best friend. We, um…we kissed in his room just before I came downstairs. He thought it would lead to more, but I turned him down and I think that bothered him because he started assuming really personal stuff, trying to get an answer out of me."

"No shit?"

"I felt nothing with Brody, Morgan. Not a damn thing. I was hoping I would feel a spark or something that would push me over the hump of my past, but…there was nothing. It didn't even feel *right*. I know this is crazy to say, but I feel like I don't belong to anyone else but the last guy I was with, and it sucks because we both wanted each other so much, but because of his life and his job, and because of my parents and my age, it's not right for us to be together. I can't have my family and have him too. Not after everything they know."

"Wow." She placed her hands on her waist. "This is some really deep shit."

"I know." I waved my hands. "Sorry to dump it all on you like this but…" A sigh escaped me, my chest feeling less heavy than it did five minutes ago. "It feels good to finally talk about it. I haven't even told Frankie about it yet. I'm waiting to fill her in in person, during Thanksgiving break. I don't want her freaking out or getting distracted, you know?"

"Yeah, I know what you mean. Well, I'm glad you told me! And you know what—it is what it is! It's life! I think you chose wisely. You need your parents. And, you know, just because you want to move on, it doesn't mean that it has to be with Brody. It's only been a few weeks, girl. You still need time to heal. Give yourself that time." She hooked her arm through mine, starting up our walk again. "I would never judge you over something like that. Ever."

I smiled up at her. I was glad.

We made it to our dorm and both of us changed into pajamas. We were done for the night. I didn't have it in me to check my phone or text Frankie back about how awful I was at the party, so I curled up beneath my blankets and was glad Morgan shut the lights off and did the same after texting Gina to let her know we'd left.

I felt bad about that too, but luckily Gina said another teammate of ours, Claudia, had shown up, and Claudia was pretty nice and good friends with Gina.

We laid in silence for a moment, and I thought Morgan had fallen asleep, until she called my name.

"Yeah?" I murmured.

"I know you said he wanted you, but do you think he was in love with you? The guy you were with?"

"I don't know," I answered honestly. "He sometimes looked at me like he adored me. He even told me he wasn't sure how he was going to move past me...but he never said anything about being *in love*. Did he love me? Yes. But I don't know about him falling *that* hard for me."

"Hmm."

"What's that for?"

"I don't know. I guess...well, what I'm thinking is that he's keeping the distance for your own good. Not to hurt you, but to give you a chance at better things. I'm sure you probably think he's being selfish by not calling or texting, but maybe he's being *selfless* by allowing you the chance to live your life instead of setting you back. A selfish man would have kept you around and not given a damn what your parents had to say. A selfish man would have stopped you from living your life, but instead he set you free."

Wow. I had no words. Literally, none. Morgan, all though a goofball, was almost like Buddha. She was wise and real and genuine and I loved that about her.

"Anyway, good night. We have workouts in the morning. You know how that goes."

"Yeah." I forced a small, quiet laugh. "Good night, Morgan."

Morgan's snoring started up minutes later. I should have been sleeping too, but all I could think about was what she'd said. She'd hit the nail right on the head. It was almost like she'd known Cane personally.

Cane told me repeatedly that he wanted me to live my life...so why the hell wasn't I doing that already?

CHAPTER TWENTY-TWO

CANE

Work was kicking my ass. My personal life was too.

I had meeting after meeting, flights from city to city, and on top of that, my mother and sister were up my ass like never before.

I guess I couldn't complain too much. Mama had just gotten out two weeks ago and was doing good so far. She put a lot of time into baking again and I was glad she was happy doing it, but having her call me every three to four hours, asking me to send her some money to buy more supplies that were just going to sit around in the kitchen, was exhausting. And I couldn't forget Lora, who loved manicures and pedicures and massages and shopping sprees.

And there was Kelly…but that had been handled for the most part. Ever since I told her I knew she was a patient at Polly Heights, she'd kept her distance, but it didn't stop her from calling or texting and asking if she could visit the office or my home. I never responded to any of them, hoping she'd eventually give up and disappear.

There was a tap on my door and I called for the person to come in. Cora trotted in with a manila folder in hand. "I have your contract for Monhagen ready to go," she announced, meeting up to my desk and placing it on top of the piled paperwork. "Do you want me to get some of the others out of your way?" She looked at several of the signed papers spread across my desk. "Yes, please, but be sure to look over them for me, will you? My damn eyes are starting to cross with this new deal."

She laughed, taking some of the papers. "Of course, sir. And new deals are a good thing."

"I agree. Oh—before you go, can you clear my schedule for the rest of the day? I have someone to meet in two hours but I'm not sure how long I'll be with them."

"Sure. Would you like everything pushed to tomorrow, same times?"

"No. Let's push everything to next week if we can. Important seminar, remember?"

Cora gave a quick nod, tucking the papers under her arms and leaving the office. I was stressed from it all, but I refused to let the stress get to me.

After failing to close the deal with Zheng, many of my investors began to draw back. To hold onto the few that still had hope in my business, I had to pull a few tricks out of my sleeve and make promises that I'd hoped would pay off.

For the most part, it had worked. I did what I had to do to keep my business afloat. Were the things I did fair? No. It caused me to lose a good chunk of money, but at the end of the day, it had to be done.

My phone buzzed as I pushed out of my chair, going for the carafe of coffee on the stand. After pouring myself a mug, I took a glance at the screen.

Kelly was calling. I hit the decline button, sipping the coffee and dropping in my seat again.

After signing off on a few papers, my phone buzzed again, but this time it was a text from Lora.

Lora: Since you won't be here tomorrow, can I go to your place to use the hot tub and watch movies?

Me: I hardly ever use the hot tub, Lora. Have fun. But no bullshit.

Lora: Yeah, whatever. Ready for ur flight?

Me: Still can't believe you got me into doing this shit.

Lora: Oh, shush. You'll be thanking me later. I'm tired of your wallowing. Plus this is the perfect time to build back up and get what you want!

I shook my head, sipping my coffee. My eyes shifted over to the sofa by the window. It was the last place I'd shared with Kandy. I don't know why I hadn't gotten rid of the damn thing yet, considering it was from Kelly.

Funny thing was Mindy sent the flash drive to my office several weeks after my incident with Derek. I rolled it between my fingers, stared at it all day, before caving and plugging it in to watch it.

I could understand why D was so pissed. I'd fucked Kandy on that couch like my life depended on it. From any man's perspective, it seemed I was hurting her, but truthfully, I was giving her my all, a piece of myself that no one else would ever have.

I hadn't spoken to Kandy in weeks, and that alone tore me up inside. I avoided sharing phone calls and text messages with her because I knew it would only lead us to regrets, and she deserved more than that. I didn't have it in me to give her false promises, so saying nothing was better. Still, I missed the hell out of her.

Hell, I missed the whole family, and maybe the decision I'd made a few days ago wasn't a wise one, but it was happening. There was a chance it could fuck everything up and put me back at square one, but it had to be done.

CHAPTER TWENTY-THREE

KANDY

My phone buzzed constantly the day after the party, and even the day after that. It was a good thing it was the weekend. I had no reason to bump into Brody. No classes to go to and MPA meetings were only scheduled during the weekdays. Speaking of, I wasn't looking forward to that following Monday. We had a meeting, and I was thinking about being a no-show.

Saturday was a free day, so I spent that time lounging in the study room with Morgan, where there were bean bags and recliners and ottomans, to read a new book I'd picked up from the book store.

"Hey, you guys hear about the thing happening tomorrow at DeBartolo?" Morgan asked, plucking an earphone out and looking between Gina and me.

"No—what thing?" Gina skimmed through her textbook, a pen tucked behind her ear.

"I don't know. Supposedly, it's for students who are striving for a brighter future and want to run their own e-commerce or business. It sounds cool. After this whole college thing is over, I would like to open up my own daycare center and maybe even sell baby clothes online. I used to knit with my mom."

"Really?" I asked. "You, Morgan Page, running a day care and making baby clothes?"

"Like, with actual kids in it?" Gina egged on.

"Yes, with kids!" Morgan flailed her hands. "I love kids, believe it or not!"

"Gotta tell you, darlin', I don't see you as a kid-loving person," Gina teased.

"First of all, screw you," Morgan said with a middle finger pointed in her direction, fighting a smile, "and second of all, I do love kids! I'm majoring in early childhood development and everything. Please come with me, guys! It's only supposed to be for an hour. We don't have practice tomorrow morning either, so it's a win."

Gina groaned. I shrugged. I had nothing better to do anyway. "I'll go with you," I said.

"I guess I will too," Gina muttered. "But if it's borin', I'm walkin' out. Not even kiddin'."

"Yes! Okay, deal!"

Sure enough, the next day, Morgan, Gina, and I were walking up the steps that led to the DeBartolo Performing Arts Center. I tugged on the collar of my coat, relieved when Gina swung the door open and a gust of heat licked my cheeks.

"Fuck, it's cold out there!" Morgan hissed. "Gonna end up freezing my damn tits and ass off at this school!"

"Might as well get used to it." Gina took off her scarf. "Just wait until it starts snowin'. You're gonna want to punch someone in the face with a cold fist."

I laughed with them as we walked down the corridor. To my surprise, the room where the program was being held was filled with more people than I thought. The rows were mostly occupied in the back and since Gina and I weren't that into the program to begin with, we let Morgan choose where to sit. Big mistake. She took the first row on the left, right in the damn front.

I read over the pamphlet that was placed on my seat. It didn't say much, just had the name of the program listed at the top and a stock image of a woman smiling way too hard while typing on a laptop beneath it. What had Morgan dragged us to?

Sighing, I placed the pamphlet on my lap to pull my cellphone out of my coat pocket, needing to return my text to Frankie. We were both excited. We would be seeing each other in a month for Thanksgiving and I couldn't wait to squeeze the life out of her and play catch up.

Just as I'd send my text, I heard deep, boastful voices.

I glanced over my shoulder at the door, spotting Leo coming into the room. Trailing behind him was Brody.

"Oh, shit." I ducked my head.

"What's wrong?" Gina asked.

"Brody's here," I mumbled, keeping my head low.

"Oh...*shit*." Morgan looked over her shoulder. "He's taking a seat in the back. No point in hiding though. He's staring right at you."

"Figures." I sighed.

I sat up higher in my chair, keeping my focus on the podium up front instead. I was glad a young woman walked behind it a few minutes later, starting up the program with introductions.

During the woman's speech, I could feel eyes on me from behind. Her voice was a buzz, but I did my best to concentrate and ignore the burning glare on the back of my head.

It was impossible.

I hadn't spoken to Brody since the night of his birthday and deep down I felt awful. He constantly sent text messages and called with no luck. He'd even left voicemails with sincere apologies, but I couldn't push myself enough to call back and talk. I knew I was going to have to face him eventually, tell him the truth. I just needed to figure out the right words to tell him.

"...He became nationally known when he was only twenty-seven years old, and is now one of the highest paid multi-millionaires in the country. Please give a warm welcome to our surprise guest, *Mr. Quinton Cane!*"

Wait...

WHAT THE FUCK?

CHAPTER TWENTY-FOUR

KANDY

If I thought my heart was beating too fast over Brody being around, it was literally about to rip right out of my chest when that name was called.

Suddenly, this program had my full attention. I picked my head up and looked to the left of the podium as my peers clapped, and couldn't believe my eyes.

Walking up the steps that led to the stage was a man I thought I would never see again.

My mouth went bone dry and my throat thickened as he crossed the stage in a white button-down dress shirt with a dark-purple tie and black dress pants. His hair was in the same style I'd always remembered, but a little messier, like he'd been running his fingers through it before coming up. His facial hair was gone. There wasn't a single trace of stubble on his face, and as badly as my heart was beating, it surprised me that I still wanted to go up there and run my fingers over his chin to feel if it was as smooth as it looked.

BREAKING MR. CANE

I fidgeted in my seat, spine stacking as I watched Quinton Cane, the first man I'd ever been in love with, step up to the podium with a bold, charming smile. He shook the announcer's hand, then faced the crowd, those piercing gray-green eyes bouncing over the audience. And then, with one simple flicker down, those eyes landed on mine.

My breaths faltered, palms sweating like mad. My blood felt like it'd run cold, my lips parting, unable to form words. Truly, I was speechless. Had he planned this seminar, just to see me? Was this some mere coincidence? Did he think we wouldn't bump into each other here? Why hadn't he told me he was coming? He had my number. *What was happening?*

Judging by the stunned expression on his face, I assumed he hadn't planned on running into me either. At least not so soon, if at all. Considering how big our campus was and that it was the weekend, the odds of running into each other were slim. But we had. Fate was a funny motherfucker, and I was tired of having her fuck with my head.

Cane spoke and introduced himself, his eyes sliding to mine every few seconds. I tried avoiding his eyes too, but after so many weeks—months that felt *endless*—it was impossible.

He looked...*different*. His eyes weren't cloudy and gray. They were clear and vibrant. He looked...clean, like he'd changed his look purposely, just for a fresh start.

My mind circled back to all the things I knew about him.

Was Kelly still in the picture? Was she here right now for the program? I looked around the auditorium, but didn't see any sign of her. *That's good.*

Time ticked by slowly, and Cane spoke carefully and diligently, but it didn't stop him from finding me in the crowd and speaking while holding my eyes. To anyone else, it would have looked like he'd just chosen someone to focus on, while talking about business and life and how to be confident, but to me, he was trying to tell me something—maybe even *beg* for something. It was almost like he was…apologizing.

After a while, I couldn't sit in that large room, listening to his deep voice bounce off every hollow corner, crawling under the thin layers of my skin and seeping it's way back into my soul. Instead, I pushed out of my seat, passing a quick whisper to Gina to let her know I was going to the restroom.

I dashed down the aisle, purposely avoiding Brody's eyes too. I knew he was watching me. I could feel the heat of his eyes on me like lava.

I hustled out the open door and marched down the hallway until I found the women's restroom.

"Holy shit," I gasped, like I'd been drowning before and had finally resurfaced. "Holy shit. Holy shit." I paced the bathroom, squeezing my eyes shut, grateful no one was in there. *This can't be real.* No way. I thought I'd never see him again. Out of all the places he could be, he was at my college? Unbelievable. He had to have planned this.

I needed to calm down.

I refused to go back into the auditorium until it was over. After turning on the faucet, dipping my hands beneath the stream of water, and swiping two wet fingers under my eyes, I snatched out a paper towel from the holder, dried my hands and face, and then walked out of the bathroom, hoping to linger in the hall until it was over.

I should have stayed where I was because standing across the hall, waiting for me to come out, was Brody. He picked his head up quickly when he heard my steps. "Kandy," he sighed.

I froze in my tracks as he came closer.

"How are you?" he asked with a forced smile. His eyes were filled with so much remorse that I wanted to punch myself for doing that to him. Don't get me wrong, there was relief and hope, but more guilt masking his features than anything.

"I—I'm good," I murmured.

"That seminar is pretty boring, huh?" he laughed, pointing a thumb back at the open door.

I shrugged. "Kinda. Why'd you come anyway? Doesn't seem like your kind of thing."

"Leo dragged me to it. You know how that goes."

"Morgan dragged me here too, so yep. I know all about it."

He put on a smile. Took another step closer. "Listen, Kandy, I'm really, really sorry about the other night. I shouldn't have been so forward like that. I should have backed off. I think I pushed you too far and made you remember some things you didn't want to remember and if I did, I'm sorry."

"Brody, it's okay. Really. I should be the one apologizing."

"Apologizing?" He looked stumped. "For what? You did nothing wrong."

"No, I did." I looked at the door where the seminar was being held. I could still hear Cane talking, and my belly twisted into a knot. "I shouldn't have led you on like that. I shouldn't have kissed you if I wasn't ready. It was wrong of me to do that."

"Wrong?" He smiled crookedly. "I liked the kiss, Kandy. More than you know."

The body of students in the auditorium cheered and I couldn't hear Cane's voice anymore.

Brody came toward me and tipped my chin. "I don't regret anything except making you uncomfortable that night." He studied my eyes. "I'm sorry," he pleaded.

I looked up. "There's no need to be sorry. It's fine."

"I was too pushy, I know it."

Just as he'd said that, I heard footsteps. I looked toward the door and immediately wanted to snatch myself away from Brody. It wasn't Morgan or Gina coming to check on me.

Cane was walking through the door, and his eyes were right on us. In an instant, his nostrils flared, his eyes shifting down to the hand Brody had on my chin. He didn't stop walking, though. No, he came toward us, shoulders broad and chin in the air. His eyebrows had stitched together along the way, his glare still on the hand touching me.

Fuck. What. Is. Happening?

I was trapped between the present and the past and it made my lungs feel too small for my own body.

"Kandy," Cane greeted, and Brody finally pulled his hand away, which made Cane look at him. "You are?"

"Oh, I'm Brody, sir. Brody Hawks. Football player here." Brody extended his arm, offering a hand. Cane took it and shook firmly. Probably a little too firmly. Brody put on an uneasy smile, but I could tell he wanted to frown by the death grip. "I, uh, liked your speech in there. Very inspiring."

"How would you know it was inspiring if you were out here flirting?"

Brody finally gave him the frown he'd been holding back on. "I...didn't realize you'd noticed. I apologize if my absence offended you, sir."

Cane ignored his remark, putting his attention on me. "Kandy Cane," he murmured, almost dreamily, and my belly flipped. "You look well."

I sucked in a breath through my teeth. "Thanks, I guess."

"You guys know each other?" Brody asked hesitantly, taking a slight step sideways.

"He's my dad's friend," I filled in quickly, before Cane could say something crazy, like he was the man who had my virginity in his back pocket.

"Oh—that's cool! I didn't know your dad had a millionaire friend!"

Cane grimaced then, his nostrils flaring. "Brody, would you give me and Kandy a second? I would like to talk to her—catch up on a few things. I haven't had the chance to speak to her much since school started."

"Oh, yeah. Sure, man! No problem."

I nodded when Brody looked my way to make sure it was okay

to leave us alone. "We'll talk more later," I told him as he started walking off.

Cane and I watched him walk away, and when Brody entered the auditorium again, Cane stared down at me. "Who is he to you?"

"A friend," I stated.

"A *boyfriend*?"

I frowned up at him, narrowing my eyes. "How's your girlfriend Kelly?" I countered, and at that, deep lines formed on his forehead.

He sighed, not bothering to answer the question.

"Still around, I assume."

"Kandy. Cut it out. She's not my fucking girlfriend."

"Why are you here, Cane? Of all the places you could be, you come here? *Why?*"

"They invited me to speak."

"Did they invite you, or did you hear about it and shove your way in just to show up and fuck with my head?" I spat.

"I didn't come here to fuck with your head, Kandy. Yes, I heard about this opportunity and wanted it, in hopes of seeing you, but is that so bad? I haven't spoken to you in months!"

"Well, who's fault is that? You can't just prance your way onto my campus and interrupt my life like this, let alone scare off my friends!"

"He was touching you. I had no choice but to interrupt."

I took a step closer. "What do you think this is? A fucking game? I don't belong to you anymore, Cane. For all you know, I'm free to touch by anyone."

His throat bobbed, jaw ticking. "We need to talk somewhere private."

I folded my arms. "I don't think that's wise. Wouldn't want to get caught alone with a *student*, would you? Think of how much it would damage your reputation."

Cane grabbed my arm and slid his fingers down the inside of it until it locked around my wrist. "I don't give a fuck about any of that right now. I'm not leaving until you understand why I'm here. Walk with me."

It wasn't a request. It was going to happen, whether I liked it or not. He clutched my hand and twisted me around with him, leading the way down the hall. We passed several rooms until one became available. This room was darker inside than the rest of them, but the door was unlocked. He pushed it open and walked right in, looking around the corner to make sure it was vacant.

He shut the door behind us, locking it, then walking to a corner away from the window to get out of plain sight.

The room smelled like old paper and fresh wood. I took a look around, noticing several shelves, and came to the realization that this was a small library. A small sliver of light poured through the rectangular window above the shelf on the wall left of us, and the milky light revealed every angle and curve of Cane's face. His strong jaw and chin, the sharpness of his nose, the dip above his upper lip, the smooth forehead, and even the light brown wisps of his eyebrows.

He looked unreal, ghostly, like a figment of my imagination, and a part of me wondered if I was so delusional that I was dreaming about him right now.

"I know I have no excuse," he started. "And I know that whatever I say won't be enough to justify not communicating with you or reaching out enough. But…my hands have been full, Kandy. I swear it—and not just with Kelly, but with everything. My life took a turn that night your father found out about us and then all of this crazy stuff started happening all at once." He took a step toward me. I crossed my arms, doing my best to fight whatever emotion was trying to scratch the surface to forgive him.

"Am I supposed to care?" I grumbled.

"No. But I'm telling you anyway." He held my upper arms, leaving me no choice but to meet his eyes. Beneath the moonlight they were shimmery and desperate and my chest tightened out of pity. "I miss the fuck out of you, Kandy. I do. I miss you so much that it's hard to concentrate some nights. I think about you every damn day, wonder what you're doing, *how* you're doing. I know it's useless to wonder but it still happens. A lot."

I drew my bottom lip in, biting into it, refusing to cave.

"I just…I wanted you to have a chance at something new. I wanted you to see that there *are* other options out there besides me. It's no excuse, I know. We were in muddy waters and still kind of are, but I still should have called to check on you a few times. I just…didn't feel like it was my place to call anymore. Plus, we promised to move on, right? We agreed."

"Yeah, that was before everything went to shit, Cane!" I finally had the strength to pull away. "I was worried *sick* about you, don't you realize that? Not only that, but I went through what happened in Georgia alone! I thought that if I didn't have my parents to talk to about it, I would at least have you to tell me that things would be okay and return to normal, but you didn't! You weren't there and that…that *hurt* me." My voice cracked, my chest weighed down with every emotion I'd been trying to fight. "I can't tell you how many nights I've cried, wishing you'd call me. Wishing you'd say something to me without making it feel like what we did never happened!"

He stared at me, eyes hard, still shimmering.

"I know what we did messed things up. I know that it probably caused a few things to change in your life, but after that one empty call, nothing else, Cane?"

He opened his mouth to speak, and I waited for the words to pour out, but nothing happened. There was only silence. I huffed a laugh, swiping the stray tears away that'd run down my cheeks.

"Yeah," I laughed dryly. "Just keep being quiet. It's what you're good at."

When he didn't say anything to that, irritation swallowed me whole. I scoffed, waving my hands in defeat and going for the door. I didn't have time for his shit.

"You wasted your time coming here. Just leave me alone."

Before I could make it to the door, his hand caught mine and that same hand spun me around. His thick arm locked around my waist and reeled me in to his large body. His head fell down and our mouths were left with no choice but to connect.

His smooth, warm lips pressed to mine, and I wedged a hand between us, my palm flat on his chest, ready to shove him away, fight him off and pretend I didn't care, but I was helpless. Stuck. Torn. Caving, slowly but surely.

This. This wasn't a dream. It couldn't be. I could feel him *everywhere.* This was what I'd missed—what I'd longed for, and it pissed me off knowing it.

My belly was slowly unknotting, the emotions running through me in a passionate frenzy. I ran my fingers through his hair and over his chest and everywhere else I could grasp. I'd hoped this was real, and not some dream. I'd hoped this was happening, and that he was here and he was mine and that this moment would never end.

I didn't care if it was happening in a library full of old books and a silvery moon revealing us.

There was only us.

Us. Again.

I couldn't believe I'd missed this so much.

He picked me up in his arms and carried me across the room to a desk. When my bottom landed on it, he shoved himself between my thighs, knocking some of the pens and supplies onto the floor as he placed his palm flat on the desk.

"Fuck, I've missed you," he rasped on the hollow of my neck. His breath was warm and tickled my skin. I wanted his mouth again, so I ducked my head, meshing our lips together and moaning when his tongue skimmed my upper lip and then his mouth claimed mine all over again. The kiss broke once more. We both gasped, in dire need of air.

"I didn't mean to hurt you," he groaned.

"But you did hurt me," I whispered back. "When I needed you most."

"I know but...*fuck*. We aren't good for each other, Kandy."

"If you think that," I breathed on his mouth, "then why come here? Why bother showing up and hoping to see me?"

He pulled his head back, and drew himself away just enough to look into my eyes. "I don't know how to forget about you," he confessed. "I don't know how to make the memories stop. You were apart of my life for so long and then you just disappeared and I don't know how to cope with that. I know it didn't have to be that way but I thought it would be the best way for you too. For all of us. I'm fucking stupid, I know." His forehead dropped on top of my shoulder and I let out a sigh. He was quiet a moment, a noise forming in his throat, as if hesitant to say what was next. "My sister is back in Atlanta. My mother is out of rehab and living with my sister in an apartment. And my father...he gets out of prison in a month or two."

His last sentence caused me to frown. "What?" I gasped, forcing his head up to see his eyes.

"He sent my sister this fucked up letter," he went on, jaw flexed. "Said he was coming for my company. I've been doing all I can to make sure that he doesn't come anywhere near it. So much that it has left me with hardly any time to do anything. I've got my family back and only get to see them twice a week, if that."

"Wow...I—I'm sorry. I didn't know things had gotten this bad."

His lips pressed. "On top of all that shit, there's Kelly, who won't back off...but I think I know a way to get her out of the picture."

"Really?" I asked, and that made me hopeful. "How?"

"It will lead me back to my old roots, lots of blackmailing, but I'm willing to do it if it means I've gotten her out of my hair for good."

"Your old roots?" My brows dipped. "What's that supposed to mean?"

His chin lifted, eyes cloudy as they bore into mine. "It means that I have a bad past, Kandy, and that I've done some fucked up things to get to where I am."

I tried to swallow, but the lump was dry going down. "Things like what?"

"A lot of shit." He pulled a hand up to pinch the bridge of his nose. "Forgive me for not being there for you enough. I'm here now. Let me make it up to you."

"Make it up to me how?"

"I'll be flying out tomorrow night. Let me take you to lunch or something before that—whatever fits your schedule."

I chewed on my bottom lip, weighing my options. We had conditioning tomorrow, but it was only for two hours. After that, Morgan and Gina and I had planned to go to the mall. I could pass on it. Pretend I was sick or something.

"Okay. Fine. We can do lunch, but you can't pick me up on campus. I don't want anyone seeing us. I'll meet you at the gas station that's not too far away."

"Okay. That'll work."

I couldn't believe we were still sneaking around, but it would have been strange for my peers to see me getting in the car with an older man. It would cause rumors. Whispers. The last thing I wanted was more fire under mine or Cane's ass.

"What if I hadn't come to the seminar?" I asked.

He smiled. "I believe there is a reason you did."

"But what if I hadn't?"

"Then I would have found you. I wasn't going to leave this state without seeing you first."

My heart boomed.

Bringing his hand up, he cupped one side of my face, and I couldn't help myself by nuzzling my cheek into his palm and closing my eyes. I missed his touch so much. His cologne and powerful body heat.

His lips came down on mine, and I think I missed that the

most. His gentle, deep, intoxicating kisses. His tongue that teased me until I sighed, and how his mouth always tasted like a trace of spearmint and cigarettes.

"Seminar will be ending soon. They'll be looking for me," he mumbled on my lips.

"I know." I'd said it, but my hold tightened around the back of his neck. I didn't want to let go. Not again.

He chuckled. "You have no idea how much I've missed you. Did you miss me?"

"Every fucking day."

Another deep chuckle. It hit me right in the core. It was sultry and deep and so damn delicious that I wanted to rip his clothes off and tell him to take me right there. Right now.

But as eager as I was, I knew we had tomorrow. He had to go. Our time was limited and my friends would start looking for me if I didn't show.

He finally found the will to pull away, and I didn't put up a fight. I dropped my arms, allowing him to stand up straight between my legs. His cock had hardened, digging into the inside of my thigh. "You still know how to drive me crazy."

I fought a smile and stroked his chin. It was as smooth as I imagined. "Get back to the seminar. I'll wait it out here for a while."

He blinked a few times, letting out a short sigh. "Tomorrow?"

"Yes. Tomorrow."

He gave me a half smile, then leaned forward to drop a kiss on my forehead. Afterward, he drew back, took a few seconds to collect himself, and then walked to the door. He looked over his shoulder at me, a brief glance, and then he twisted the knob, walking out and going back to the auditorium.

I watched him go until I could no longer see him through the window, and then I closed my eyes, inhaling deeply and letting it go.

Hopping off the desk, I walked out of the room. On my way

back, I spotted Morgan and Gina by the restroom. Gina turned her head when she heard me coming, relief taking hold of her. "There you are! I thought you fell in the toilet or something, girl! Where'd you go?"

"Just looking around," I told her with a shrug. "I've never seen this building before. I like the architecture."

"Oh, yeah." Gina nodded, taking a look up at the arched ceiling. "That's one of the best things about this school. The architecture." I was glad she took the bait.

"Yeah, well that program is a big yawn fest. You ladies ready to go?" Morgan asked, turning toward the door. Gina and I nodded and we left, but before we walked out the door, I looked over my shoulder.

Through it, I could see a corner of the stage. Cane stood there, his hands in front of him, and was looking right out of the door, watching me go.

I started to smile, but stopped when my eyes dropped down, and I noticed Brody looking at me. His eyes were narrowed as he focused on me for a bit, and then swung his line of vision back to the stage to look at Cane.

I hurried out of the building and didn't look back again.

CHAPTER TWENTY-FIVE

CANE

I had no idea what the fuck I was doing.

I was stupid, yes, but I'd always been a moron when it came to Kandy. When it came to her, my mind ran in circles, like a dog chasing its own tail. It wasn't smart of me to fly here and take this opportunity just to see her and it damn sure wasn't smart of me to shorten my speech at the seminar and walk out, just to get the chance to talk to her. Who would have known it would be so easy? That she'd show up in the place I would be?

When I walked out and saw that boy with his hands on her, my morals went flying out the door. My heart boomed and my fists wanted so badly to clench, or better yet yank him by the collar and shove him away.

He had his hands on Kandy. *My Kandy.* That shit didn't sit well with me at all, so yes, I whisked her off to a room and kissed her in the dark. Yes, I begged for her forgiveness and held her and kissed her. I needed her to remember what was important—that she was always going to be mine and there wasn't anyone getting in the way of that.

She'd told me to meet her at noon, and I was parked at the gas station, waiting for her to arrive. I checked the dashboard for the time. 12:34 p.m. Maybe she'd changed her mind.

Shit, could I blame her? I'd gone weeks without speaking to her. She had plenty of time to forget about me. It may have only been a maximum of eight weeks, but people changed when something bad happened. Hopes failed and dreams crashed like planes and as humans, our only defense is to detach ourselves from the situation.

Had she detached herself from the idea of me?

I waited ten more minutes, ready to throw in the towel. I push-started the car and grabbed my phone, about to text her, but then someone knocked on the passenger window.

"Shit," I hissed, looking through the window, spotting Kandy on the other side. She was waving with a soft smile. I unlocked the doors and she opened it right away, sliding right in. "Scared the shit out of me," I told her, chuckling lightly.

"Oh—sorry!" she snorted.

"What took you so long?"

"I had to walk from the opposite side of campus. The walk was longer than I thought."

"Well, I'm glad you showed up."

She put on a bashful grin. "I'm glad too."

I grabbed the wheel with one hand, putting the car in gear with the other. "I thought it would be best to have lunch at my hotel. It's a little ways from campus, but there shouldn't be any students there. We can walk through the back to be safe, though. How does that sound?"

"Good...but I hate that we still have to sneak around. So dumb." She continued to smile.

My hotel was a twenty-minute drive away. During it, I could tell she was anxious. I was too nervous to comfort her. Instead, I asked her how her day was going so far—small talk, which I hated doing with her because it didn't feel right.

It was fucking with my head. For some reason, after seeing her with that boy in the hallway, I felt like I had to *win* her back. Fucking ridiculous considering I was a grown-ass man and he was just a boy. It was a petty thought, but it was getting to me. It hit me that yes, she could move on from all of this and I thought I'd wanted her to...until I'd seen her with someone else.

When I parked in the hotel lot, I walked around to open her door and led the way inside. She kept close by, peering around like a hawk, like someone would notice her.

"Relax, Kandy," I told her, pushing the button for the elevator. "The prices of these hotel rooms cost triple what a college student pays for rent." I smiled down at her, grabbing her hand, and she nodded, exhaling.

"You're right."

I smirked. "When am I not right?"

She looked up at me, head cocking, ready to challenge that statement. "When you're being a dick," she answered.

"Here you go with the name calling," I chuckled, and she bit a grin.

The elevator took us up to the top floor, and I pressed a hand to her upper back as we walked to my room. With one swipe of my key card, we were in. She was mesmerized before she could even get inside.

"Holy shit! This is where you're staying?" Her eyes were wide with wonder, her mouth agape as she shrugged out of her coat.

"Temporarily." I shut the door behind us and took my jacket off.

She turned, her ponytail flipping with her. "And you said you're leaving tomorrow?"

"Yep. Tomorrow morning."

"Oh." A shadow of sadness ran across her face, but she brushed it off with ease, turning to soak it all in. "I've never been in a penthouse before."

"They're pretty spectacular." I tucked my hands in my pockets as she flitted about, walking past the furniture and running her fingers over the leather. She went to one of the doors, pushing it open. "Nice, spacious bedroom. Beautiful duvet and glorious canopy."

"Sounds like someone has been watching too many home improvement shows?"

She giggled. "It gets pretty boring here. I watch them with my roommate. Gives me ideas of how I'd like my future house to look."

She was fucking adorable. I missed that.

She came back and stopped at the wet bar. "Been drinking?" she asked, picking up the half-empty bottle of bourbon.

"Did a little drinking last night when I got back from the seminar."

"Why?" The skin around her eyes tightened.

"Because reality decided to punch me in my face, yet again." I took a step toward her as she placed the bottle back down.

"When you say reality punched you in the face, what do you mean by that?" Her voice was soft. It seemed she wanted the answer, but was also afraid to have it.

"It means that during those weeks when I didn't call or text, thinking I was helping you, you were getting to know someone else." My jaw clenched. "He had his hands on you and I saw the way he looked at you, like something intimate had already happened between you two." I was getting angry just thinking about it. My teeth clenched and unclenched, but I kept a level head for her. "I realized that if I hadn't come in when I did, it may have been too late. Hell, it's probably already too late."

She didn't say a word, just stared at me. Only, she didn't stare like before, where she seemed to admire everything about me, the sound of my voice, and the way that I looked at her. No, she stared like she was confused and surprised and slightly enamored.

"I don't know why I thought I was doing both of us a favor," I went on, head shaking. I lowered my gaze, studying the black Vans on her feet instead. "Maybe it's because I know I'm no good for you, Kandy. And things are going to keep happening in my life and getting worse and I don't want you anywhere near it. I'm a fuck-up and a betrayer, but I feel like a piece of myself is missing without you, so being right here, right now, with you is...." I dragged a palm over my face. "Fuck. My sister has gotten into my fucking head. She's the reason I'm even here, doing this." I looked up and she was still staring. "Damn it, why aren't you stopping me from saying this shit? Tell me to shut up or something!"

"What were you going to say?" she murmured, taking a step forward. "Being with me right here, right now is what?"

I met her eyes, and they were damp. "Right," I answered, dropping my hand, as if all hope were lost. "Being with you right here, right now feels right. And before you try to leave or turn it down, I want you to know something." I took another step toward her, looking her deep in the eyes. "I want you to know that I don't give a fuck what anyone says or how much society is against us. What we had, as fucked up as it may have been, felt right and yes, I have my regrets, and I do wish our situation had been different, but when I think about that stuff, none of the regrets include loving you."

A tear slid down her cheek in an instant. She only stared, and I was sure I'd fucked things up or said the wrong thing. I figured maybe she'd felt the complete opposite and hated my fucking guts now. She'd had time to develop the hate, after all. "Look, Kandy, I understand if you don't want to be here. I can take you back—"

"No," she breathed, rushing my way. "Now is when you shut up and show me how much you really love me." Our bodies collided and as she threw herself at me, I caught her in my arms, groaning when her lips found mine.

With her in my arms, my actions couldn't be controlled. I picked her up, gripping her ass in my hands and carrying her across the penthouse to the bedroom.

We kissed hard, sucked and licked and nipped. Her moans were breathy and sweet, while mine were deep and guttural.

"Fuck," I groaned behind her lips while she moaned. "Fuck, baby, I've missed you." My knees hit the edge of the mattress, causing me to fall forward. We landed on the bed, and she went straight for my shirt, ripping at the buttons. I went for her T-shirt, tugging it over her head and then unbuttoning her jeans. I slid them down to her ankles, wasting no time burying myself between her legs again, then devouring the sweet lips I missed so much.

Not many words needed to be spoken. We both wanted the same thing. It was only two months, but it felt like it'd been a century. We groped and snatched and tore at each other's clothes, fumbling over one another until we were both bare.

I pushed her to the center of the bed, my cock hard and anxious, and pressed the tip to the entrance of her pussy. Her eyes found mine and she clutched my face, closing her eyes and bringing my head down to kiss her. With the ease of kiss, I slowly plunged into her. The thrust was long and powerful and she gasped loudly, dropping a hand to dig her nails into my shoulder.

"Cane," she moaned as I drew back. I pushed forward again, picking up one of her legs and pressing her knee to her chest, my other hand cupped the back of her neck, and my cock had a mind of it's own. Looking down, I watched as my cock slid in and out of her beautiful, wet pussy.

"Shit, I've missed this," I groaned.

"Swear," she whimpered.

"Swear it on my life, baby." I dropped my face, burying it in the crook of her neck. "I've missed this. Us. You and me. I missed having your tight, wet pussy wrapped around my cock." She moaned louder when I provided another stroke.

"Tell me what you've missed," I demanded.

"Everything." Her breath was warm as it ran over my chin. "I missed your hands, and how they held me like this," she panted, sliding a palm down my arm. "I missed your mouth, and how ours were like magnets when we were close like this." I sighed, swelling up inside her. Her voice was going to be my undoing. "I miss your cock, and how good it makes me feel. How big you feel inside my pussy. Sometimes I feel too small for you, but I'll take everything you give me because I need it. I love it and miss it so much." She sighed on my mouth, and I couldn't help myself. I picked up my pace, my grip around the back of her neck tightening.

Her breathing picked up with every rapid thrust, her beautiful tits bouncing with the momentum. I dropped her knee, wrapped both hands around her thin waist, and forced her legs around either side of mine. At this angle, her pussy was even tighter around my cock.

I was so fucking hard inside her that it was becoming unbearable—too much to hold back. She was right. She was too small for me. It took everything in me not to come on the spot when I first broke through.

I stared down at her, watching her writhe and bite into her bottom lip. Her tits kept bouncing and her brown nipples were erect, dying to be sucked. I dropped my head, latching my mouth around it, sucking like my life depended on it.

"Shit," I rumbled around her nipple. "I'm about to come." Fire built up inside me, memories replaying in my head. Memories of all the things I missed. The lake house, the tenderness, the fiery passion only we could conjure.

With several more deep strokes, I came. I came hard and swift and there was no stopping it.

"Oh, shit." My mouth was on her chest, a hard shudder taking over me with every gush of release.

Moaning, she ran her nimble fingers through my hair. I couldn't remember the last time I'd come like that. Shit—the last time it'd happened was with her, on the sofa in my office. I hadn't touched a woman since. I couldn't bring myself to do anything with anyone else.

I picked my head up and she was already staring down at me.

"Not done," I mumbled, pulling out and bringing my face between her legs. I lowered a hand, dipping a finger between her folds and sliding it down to her pussy. She clenched around my finger when I pressed my thumb down on her clit. "You like that?" I murmured, and she nodded, clutching the sheets.

"I need it," she moaned.

"Need what, baby? Tell me what you need."

"I need you to make me come," she begged. "It's been so long."

That was all she had to say. I kept a finger inside her and leaned forward, sealing my mouth around her clit. She let out a shrill gasp, her fingers going straight for my hair to clutch it. I didn't stop. I knew her clit was her trigger spot so I rolled my tongue over it repeatedly, which made her moans come out heavier. I dipped another finger inside and that'd truly tipped her over the edge.

"Oh, Cane!" she cried out. Her slick cunt tightened around my fingers and she worked her hips in small circles until she came. She squealed next, and as badly as I wanted to smile with satisfaction, I refused to stop giving this woman all the pleasure I owed. She came in a matter of seconds, gripping my hair tight.

When she was over the high, her hips fell like dead weight and she let out a soft gasp.

I pulled my mouth and fingers away, gazing up at her. She'd thrown an arm over her forehead, and as I rose between her legs, she focused on me. I brought those same fingers to my mouth and sucked the cum away. It was a combination of both of us, the taste of it pure, illicit perfection.

She smiled, covering her eyes. "I can't believe you just did that." Humor laced her voice.

I lay beside her, grabbing her by the waist and bringing her head to my chest. "Missed that," I breathed in her hair.

"Me too."

Silence filled the air. There was a lot running through my mind, but yesterday during the seminar got to me the most.

"The boy who was touching you…is it serious with him?"

"No," she answered, and she almost sounded sad about it.

I picked her head up, forcing her eyes on me. "Do you like him?"

She stared into my eyes, and before she even responded, I already knew the answer. "He's a good guy. A really good guy, actually."

"How so?" She tried to pull away, but I kept her chin trapped between my fingers. "How so, Kandy?"

"I don't know, he just is. He does little things that any sane girl would kill to have."

"Things like what?"

"He's attentive and caring. Patient. He holds doors and offers to buy me lunch, and apologizes way too much, even when he really didn't do anything wrong. We're not together, and I feel bad that we aren't because he's such a nice guy." Her eyes fell. "He's the complete opposite of you," she whispered. "And I think that's why I can't bring myself to want him."

Wow. That had truly shocked me to hear.

"Damn." I released her chin and she dropped her head, placing her cheek on my chest again. "Is that a bad thing? Him being the opposite of me?"

"Kind of. For one, being around him made me realize that I'm not ready to move on yet." She ran the pad of her forefinger over my ribcage, drawing the shape of a heart. "And two, because kissing him didn't feel anything like kissing you."

"You kissed him?" I frowned, grabbing her chin and putting her eyes on mine again.

"You shouldn't be so surprised. I was trying to move on." Her voice was light.

My nostrils flared, but deep down, I knew I couldn't be too upset. I'd allowed this to happen. Still, it didn't stop me from being a possessive asshole.

I leaned forward, cupping her ass in my hand and shifting her up just enough until her lips were hovering above mine. My other hand wrapped around the back of her head, my fingers getting tangled in the loose strands that'd fallen out of her ponytail, and I kissed her.

I kissed her hard and deep and she moaned, body melting into my grasp. I kissed her until my lips were raw and almost numb. "He doesn't have shit on me," I growled. "Kissing him didn't feel like *this* because he doesn't know what you like."

She let out a sharp breath, pushing her groin into mine.

"I know what you like." I brushed my lips across hers, teasing. "I know what you need." I kissed her once then tugged on her hair to force her mouth away, and she made a noise of defeat. "I know what riles you up and what keeps you sane. You are mine. Always will be. No matter the situation, no matter how fucked up life gets. *Mine*. Do you understand?" I kissed her harder, sliding my tongue over her lips before plunging it through. Her body was lax, her breaths intense and quick as our tongues collided. Blood pumped between my legs, bringing my cock to life all over again. Fuck, she drove me crazy.

She sucked on my bottom lip and my hardening cock twitched, eager to be inside her again. She then looked up at me with a face so angelic, it made my heart boom, knowing I probably wasn't worthy of a presence like hers, but was also too damn stubborn to let this angel go.

When our mouths parted, they hovered. Hovered, but hardly touched.

"I will always be yours," she whispered.

And I knew she'd meant it.

CHAPTER TWENTY-SIX

KANDY

Cane ordered room service for lunch. Hot sandwiches and Mountain Dew were on the menu and I was glad he'd remembered my favorite soda.

There was a reason I'd taken so long to meet him at the gas station. I had contemplated before going. I literally paced my dorm room, after pretending I didn't feel up to par to shop with Morgan and Gina, debating whether or not to meet Cane. I weighed the pros and the cons repeatedly, and somehow the pros outweighed them.

I met him because I knew I would regret not going to see him. It was a good thing I showed up when I did too. I could tell he'd gotten tired of waiting.

We lounged around on his bed, the perfect lazy Sunday. He'd answered a few business calls, but I didn't mind. I was just happy to be around him.

"So how was it your sister's idea for you to come here?" I asked when he sat in the chair across the room. I was laying belly-flat on the bed, my phone in hand, waiting for an email to show up to tell me my grade for a quiz we had the past Friday.

"Oh." He smirked, spreading his legs apart and sliding his palms over the thighs of his pants. "Well, she's the one who told me about the seminar. I've told her quite a few things about you. She's also a persistent little shit, kept pushing me for answers. I told her what school you went to, how I'd probably never see you again because you were so far away, and the whole thing with your parents knowing." He shrugged. "Then, a couple weeks later, she tells me about the seminar, and how they were looking for business owners to come speak and share their personal success stories."

"Really?" I smiled, amused.

"Yep. She sent the link to me in an email, but before that she signed me up without my permission. I was annoyed at first…but the idea of seeing you again grew on me." He laughed. "If you can't tell, my sister is fascinated with the idea of you. She also doesn't care about consequences."

"I can see that," I laughed with him. "Why is she so fascinated?"

"Because for one, she knows you are years younger than me. She also got a kick out of the whole *best friend's daughter* thing—said it sounded like something out of a book or from a soap opera."

I grinned. Now that I thought about it, it did seem like it.

"And also because there are times when she'll catch me thinking about you," he continued, voice softer.

"How?"

"I don't know. Just by little things. Like over dinner with her and my mother. I'd space out a little, and somehow she just knew who I was thinking about. She said she'd never seen 'love' on me before. Apparently to her, love looks weird on me."

I broke out in a laugh, dropping my phone and sitting up. "Is it true that you love me that much?" I asked, my voice gentler. "So much that you came all the way here, spoke to a bunch of students who have probably already forgotten about your speech, just to see me?"

Cane sighed and held my eyes for a split second. He pushed to a stand, walking toward the bed. When he stopped on my side, he looked down with warm eyes.

"I lost my best friend because I couldn't stay away from you. In the beginning, I thought it was an addiction, you know? Addicted to the risk of it—the temptation. The thrill. I figured, maybe if I went a while without seeing you, I could detox and forget about what we had. That didn't even come close to happening. Every day felt more painful than the last. We spent that time together at the lake house and I can't forget it. I can't forget how perfect it was, or how you were there for me, and would have done literally anything for me. I can't forget holding you in my arms, or caressing you in your sleep." He placed a hand on the side of my face then used the pads of his fingers to gently caress the skin behind my ear. "I can't forget your voice or these pouty, pink lips," he went on, thumb skimming over my mouth. "I can't forget you, Kandy. I've tried, but it's not possible."

I gazed up at him as he wrapped a loving hand around the back of my neck. I threw my legs back and pushed up on my knees on the bed, coming face-to-face with him.

"I can't forget you either. No matter how hard I try...I can't." My chest bumped his. "I need you, Cane." I slid a hand down his arm, clutching a loop on the back of his pants.

"You need me?" he groaned.

"Yes."

"I need you too."

I dropped my hand, running my fingertips over his zipper. I felt him twitch in his pants and he groaned, looking at me through hooded eyes.

"Did your pussy ache while thinking about me?"

"Yes," I breathed.

"How often did you think of me?"

"Every day and every night."

He groaned again, a satisfied, guttural noise that made my skin hum and my body tingle. "Did you play with yourself when you missed me?" The tip of his nosed brushed across my cheek before trailing down my jawline.

"Sometimes," I admitted, and the thought of it made me flush. It only happened in the showers. It was the only time I had privacy, and even so, I had to do it quietly. I thought about the shower, and how the water ran over my breasts and dampened my fingers just enough for me to slide a finger into my pussy.

He grabbed the ends of my hair, tugging lightly. "Tell me what you did."

"I played with myself," I whispered on his lips. "With my pussy."

"Mmm." He groaned. "What else?"

"I would close my eyes and press my back to the wall," I continued, "and I would think about those moments we shared in the lake house, or even when I sucked your cock in the movie room in Destin. I even think about when you finger-fucked me for the very first time at your house, when we were alone and it felt so wrong and right." I drew in a breath as his nostrils flared, eyes blazing with hunger.

"You want to know what I thought about?" He pressed his hands on my shoulders, forcing me to lie down before climbing between my legs. I was only in my panties, and he tucked his fingers beneath the straps at my waist, wrenching them down to my ankles. When they were gone, he fiddled with the button of his pants.

"What?" I asked as he pushed his pants and briefs down next, just enough to pull his large cock and balls out.

"I thought about the sounds of your moans when I first put my cock inside you." He turned me on my side, gripping himself with one hand while lifting the bottom of my thigh with the other to push the head of his cock into my pussy. As he did, I couldn't hold back on the moan that had built up inside me. "I thought about how tight you felt when I first broke you in. How you dug your fingernails into my skin because I was too much for you—too big for your virgin pussy." He thrust forward, and then drew back, and an impatient sigh escaped me. "I thought there was no way in hell I was going to last for long when you were so fucking tight. And when you clenched your pussy around my dick...*fuck*," he rasped, and the deepness in his tone made my pussy throb.

He released a ragged sigh, gripping my hip and giving a relentless stroke. Then he picked up his pace, going primal for several seconds and taking what he needed while my breaths became tattered and hasty with each rapid thrust. It felt so good, but it was also torture. He was teasing me. Playing with my body, my mind, and I loved it. I loved it so damn much.

"But my favorite thought..." he went on, voice tight like he was close. He decreased the momentum to pull his hand off my thigh and slide it up to my chest. When he wrapped his hand around my throat, lightly locking and resting his fingers at my pulse, I quivered with lust. "...is when I wrapped my hand around your throat like this while fucking you, and you were left with no choice but to come all over my cock." He leaned down, stealing a full, savory kiss from my lips, his hand still fixed around my throat. "That's when I realized how perfect we were together." Another kiss, and a little tongue that sent me spiraling into a reckless moan. "That's when I realized that you truly are *mine*, Kandy."

"Oh my God, Cane," I breathed, holding his face and devouring his lips again. I couldn't control my body. I was close and didn't know how to handle the rush.

"Come for me, baby," he demanded gruffly on my lips. "Wanna feel your pussy soak my cock all over again."

His voice was dangerous. I trembled, feeling a wave of pleasure ride through my entire body. It rocked me hard, and went straight to my core. I held Cane's face tighter, sucked on his bottom lip as he plunged even deeper, and then I came. I came for him, like he'd wanted me to, and when he felt my juices coating the length of him, his groan was ravenous.

"Oh, fuck," he moaned. "That's exactly what I wanted, baby." He pulled his hand from my throat and worked his hips in rapid thunder. Slapping noises bounced off the walls, blood rushed to my ears. My pussy savored every single penetrating move. A raucous groan ripped through him and he stilled on top of me, hanging his head and crushing my mouth with his like his life depended on it.

We both sighed and whimpered behind the rough kiss. I clenched and released and he throbbed and twitched, spilling all he had within me.

He shifted back so I could drop my leg and lay flat on my back, then maneuvered between my legs, pressing his forehead down on mine. "Wish I could stay like this with you forever."

"I know. Me too." My heart sank when I realized that in only a few hours, I would have to go. I didn't want anyone asking questions about where I'd been either. I was going to have to leave soon, even though I really, really didn't want to. I wanted to stay with him. "Will I see you again soon?" I asked.

"Of course you will."

"I'll be back in Georgia for Thanksgiving break. Maybe we can meet up while I'm there."

"We can. I should be home for Thanksgiving. My mother is cooking—wants me to be there to *revive* the family...whatever that means," he laughed, picking up his head.

"Does she know about Kelly?"

"No, she doesn't, and I'd prefer if it stayed that way. I moved my sister into a place as soon as I could. She was there for a while, hated Kelly's guts whenever she just so happened to stop by. I don't want her meeting my mother at all." He made a face and looked away.

"What's wrong?"

"I don't know. The whole thing with Kelly is fucking weird." He pushed up and rolled onto his back. I sat up, placing my cheek in my hand and balancing my elbow on the mattress. "I had someone do some digging on her after finding out my office was bugged. Had it cleaned out and then hired this guy to get some information about her and her family. It is true that her father is a wealthy man and her parents are still married. They live in Florida now, moved sometime last year, but were Georgia residents for years." He frowned again. "But the investigator told me she'd spent four months in a rehabilitation facility, and before that, spent six years visiting a behavioral therapist in a certified clinic."

"What?" I gasped, eyes expanding. "For what?"

"Not sure yet. He's getting into that now, digging a little deeper. But the thing that fucks with my head the most is that she was checked into the same rehabilitation facility my mother attended. It's almost like she'd *planned* to get to know me. Almost like she'd been watching my every move, waiting for my visits. Waiting to run into me. I met her at that very clinic. I saw her around, but she wasn't in scrubs or anything, like the others. She wore the clothes she wears now. Fancy shit. When I first met her, she told me she was there visiting a family member, not that she was a patient seeking therapy. She lied."

"I don't get it. How could she wear regular clothes if she was a patient?"

"For most rehabs, they have a thirty day program for their patients, where they can come back and do group therapy or one-on-one therapy sessions. For that, the patient can wear whatever they want because the program is optional. From the dates I was shown, and by doing the math, I'm assuming she was doing her thirty-day therapy sessions around the time I had checked my mother in."

"That is fucking insane!"

"It really is. Which makes this much worse than it already is. I don't just have a desperate woman coming after me and jeopardizing my business, I have a desperate woman with deep baggage coming after me. Not only that, if she was with a behavioral therapist, I'm certain she has a mental case as well. Her behavior isn't normal, and I remember talking to her mother once when she'd called and Kelly was in the shower. Her mom told me to make sure I called her if anything seemed off with her daughter. I had asked what she'd meant by it, but she didn't go into great detail, just told me to call if something didn't feel right."

I sat up then, looking down at him. "Cane, this is serious then. You said you had a way to take care of it. Said you'd have to go back to your old roots. What exactly are you going to do?"

His eyes flashed up to meet mine, but he pulled them away just as quickly. He sat up and climbed off the bed, picking up his briefs and then his pants. "There are people who are good at intimidating others. Lora knows a lot of them. In my position, and with my career and my business on the line, I can't do what I really want to do to get her out of the picture, but the people I know can. They can put a scare into Kelly, have her back off for good. They used to do stuff like that for me all the time, but it was for more serious matters. I'm just not sure if I really want to go that route."

"Why not?"

"Though she is a pest, it's not like she's threatening to physically harm any of us. She just wants everything to go her way. With these people, everything could backfire. It's too big of a risk."

"God, Cane. You make it sound like you're going to *kill* her or something."

He gave me a warning look, and for a moment I froze...until he shook his head. "I would never kill anyone," he mumbled, eyes falling. His eyelashes created small, wispy shadows on his cheekbones. "But I have no problem ruining someone's life for trying to ruin mine. Because of her, I almost had to sell my company. They were trying to get someone to buy half of it, make me co-owner, push me out of the picture and turn it into this stupid trade with obligations I didn't like. I refused, so I busted my ass and made deals I'm not proud of to make sure it didn't happen."

I climbed off the bed to stand in front of him. "Well, it's okay. You didn't sell it, and things are getting better now, right? As long as you are safe in the end and no one is harmed, I don't care what you do. Do what you have to in order to make this work."

He studied my face a brief moment. "What about your parents?"

I frowned a little, backing away enough to see his whole face. "What about them?"

"I'm not allowed to come around them anymore. They've made that perfectly clear. Your father threatened that if I ever came near you again, he'd kill me this time. Probably not kill me, but beat my ass to a pulp. I don't want you to have to sneak around with me. You shouldn't have to go through that shit. You're too young and shouldn't be a secret, Kandy."

"My parents don't understand what we have." I grabbed his hands. "They don't understand how much I truly love you. They never will, Cane. I was trying to keep the distance with you too because I thought I had to choose…but I shouldn't have to. My heart hurts when I force myself to try and forget about you."

"Kandy." He exhaled, giving me a sincere once-over while squeezing my hands. "My Kandy."

"What?" I asked, blushing.

He tipped my chin, bringing my eyes to his again. "I don't want to hurt you anymore than I already have. I would never make you choose." He exhaled. "But if this is what you want, for things to be private until we settle all of the shit around us, so be it. But I think you deserve better than to be a secret."

"I don't mind being your secret. Just…promise not to let me go again."

He cradled my face, dropping his lips on my forehead. He wrapped his fingers around the back of my neck and I looked up into his beautiful green-flecked eyes. "I will never let you go again. Do you hear me?"

I nodded.

"Never," he asserted. "What we have will be complicated. You know that, right?"

"Yes…but it's been complicated from the start." I put on a sad smile and his eyes softened, like he knew all to well what I was getting at. "As long as I know you're there, I'll be okay."

I suppose my response was good enough for him because he nodded and placed a kiss on my cheek. I wanted him to know that I could handle it this time. Even though I had my doubts, and what he'd told me about Kelly made things even more complicated, I was willing. I missed him too much. Craved him too much.

I'd let my parents down once before for wanting Cane. But they already knew how much I wanted him now. Just because things had blown out of proportion, it didn't mean it would stop my desire for him.

Suddenly, all of these questions came to me, hitting me like a train. Why did I have to fight it? Why did I have to deny myself happiness and pleasure? Was I being selfish for wanting him so badly? Was it wrong to love him the way I did? I wasn't sure, and as we got dressed and he drove me back to the campus, I kept thinking about it.

Loving him was wrong…but at this point in my life, I didn't care about being right anymore. I would have done anything for Cane, and by him showing up and coming to my school, I realized he would do anything for me too. We'd had a small setback, but we'd found our way to each other again.

Fate hadn't been against us. Fate was with us. I could feel it.

We'd sacrificed so much for the sake of other people's happiness. It wasn't fair that we had to give up on each other, just to keep others content.

Cane kissed me long and hard before letting me out of the car. Our hot breaths mingled when I gasped and his fingers lightly tickled the hairs at the nape of my neck. This kiss completed me—almost like it was set in stone that we were going to do this...*again*.

"I'll text you," he told me as I opened the car door.

"Okay." I smiled at him, but before I got out, I leaned in for another kiss. I loved the softness of his supple mouth, the way his breath ran over my upper lip and my nose. I got out of the car and gave him one last wave goodbye before walking off. He had a flight at four in the morning and I knew he needed rest. After all, it was nearing 10:00 p.m. I had definitely broken the Sunday night curfew, but I didn't care. It was worth it with him, plus I was sure I could convince Henley that I was studying and got caught up.

When I made it to the door of my building, he drove away slowly. I watched him go, and then grabbed the handle to open the door to my building, but a deep voice called after me, stopping me in my tracks.

I gasped, turning toward the darkness. The shadow got nearer, and when it came into the light, I caught sight of the brown skin and whiskey eyes.

"So it's him," Brody said, frowning up at me. His head swayed and my heart dropped to my stomach.

"Brody...w-what are you doing here?"

"I came to see you, talk about a few things, but I guess I shouldn't have. You were gone all day. I know, because I came by earlier to see if you were around and you weren't. I assume you were spending the day with *him*." He scoffed, looking back at the parking lot with a grimace like Cane's car was still there. "He's the guy you can't get over? Didn't you say he's your dad's friend?"

"He *was* my dad's friend," I emphasized.

"What happened with that, huh? Did you fuck it up by *fucking* him? They must be ashamed of you."

I blinked hard when my eyes prickled with emotion. Most of the emotion was out of anger. How could he say something so rude?

"Brody, I—" I clamped my mouth shut for a second. "Are you going to tell anyone?"

He shrugged hard, his shoulders nearly touching his ears. "It is what it is. I mean, I get it. He's rich. He's nice looking. He probably buys you whatever you want. I bet he's a real catch. Kind of like a sugar daddy, right?" He laughed, a bitter laugh that cut me deep. "Whatever though. You're better off with him." He turned his back, but kept his eyes over his shoulder to glare at me. "I'm not into *sluts* who fuck their family members' friends anyway."

He walked off, way too fast for me to even utter a word or try and stop him. He vanished into the darkness and I felt like I'd been shot right in the chest by a cannon. Brody had never spoken to me that way. Ever. I almost started to chase after him, but what would that have solved? He would still be upset with me about it. And it wouldn't make me want him any more or Cane any less.

I went inside before I could let his words get to me, heading straight up to my room and thanking the heavens that Morgan wasn't around. She must've been with Gina. I grabbed my shower caddy and towel and went for the showers. I thought I was doing fine—that his words meant nothing and his opinion didn't matter—until I realized I was washing so roughly with my loofa that my skin became sensitive and red.

Slut.

I'd used that word many times in a conversation with Frankie when we talked about girls in high school who wanted all the attention at parties...but never had it been used on me. At least, not spat right at my face like that. It was an ugly word. Cruel and insensitive and I vowed to never use it again because yes, it did hurt.

I finished up and went back to my room, got dressed, and tried to catch up on homework. It was useless because when I thought about what Brody had said, I realized he was right.

Only a slut would be okay with sneaking around with a man who was nearly twice her age.

Only a slut would fuck her father's best friend, ruin everything, and *still* choose him afterward.

CHAPTER TWENTY-SEVEN

KANDY

Despite how low I felt and how much the guilt was eating me alive when I had to go to class and see Brody—only to have him completely disregard me—I couldn't help being happy when the time came for me to go back home for winter break.

I had my suitcase packed, my phone in hand, ready to go to the airport and fly home. Morgan had already left, and Gina was driving home so she offered to take me to the airport before making the trip. I hugged her around the neck when she dropped me off, and then made my way to the line to check in.

It was a quick flight, and though the bad memories were trying to resurface and remind me that I'd left from a broken home, I was ecstatic to see my parents after so long. I was even happier to see them both standing at the front of the airport, waiting for me.

Dad spotted me first, and instead of getting the scowl or disgusted look I kept imagining he would give, I got a warm, comforting smile.

He opened up his arms and I rushed into them, burying my

face in his chest. I missed that the most. The protection he always provided. How I always felt so safe in his arms. When I was little, I loved the way my Dad smelled. His smell reminded me of a safe place. Of home.

"Hey, kid." He kissed the top of my head.

"Hi, Dad."

I pulled back, but kept my hands pinned just below his ribs. I scanned him quickly, trying not to make it too noticeable. He looked really good, unlike the last time I saw him, when his eyes were filled with fear and horror and a hint of repulsion. "How are you?" I asked.

"Happy now that you're home." He smiled then passed me over to Mom who nearly squeezed the life out of me.

"My sweet girl," she cooed over my shoulder. She drew back, looking me all over, rubbing my hair, squeezing my cheeks. I laughed, playfully swatting her hand away. "You look like you haven't slept in ages, Kandy. Are you tired? Hungry? We can get you something to eat and let you rest. I read something somewhere that the first year is always the roughest. I had a hard time getting used to the college life myself."

"Babe," Dad chuckled, wrapping an arm around me. "Will you calm down? She's fine."

Mom inhaled before exhaling, shrugging. "Well, come on. Let's get some lunch and catch up. All of us." She joined Dad, throwing an arm around his waist and walking. We'd made it to the car, where we decided we would eat at one of our favorite restaurants in the city. They served the best steak burgers—not too greasy, not too dry—and I couldn't forget to mention the seasoned steak fries.

"Gah, I missed these burgers," I groaned after taking a bite. I was settled in my booth, a chocolate milkshake, a load of fries, and a double steak burger in front of me.

Dad laughed. "Got tired of eating noodles and pizza, huh?"

"Oh my gosh, like you wouldn't believe!" I exclaimed. "I'm

pretty sure I would have turned into a walking slice of pizza if this break hadn't happened."

They both laughed.

"Well, eat up," Mom insisted. "There's more where it came from."

When lunch was wrapped up, I was pleased that it was easy-going and not at all awkward. It was almost like what had happened three months ago had never even occurred.

When we got home, we settled at the table with a pack of Oreos and milk as our dessert. Dad talked about work and how he was looking at signing up for the Sheriff's position since the current one was thinking about retiring the following year. Mom talked about her job at a new law firm. She still worked the divorce lane, but wanted to switch to criminal justice after what Dad had gone through. She loved her new firm much better though.

Catching up, laughing, and spending time with my parents was amazing, but even so, I could still feel a bit of disconnect.

I caught the small glances Mom would give Dad when he would get a little too quiet. I noticed how she'd changed the subject when Dad asked if I'd met anyone new on campus. By *new*, I was sure he was asking if I'd met any boys. I had told Mom about a guy that was interested in me, but told her I didn't feel the same for him. She told me to give it a chance, but that didn't turn out so well, considering Brody now thought of me as a slut. I wondered if she'd told Dad about Brody.

"So, I did well on an essay I had," I said, dipping an Oreo in a tall glass of milk. I liked to hold the cookie in the milk until it was mostly soggy, but the end, where my fingertips were, still had a little bit of crunch. It was the best. "A lot of people didn't do so well and have to retake it when break is over, but I nailed it."

I popped it into my mouth as Dad asked, "Oh really?"

"Yep." I pulled my phone out and went to my browser where my grades were already waiting. I slid the phone across the table to him and he picked it up, reading the screen.

"Wow." His eyes expanded as he focused on the screen.

"Let me see that." Mom took the phone from him, studying the screen. Her eyes widened and she lifted her head, sliding the phone across the table and smiling at me. "Wow is right! I'm proud of you, honey!"

I smiled, dipping another Oreo into my milk. "Will it be okay if I go to Frankie's tomorrow? I haven't seen her since the summer, plus I miss driving Bubby. I know she's missed me too." I grinned.

"Kandy, you know you don't have to ask to see Frankie," Mom said.

"You don't have to ask to do anything anymore. You're in college now," Dad said. "Your car is still in the garage. After seeing that grade, I think you deserve a little fun. But don't get too carried away," he teased with a chuckle. Though he was kidding, I had a feeling his last statement held a deeper meaning.

Mom cleared her throat and reached for the Oreos as a distraction. Dad pulled his gaze away from me, clearing his throat as well.

Shit. I spoke too soon. *There goes the awkwardness.*

"Yeah, I won't," I muttered. *Silence.*

"I, um…I'm going to hit the shower. Got an early morning." Dad stood and walked around the table to drop a kiss on my temple. "Night, my girl."

"Yeah, good night," I murmured, forcing a smile.

Through the corner of my eye I watched him go, then looked up at Mom who was chewing her cookie. "He used the wrong words," she stated. "He didn't mean anything by it." It was just like her to defend him.

Dad was never good with words, I knew that, but it didn't stop things from taking a hard left turn. Even while sitting across from Mom, I felt scrutinized by her, like she was wondering if I'd actually go to Frankie's or somewhere else…like with Cane.

"It's fine," I lied. "I'm going to call it a night, too. Unpack and unwind a little."

"Yeah, yeah, go," she insisted, like even she felt out of place. I forced a smile at my mother before pushing out of the chair and leaving the kitchen.

I went upstairs but before I got to my room, I spotted Dad in the loft section, sitting on the recliner. His head lifted and he spotted me. I put on a smile for him, hoping he'd warm up to it.

He didn't.

Not much.

His smile was faint.

I jerked my gaze away and went to my room, shutting the door behind me. My first instinct was to text someone whom I knew would make me feel better. Someone who would accept me and not make me feel so out of place.

I went to Cane's name and sent him a text, saying 'hey'. Cane and I had texted one another back and forth since his surprise visit at Notre Dame. He wasn't usually quick about it, but he returned my text messages and calls whenever he could and that was all that mattered. He was dealing with a lot, so I could understand the delays.

I took a quick shower, changed into pajamas, and checked my phone. He'd sent a message back and my heart boomed.

Cane: How's my Kandy?

Me: I'm good.

The bubbles bounced instantly. I was glad he was still around to chat.

Cane: You sure? You already in town?

Me: Yeah, I'm sure. And yep, got here around 12.

Cane: In Washington, but coming home tomorrow. Want to see you.

I chewed on my bottom lip, my thumb hovering over the screen. I wanted to see him too, I really did, but it felt too soon.

Me: Can we do the day after?

Cane: Sure. What's wrong?

Me: My dad is watching a lot. I think he knows I'm going to make an attempt to see you.

Cane: how would he know that?

Me: I don't know. He's acting weird, though.

Cane: weird how?

Me: like…he's still ashamed of me, I guess. Or maybe he knows I'm going to see you while I'm here. Idk.

Cane: Stop Kandy. He's not ashamed of you.

I stared at my screen until my vision went blurry. I didn't want to say anything else. I shut the screen off and sat on the bed, staring at the pink lamp on my nightstand. My phone buzzed in my hand again and it was another message from Cane.

Cane: I told you this would be complicated. I feel like shit too, but you told me this was what you wanted. We agreed. We don't have to do this if it doesn't feel right to you.

That was the thing: it did feel right. I didn't like the odd looks and gawking, but I liked the reward, which was Cane. I liked the butterflies that rushed to my belly when he'd text or call. I liked the deepness in his voice when he told me he missed me. Needed me. Couldn't wait to see me.

I couldn't stand the heavy feeling on my chest or in my heart. It'd only been three months. I knew it wasn't enough time for my parents to get past what had happened, but I had hoped that they would at least avoid going near the topic.

The dirty deed I'd done was going to haunt my family for a long, long time. It was going to be worse for me because I didn't want to move forward.

My life was a complicated mess.

Me: It feels right. Will I be able to come to your house the day after tomorrow?

Cane: Of course. I'll work from home that day, just for you.

Me: Okay. I'll see you then.

Cane: Okay.

Cane: When I kiss you, things won't feel so complicated, I promise. See you Wednesday, Bits.

I bit a smile, shaking my head. He always knew what to say to pull me out of my own head. Just as I plugged my phone into the charger, there was a knock on the door.

"Come in," I called.

Dad walked in, and I straightened up with haste, brows drawing together. I wasn't expecting it to be him. It wasn't his usual code of knock. "Dad? What's up?"

He stepped into the room, giving a sympathetic smile. "I need to apologize to you…"

"For what?"

"I just…I don't want you to feel out of place in your own home. I shouldn't have said what I did in the kitchen. I—" He opened his mouth, but clamped it shut just as quickly. "I'm trying to move past it. I want us to go back to how it was before. I don't want you to feel like you can't talk to me or that you're walking on eggshells around me."

"I—I don't," I lied. I don't know why I wasn't telling the truth. The fact of the matter was that I did feel out of place in my own home. I was happy to be back, yes, but not for moments like what had just happened in the kitchen.

His eyes softened. "What I was trying to say down there was that I don't mind you having fun…just…be careful."

"I will, Dad."

He dropped his eyes to the floor. An awkward silence filled the room as he shifted from one foot to the other. "Do you still talk to him?" he asked, slowly dragging his eyes back up. I noticed his grip was tighter around the doorknob, his lips pinching together. The possibility of me still talking to Cane was tipping him over the edge. I couldn't be dumb enough to tell him yes. Yes, I still talked to Cane. Still wanted my dad's ex-best friend. Still enjoyed having sex with him…

"No," I answered, and his eyes widened a bit, his shoulders slumping. His grip on the doorknob went slack.

"Oh. Well, I guess that's good. We can all move past this then."

I nodded, smashing my lips together.

"Okay, well, thank you for telling me and um…if there's ever anything you want to talk about, you can talk to me. I may not be the best at talking, but I'm good at listening."

I nodded, smiling a bit. "I know, Dad."

"Okay." He took a few steps back until he was in the hallway. "Goodnight."

"Night," I whispered.

When he left, shutting the door behind him, I shut off my lamp and rolled over, staring out of the window. I needed the night to be over so tomorrow could deliver me a less awkward day.

This will be complicated, but it will be okay, I told myself. *Your heart knows what she wants…even if that makes her a traitor.*

CHAPTER TWENTY-EIGHT

CANE

When Kandy showed up at my house the day after I got back from Washington, something seemed off with her. She still smiled when she saw me, and her eyes still sparkled with adoration. She kissed me when she walked into my arms, but even though her eyes had sparkled, they were sad. She had this defeated look on her face, like she wanted to be there with me, but also felt bad for it. I could tell right away the guilt was eating her alive, probably because she'd been around Derek and spent a lot of time around him since being home.

"Everything okay?" I asked, letting her into the house.

She nodded when I shut the door, releasing a sigh. "Yeah. Fine."

"Doesn't seem like it. You look like someone hurt your feelings."

"Well, maybe they did." She shrugged and turned, walking down the hallway, her keys jangling. I followed her to the kitchen, tucking the tips of my fingers into my front pockets.

"Who did?" I took a step toward her. "Tell me now, and I'll set them straight for you." I was teasing, but she frowned and peered up at me. I clearly wasn't helping with lifting her spirits.

"It's been more than twenty-four hours and I can't stop thinking about it..."

"About what?" I asked.

"He asked me if was still talking to you," she murmured when I wrapped my hands around her upper arms and rubbed them. "The first night I got back."

"Oh yeah?"

"Yes. And I told him that I don't."

"Oh." I guess I couldn't blame her for that one. Yes, we cared about each other, wanted to be together, but now wasn't the time to make matters worse.

"Are you mad?" she asked, and her voice, the naivety swimming in her eyes and masking her face, hurt me to witness. My girl was hurting and I didn't like it one bit.

"How could I be mad? I understand why you told him that. What happened is still fresh and he probably wouldn't take it lightly if he knew the truth." She nodded, about to lower her gaze, but I tipped her chin back up with my forefinger. "What can I do to help?"

She looked away, sighing. Then her eyes shifted up to lock with mine. "Are you sure we should keep doing this?" she asked. "I mean, you have a lot on the line, Cane. And Kelly is still around. Maybe not here, but she's around and will probably be back if she catches wind that I've been here. I'm worried the fucking house might be bugged now too." She looked around nervously and I shook my head, smirking.

"Kandy, as soon as I found out she wired my office, I had my whole house checked and I've paid for more security. Nothing was found."

"How did you find out about the video?"

"Mindy mailed me the USB flash drive, along with a note asking me to kindly stay away from you, them, and to never contact you again."

"Wow." She huffed. "She didn't tell me that."

"Of course not. She was trying to protect you." I sighed. "Kind of blows my mind that they think I'm some kind of predator now." I focused on her. "Do you think that?"

"What!" she shrieked. "No! How could I ever think that, Cane?" she grabbed my wrists, squeezing lightly. "I love you—I've loved you for the majority of my life. You never looked at me in 'that' way until I came onto you. I remember. Of course you're not a predator."

I sighed and she linked her arms around my waist. I brought a hand down to tilt her chin again. Her eyes locked on my mouth, as mine did hers. A soft smile tipped the edges of her lips, like she knew what was coming.

I kissed her, breathing raggedly through my nose, loving the smoothness of her lips. They were pouty before, especially with her gloomy mood.

Grabbing her by the hips, I picked her up and she moaned and smiled, slinking her legs around my waist. I carried her to the island counter, maneuvering between her legs. My palms slid down her waist, curling around to grip her plump ass.

She moaned against my mouth, lips parting and panting wildly. "Cane," she moaned.

I stole another kiss. "I told you that when I kissed you, things wouldn't feel so complicated."

She grinned and pressed her forehead to mine, the apple of both cheeks turning a light shade of red. "I love it," she murmured, then clasped her hands around the back of my neck, pulling me forward for another embrace.

I could have stayed like this forever—really I could have. Yes, I had business to tend to and papers that needed signing. I had three conference calls lined up, but none of that felt as important as being with her. I held her tight to my body, my cock aching to be inside her again. I wanted to tear her clothes off and work my way inside her, but there was something about this kiss that proved to me that maybe we weren't so complicated after all.

"Well, fuck her on the counter, why don't you!" a voice came from my left and I snatched my lips away.

Kandy gasped, turning her head and tugging her T-shirt down where I had slid my hand up to palm her breast.

We both looked at Lora, who was grinning like a fucking loon. I stepped back and Kandy slid off the counter, fighting the biggest blush I'd ever seen.

"Lora," I breathed. "What the hell are you doing here?"

"I told you I was coming by to use the hot tub again, Q." She had a tote bag on her shoulder, and indeed, she was wearing a swimsuit cover-up. Lora had a hot tub where she lived, but she didn't like staying around the apartment for too long. Apparently she needed an escape from Mama's overbearing ways. "But, of course, when it comes to mouth-fucking someone, it's easy to forget shit like that," Lora went on.

She walked by the opposite side of the counter, dropping her bag on the middle of the four-top table in the corner. She walked to the fridge and opened it while Kandy stepped closer to me, tucking loose strands of hair behind her ear.

"She's your sister," Kandy whispered.

I looked down and nodded, and Lora turned back around, smirking at us. "Cane, I have to admit, she's fucking adorable. That family photo didn't do her any justice."

I rolled my eyes. "Go to the hot tub, Lora." I reached for Kandy's hand, ready to leave the kitchen and take her someplace more private, but Lora yelled, "Wait! I want to talk to her."

"She's having a rough day. I'm sure the last thing she wants is to be hounded with questions from someone like you."

Lora gasped, pressing a hand to her chest. "Someone like *me*? What a dick-ish thing to say! I am one of the best people on this fucking earth."

Kandy laughed a little.

"See, she thinks I'm funny. And besides," Lora went on, opening the bottle of water in her hand, "she's a grown woman. Let her speak for herself."

I looked down at Kandy who shrugged and continued to smile. See, this was the only downfall of having family around. They invaded my space, my privacy—everything. Though I was grateful to have them back in sound mind and body, they were really starting to get on my fucking nerves.

Honestly, it was Lora bugging me more than my mother. My mother had her own hobbies. She attended AA meetings, still sought therapy, was learning how to crochet, and was constantly baking to take her mind off of old habits. Lora on the other hand, didn't have shit to do other than annoy me.

"You want to talk with her? You don't have to if you don't feel like it," I urged, looking at Kandy.

"No." She smiled at me then put her focus on Lora. "It's okay. I've always wanted to meet her."

"How fucking sweet." Lora put on a shit-eating grin and I narrowed my eyes at her.

"Don't say or do anything stupid, Lora. I mean it."

"What?" She threw her hands in the air, a guilt-free gesture, but her eyes were too sparkly, her smile mischievous. "I just want to get to know the girl who has my brother wrapped around her young, little finger. Is that so bad?"

"Yeah, yeah. Whatever." I gave Kandy my attention. "I'll be in the office in the den," I told her.

"Okay," she murmured.

Lora placed her water bottle down and walked around the counter to meet with Kandy. "I'm not big on formalities or introductions, so yes, I'm Lora, Q's sister, and you're Kandy, Q's obsession. Nice to finally meet you!"

I groaned, pinching the bridge of my nose and walking out of the kitchen. "No stupid shit, Lora! I mean it!" I yelled over my shoulder on the way out, just as Kandy broke out in a laugh.

CHAPTER TWENTY-NINE

KANDY

I could understand why Cane was so nervous about leaving me alone with Lora. She had no filter whatsoever. She asked me to come out to the deck with her. While she relaxed in the hot tub, I sat on one of the pool chairs, my legs crossed, watching as she sipped from a bottle of wine. Yes, the actual bottle. Apparently she'd had a rough week and needed to unwind.

I thought it was strange she wanted to use the hot tub before we came out, but of all the times I'd been to Cane's house, I'd never really given much notice to the smaller hot tub that was sectioned off by a glass door and glass windows. I always thought it was a pool house or a garden room, neither of which intrigued me.

The windows had fogged up a lot when she started the heated pool. "So tell me, Kandy Jennings," she sighed. "Why do you like Cane so much? He told me you're nineteen. God—I remember those days," she sighed. "So young. So naive. I had no idea what the hell love even meant." She looked at me with eyes that I swear were just like Cane's. Calculating. Observant. Hers were grayer, which made them colder and more intimidating than his.

In fact, they had a lot of similar traits. They could have passed as twins if Lora's hair wasn't dyed a bold aqua. She had sleeves of tattoos on her arms, just like Cane. She even had one on the inside of her wrist that said RISE. Hers was in a pretty script font, more feminine than Cane's, but it was the same word and seeing it made me utterly curious about the meaning of it. Apparently, that one word was very important to them.

"For a lot of reasons," I answered as she looked me over before taking a gulp of the wine again.

"Like?" she pushed, eyes expanding.

"Like how he's always there for me—has been since we met. He's always respected me and since I can remember, him and I have had this deep understanding and connection to one another." I struggled for words, trying to find the right ones to use. It was always harder to explain why you loved someone when you were put on the spot. "He was supposed to be like family to me—I'm sure it's what you're thinking—but I never saw him as family."

"Well, what did you see him as?"

I shrugged, lowering my gaze. "Someone I knew I couldn't have."

"Shit." She took another drag from the bottle. "You are pretty fucking deep for a nineteen-year-old."

"Does my age bother you?" I tilted my head.

"Me? Psshh, not at all." She placed the bottle down then moved to the side of the hot tub closer to where I was sitting. She rested her elbows on the cement edge and smirked. "To me, age is just a number. It doesn't determine anything in life other than being able to vote and buy liquor. When love hits you, it doesn't care about age or color or even if it'll hurt. Love is fucked up, man. But it's real. There is no denying when it's present and when I look at Cane, I see that. I didn't think it was real for him—thought maybe he was in it for the lust—but seeing him just now with his hands all over you and the way he looked at you before he left the kitchen gave me all the *holy shit* feels. I have never—and I mean *never*—seen him like that with a girl and he's had so fucking many."

That made me frown. "He has?"

"Oh!" Lora clamped her mouth shut and pretended to lock her lips and throw away the key. "Not, like, a lot," she went on, and then she rapidly changed the subject to one that I really wasn't up for discussing. "Is your dad still pissed about finding out about you and Cane?"

"Oh, I'm certain."

"I heard what that skanky bitch Kelly did. I told Cane I could punch her right in the nose and make her bleed when I first saw her, but he told me to stay calm and to keep my hands to myself." She let out a ragged breath. "I hate her. I really do, and there aren't many people that I hate on this earth. She's stringing my brother along like a fucking dog, trying to get him to bend and break for her. I hate seeing him in such a bind and if she didn't know so much, I'd beat her ass."

"What does she know exactly?" I asked, hoping my question came off light and harmless.

Lora glanced at me before pulling her eyes away. "A lot of shit, Kandy Jennings."

"Like what?"

"Just…shit. She's a psychotic bitch and he needs to whack her upside that narcissistic head of hers and leave her in a ditch in the middle of nowhere." She climbed out of the hot tub, grabbing her towel and wrapping it around her, securing it at the chest. "And don't ask me what all of the shit is," she went on, like she knew the question was running through my mind. "He told me you'd be coming home for the holidays and made me promise not to say anything to you about it. I'm tipsy and shouldn't have brought it up in the first place. My bad. But…I'm sure if what you guys have is real, he'll tell you eventually. He'll have no choice."

"Is it bad?" I asked, pushing off the chair and standing.

She shrugged. "To me, not so much. But I can understand how it could be bad and a big deal for someone like you. You didn't grow up the way we did, so it'd be harder for you to understand why he did some of the things he had to do. Sometimes we did things we weren't proud of just to survive. When I think about it now, I don't blame him for taking certain routes."

Wow. Well, then I hoped what he and I had was real because now I really wanted to know. I mean, even though we'd settled with being together in private, I did have my moments of doubt. What if he could never get rid of Kelly? What if she kept coming back to tempt him and ruin him? Would I be strong enough to stay in a secret relationship with him, knowing I couldn't do anything about it? Not only that, but Cane had so many secrets and so much mystery surrounding him, it felt like every day, I was finding out something new about him.

Though I despised Kelly with a passion, she was right about one thing. Cane was a man with many, many layers, and what he had deep down probably wasn't pleasant.

I was almost afraid to find out the truth about him because a part of me knew it would determine whether we would stay together, or leave each other alone for good.

CHAPTER THIRTY

KANDY

Lora announced she was going upstairs to shower. While she did, I shuffled around in the kitchen and living room. I heard clicking coming from Cane's office and knew he was hard at work. Though I had a thousand questions running through my head, I decided to let him finish and find me when he was ready.

I went back out to the hot tub and twisted the knob to turn up the heat. There was still a chill in the air that definitely made goosebumps run across my skin, but I was certain that with the heat of the pool, it would make for a relaxing time.

I didn't have a bathing suit. At this point, I didn't care. I stripped out of my jeans and T-shirt, folding them and placing them on the chair I'd been sitting in previously. All I wore was a pair of nude panties and a bra to match.

Since being in college, I had more freedom with my wardrobe. Whenever Morgan or Gina wanted to go to the mall, I always made a pit stop at a lingerie store, hoping like a madwoman that Cane would give me another on-campus surprise and I'd be prepared the next time. It didn't happen, but wishful thinking was what got me through the long days after he'd left.

I sank into the hot tub, allowing the heat of the water to consume me. It felt amazing.

Twenty minutes passed before I heard the patio door slide open. I looked back and Cane was walking toward the pool house. He opened the door and came inside. His hair was messier, his burgundy tie undone, hanging loosely around his neck. His shirt was unbuttoned at the collar, his belt missing. God, he looked so good like this—so appetizing. A small smile swept across his lips when he spotted me, his shoulders relaxing a bit.

"Did my sister influence you?" he asked, stopping at the edge.

I smiled, probably a little too hard. "She may have."

"She has that kind of power." He looked around, like he hadn't seen the inside of this little pool house in months. "She didn't say anything crazy, did she?"

I shook my head and laughed. "No."

"Hmm." He took a step back. "It's kind of chilly today. Listening to my sister will have you as sick as a dog."

"Not at all! It feels good. You should get in with me, let go a little."

His eyebrows shifted up. "Not gonna happen."

"Come on. Please?" I begged, moving closer toward the side of the hot tub he was standing on. "Ten minutes with me in a hot tub. Think of how much fun we'd have."

He chuckled. "Very tempting, but I have more work to do. Just came out to see if you were hungry."

"Hungry for you? Yes." I smiled harder. "Come on! I dare you to get in."

His smile was coy as he looked away, like he couldn't look at me for long or he'd break out in a laugh. "Your age is showing," he said, dropping his head.

I brought a hand out of the water to flip him off.

"Fine." He stepped back and started unbuttoning the rest of his shirt. "Ten minutes."

"Really?" My heart pounded. He was going to get in. He was undressing too. *Holy shit.*

I watched carefully as he finished with the buttons of his shirt and pulled it off. During the whole process, his eyes were locked on mine. Tossing the shirt and tie aside, he kicked off his shoes and unfastened his pants, sliding out of them too. All that was left were his boxers. He came closer, bending down and sitting on the cement edge to snatch off his socks. He slinked into the hot water, eyes glued to mine.

"For the record, I've never lost a game of truth or dare," he said.

"I see that." I swam toward him, locking my arms around the back of his neck.

I studied his face, but mostly his eyes. When I looked at him, I couldn't figure out how he had so much in the world against him. I mean, his eyes were sincere, but maybe that was only for me. Because he loved me. But for the world to be fighting him and backing him into a corner seemed wrong. He was a good man. I could feel it...or maybe I was only seeing what he wanted me to see.

"Why are you looking at me like that?" he asked, lips brushing across mine.

I chewed on my bottom lip before answering. "Because...we get to do stuff like this again."

"Ah." He kissed the tip of my nose. "And I get to hold you like this? And kiss you wherever I want without anyone stopping me?"

"Yes."

"Still feels wrong to you?"

"Sometimes," I admitted.

"Yeah," he murmured. "Me too."

"Why for you?" My brows stitched together. Cane didn't need

to feel like this was wrong. He and my dad were no longer friends. Nothing was stopping him anymore, other than empty threats.

"Because when I see you, I think of D…and when I think of D, all I can remember is how much hurt was in his eyes that night he came here to confront me. I hated it—still hate it." His throat bobbed. "The respectful thing would be to stay away, show him that I do care and respect him…but that shit is hard for me when it comes to you."

I knew this topic pained him, but I couldn't help feeling satisfaction when he spoke those words. How was this man so weak for me? How could I make him lose sight of right and wrong? Make him feel guilty and bad for wanting me?

"Perhaps I've broken you," I answered.

"Broken me? How?" His brows dipped, curiosity burning deep in his eyes.

"Well, before we became a *thing*—before the lake house and the office—it was easier for you to stand by your morals. Easier for you to ignore me, keep a distance. But after becoming this," I breathed, my lips hovering over his, "maybe having me broke most of your morals—your standards. Maybe being with me leaves you broken and complete at the same time…however that works. I know exactly how that feels because sometimes I feel broken too. Like we discussed at the lake house…when we're together, it's like nothing else matters. But when we're apart, all of the demons start to pop up and reality is shoved into our faces and it's harder to breathe—harder to think clearly."

"But when we're together," he crooned, "thinking doesn't exist. And that's how it should be. When you're with someone you love, they are your escape from the madness of the real world. With you, I have broken many rules and many morals and many standards and sometimes that wears me down…but I'll be damned if it stops me from having you."

A shiver shot down my spine and goosebumps spread across my skin like wildfire. He ran a hand up my arm, but didn't question the outbreak sweeping over my skin because even he knew that his words were powerful and raw and real and they were much needed in this very moment.

Moments ago, I had my doubts. I was questioning a lot of things about us, and even though those thoughts were still whispering, his voice was louder and so much clearer.

"Is Lora still here?" I breathed on his mouth.

"No. She left to pick my mother up from an appointment."

"Good." I pulled my arms away, swimming backwards. I brought my hands behind me and unhooked my bra, latch by latch. Cane's eyes blazed with fiery hunger as he watched me, realizing what this was. He studied every movement until the bra was gone and I'd tossed it outside the pool.

"Kandy…you're testing my limits," he rumbled.

"I know." I swam closer to him, my breasts on full display. "I like testing your limits."

A feral groan came from the back of his throat and not much held him back after that. He reeled me forward, then tugged my panties down before lifting me up. Our lips locked instantly and I felt one of his hands drop to lower his boxers.

I moaned on his mouth and held on tight with one arm draped over his shoulder, as he lowered me back down, slowly entering me at a pointed angle. His lips parted, mouth wide open as my pussy wrapped around him.

"Shit," he rasped.

A moan shot out of me as he held my eyes, bouncing me up and down on his thick cock. The water was still hot and with the movements, we both had sweat prickling on our foreheads and above our upper lips but we didn't care. The water splashed between our bodies, fueling me.

I groaned as he sucked on my bottom lip. His upward thrusts were powerful and deep and they held meaning—I was his and he was mine. We were each other's broken, fucked up mess and we loved it. We loved it so much it both hurt and felt good.

"I love you," I said on his mouth.

He groaned, clutching my ass. "I love you, baby." He found my mouth again, bringing one of his hands up to hold the back of my head, tangling his fingers in the damp hair at the nape of my neck. "Love the fuck out of you," he growled on my mouth. "Don't forget it."

His voice was hypnotic and deep and struck every single nerve in my body. I was so close to the top, and when he picked up his pace, sure enough, I'd reached an all-time high.

"Oh, Cane!" I cried, holding on tighter. He kept bouncing me up and down on his cock, filling me up and leaving me empty, filling me up, and driving me crazy with the slight absence. He felt so good—too good. It blew my mind that he could do this to my body—make me feel on top of the fucking world with just one orgasm.

I squeezed my eyes shut as a heavy, primal groan built up in his chest and ripped right through him. He finally stopped lifting me up and down, and squeezed me to his toned, sculpted body, moaning as he sucked on the bend of my neck.

His cock pulsed as he released, and with each throb, his body became more and more relaxed, muscles less tense, and a sigh leaving his parted lips.

"Fuck the ten minutes," he growled. "I need more." With me still in his arms, he carried me to the stairs of the hot tub and went into the house. He took me up to his bedroom, where we showered and made out and whispered *I love you's* repeatedly, until the water ran cold.

Then after, still naked, our appetites insatiable, and our bodies still heated, Cane took me on his bed again, but before he did, he'd buried his face between my legs and ate me like I was his last meal. He devoured me whole and I came hard and swift, unable to hold back.

He slid into me with ease, cock swollen and in need, and came again, this time pulling out and grabbing my hand to yank me up swiftly and thrust his cock into my mouth.

"Hold still," he rumbled. "I want your mouth." He shoved his hips forward and let out a ragged breath as he drew back again, staring down at my mouth. As if the sight of having his cock in my mouth tipped him over the edge, he thrust forward once more and a harsh groan ripped through him. His hips stilled, his cock still deep down my throat, and with a heavy groan, he came, and I moaned as his warm cum spilled down my throat.

He shuddered, gripping the back of my head with one hand and my shoulder with the other, like he couldn't hold on tight enough while he unleashed his orgasm.

"Oh, fuck," he groaned when he was empty.

He pulled his sated cock out of my mouth and I licked my lips. Bringing a hand down, he pressed his thumb on my bottom lip, a lazy smile sweeping over his mouth. "Hungry?" he asked. "For food, I mean."

I laughed softly. "Yes."

"Okay. I'll grab your clothes and order something. Or we can cook? My mother doesn't let me live with an empty fridge anymore." He laughed, eyes softening as he stepped back. Aw. He was adorable when he spoke about his mother.

"Let's cook," I insisted.

"Okay, but I'm warning you now, if it's a burnt mess, don't be mad at me. I'm not the greatest in the kitchen. I hire people for that shit."

I laughed. "Well, that's okay. We'll see what we can whip up and you can help me with the small stuff. Good thing I watched my mom cook all those dinners she made when you used to come over."

"Ah, yeah." He went to the closet, taking out a pair of sweatpants. "Miss those dinners."

I sat on the edge of the bed, fiddling with my cuticle. "Yeah. Me too."

Cane walked to the door. "I'll go get your clothes. We'll eat then play a board game or something. How does that sound?"

"Like my kind of night." With a small smile, I watched him go, but with every step he took, my smile fell.

It was the little things—the memories we shared—that were going to be the hardest to get over, especially the ones that involved Mom and Dad.

This was hard for him—having to live a life without them and pretend nothing was wrong. Hell, it was hard for me to still have them *and* him while they were all at odds.

I was stuck in the middle of it, and even though my parents didn't know about what Cane and I had now, it still sucked to see the look on their faces while they hoped I was making better decisions.

CHAPTER THIRTY-ONE

CANE

Kandy didn't go home that night, and even though I had to wake up at six the next morning to prepare for a presentation, I was glad she'd stayed. I'd lost so much precious time with this girl. I was certain her parents were going to wonder where she was, so when she got comfortable in my bed after eating an amazing pasta dish, I told her to text her mother to let her know she was staying at Frankie's, at least. It was a lie, but the truth would have stirred shit up again and that was the last thing I wanted for her.

She seemed happy being with me, but I still noticed this look in her eyes, as if there was a lot more wrong than what she'd told me when she first arrived. I couldn't figure it out. She was happy, yes, but there was this swirl of sadness that couldn't be missed. I'd catch it during her quiet moments, like she was thinking about something that was breaking her heart. I didn't push. Just hoped she'd tell me when she was ready.

A little after midnight, she lounged on the bed with me, scrolling through her phone while I worked on my laptop. She twisted onto her stomach, yawning as she shut the screen off. "You seriously don't sleep, huh?" she mumbled, turning sideways and resting her hands under her cheeks. Her legs brushed against mine.

"Too much work to do," I answered, focused on the screen.

"You really should start letting loose, Cane. Working so hard is going to burn you out one day, don't you think?"

"I've been working hard all my life." My head turned a fraction, our eyes connecting. "It's nothing new to me. If I don't work hard, I don't see results. That goes for anything in life, honestly."

"Hmm...I guess you have a point. But still...you hardly take a vacation or give yourself time to relax. The least you can do is sleep."

I smirked as she brought two fingers up and walked them across the keyboard. She didn't press the letters, just lightly tapped over them with the pads of her fingers.

"Sure you aren't saying all this just to get my attention?"

She grinned and dropped her hand. "Maybe you should get rid of it for the night."

"I have a presentation in the morning. I'll have to be updated on all of my information..." My words were meaningless. Yes, the meeting was important, but having her seduce me was much more pleasurable.

Kandy sat up and closed the lid of my laptop, then grabbed my wrist, tugging until I was on top of her.

"I'll let you get back to work, right after you take care of me. Sound fair?" she breathed on my mouth.

"How persuasive of you," I crooned, thrusting between her legs. The only thing holding me back was my briefs and her panties. The ridge of my cock pushed on her lace-clad pussy and she moaned. I crushed her lips and swallowed that moan, one hand sliding down the outside of her thigh while the other worked on getting her panties off. When her panties were gone, I looked down and my mouth damn near watered. She'd listened to what I'd said, keeping her pussy fresh and shaved. She was pink and glistening, her hips shifting up, eager to be used.

I kissed my way down her body, leaving sweet drops on the nipples that were barely concealed by the white T-shirt she borrowed from me. I kissed between her breasts and down to her stomach. She tensed when I hovered over her pussy.

"What do you want me to do to you?" I asked, purposely breathing on her.

She shuddered, bucking her hips upward, trying to get closer to my mouth, but I made sure to keep just enough distance to make her writhe. She groaned, fed up with my teasing. I laughed.

"You know I'm not patient, Cane," she breathed.

"Your impatience satisfies me," I admitted. "Lets me know that it will be a while before you stop wanting me."

She picked the back of her head up to stare down at me, and her fingers ran through my hair as she said, "I'll never stop wanting you."

"How can you be so sure, baby?" I watched her eyes carefully.

She wanted to be serious, but when her eyes flickered down and she realized how close my mouth was to her exposed cunt, she let out a shaky breath and said, "I just know it." She dropped her hand to rest on her elbows. Still peering down at me, she asked, "Will you stop wanting me?"

I licked my lips and dropped my eyes. She was about to speak again, but I cut her sentence short, sliding the tip of my tongue through the slit of her pussy. She was fresh and sweet and fucking perfect. My tongue plunged into her cunt and she let out a heavy moan, her fingers curling in my hair.

There was no way in hell I was going to stop wanting her. How? How could I stop wanting a woman who drove me crazy? How could I stop wanting someone who brought me peace and made me whole? How could I stop wanting a woman who always felt like she belonged to me? How could I stop wanting a woman who tasted so magnificent? I watched her get riled up with just my tongue in her pussy and it was like fucking magic. Her hips rotated, shifting up and down and then round in circles, her moans becoming shrill cries.

"I'm close," she pleaded. "Cane." She clutched a handful of my hair and squeezed, grinding her pussy on my tongue, bringing herself higher and taking what she needed. I loved when she got greedy—when it became too much to bear and she was in need of release immediately.

It didn't take long for her to come. In a matter of seconds her body locked up, her grip tightened in my hair, and she was calling my name like her life depended on it.

I lapped my tongue around her delicate clit before grazing down and curling my tongue around the hole I was eager to be inside of. She shuddered with satisfaction, her body much more relaxed.

I pushed up, straining like hell in my briefs. I was about to rest between her legs, but she forced me onto my back, pressing a palm flat on my chest. I grunted as she rested on one elbow and slid the hand that was on my chest, down to my briefs.

"We're doing that now?" I inquired, voice thick, husky.

She chewed on her bottom lip then lowered her body, pulling my briefs down just enough to reveal my cock. I was hard as hell, veins bulging, head swollen. The tip glistened with cum and Kandy dropped her head, sliding her flat tongue around it and licking it away.

"Oh, fuck," I groaned. She gripped the base of my cock, suckling on the tip. It felt so fucking good, her velvety tongue swirling around the ridge of the head where it was most sensitive.

She pulled back up, pressing her body to mine, her hand still gripping my cock. With hooded eyes, I focused on hers, letting her take the lead. She kissed me once. Twice. She did it again and again until the simple pecks transitioned to deeper kisses and moans and groans and tongue locking. Through it all, she pumped my cock with ease, grip still tight, the pad of her thumb skimming over the slit, where pre-cum beaded up.

The kiss broke as she jacked my cock faster and faster, and my whole body tensed as she kept her face hovered above mine, teasing me with her mouth, knowing I wanted to kiss her, but refusing to give it to me. I knew what this was—her own sweet, twisted version of payback. I'd teased her, and now she was returning the favor in the best way possible.

Her hand ran fluidly up and down my cock. I groaned loudly the faster she went, bringing the hand that was behind her, up to her hair. I clutched it tight and she moaned, dropping her face again and crushing my lips. And with her mouth on mine, our tongues colliding and my cock begging for release, I came.

A harsh groan tore through my entire body, starting from the pit of my belly and rushing out.

"Oh, shit, baby," I growled on her mouth. I shuddered as I came, spilling all over her hand. I glanced down when she pulled her mouth away to look, and sure enough, her hand was soaked with my cum.

She looked up with a bashful smile, kissing me once more, still gently stroking my sated cock. Only she could do something so fucking filthy and make it seem like a mindless, innocent act.

"To answer your question from before," I mumbled on her lips. "I'm almost certain that I will never stop wanting you." I cupped a hand around the back of her neck, bringing her mouth down to mine again. "You're all I want, Kandy Cane. All I need."

She gently sucked on my bottom lip, making my dick spasm. "And to answer your question...ever since I can remember, you've been the only person I truly wanted. That's how I know I will never stop wanting you." Her eyes softened. "We *will* make this work."

Yeah.

I hoped so.

CHAPTER THIRTY-TWO

KANDY

Thanksgiving break went by much faster than I had anticipated.

I'd spent most of it with Cane. I constantly lied to my parents about going to hang out at Frankie's or going to shop with her. Not that it was a complete lie. "I did hang out with Frankie, even if it wasn't as often as I'd liked. She had to start working after her mom lost her job, which only made lying to my parents worse. I didn't tell them about Frankie's mom, and if Frankie stopped by, I asked her not to mention it to them.

I only had two and a half weeks of school left for the semester. I studied like hell for my exams and was so glad those two weeks flashed by. I flew back home five days before Christmas, mostly eager to be reunited with Cane.

Despite the secrets, Cane and I felt freer, which was strange.

He told me that Kelly was still around, which I hated, but understood. She wasn't around-around—more like constantly calling and texting.

He couldn't just ditch her after finding out about her being in the same rehab as his mother. It was becoming this sticky web between him and Kelly. She knew things about him, and now he knew things about her. At the moment, it was a matter of who would snitch and ruin things first. The heat of that left Cane on edge most of the time.

I noticed it during the moments when he thought I wasn't watching. His phone would buzz or ring and his jaw would flex, proving that she was most likely calling. I hated seeing him in such a dilemma, but was glad that he had me, Lora, and even his mother there to support him and push him through it.

On Christmas, I opened presents with my parents and then devoured some hot cocoa and chocolate chip pancakes. The thing I loved about Christmas was that it left us in a feel-good mood. It was a perfect day.

Unfortunately, Dad didn't get as many days off, so he went into work that afternoon. Mom had some work to do from home and had a lot to catch up on, so I dropped off my gift for Frankie, and then took the gift I'd hidden in my trunk for Cane, to him. It wasn't much. Just a tie with candy canes on it, which he got a real kick out of. The funniest part was that he wore it to work the next day and had even taken a selfie and sent it to me, just for my viewing pleasure. I couldn't lie, he was a handsome devil.

On the last night of my winter break, Cane had planned a dinner. He invited me over, and I had asked if I could bring Frankie with me. She was off that night and I missed my best friend. It would be the last time we hung out for a while, so yes, I dragged her with me. Cane was more than okay with her being there, seeing as I trusted Frankie with my life.

"So is it just sex with Cane or is it getting serious?" Frankie asked in the passenger seat. I was driving while she scrolled through her phone.

I didn't know if it was because I hadn't spent much time with her since school started, or if I was so wrapped up in Cane and hiding him that I hadn't really paid attention to her, but something seemed way off with Frankie. Her hair was no longer the spunky colors she'd loved. It was dyed black and her eyes were sadder. I'd constantly asked her what was wrong, but she would always blame it on her mom losing her dream job and not making enough money, and how tired she was, but it felt like something much deeper to me. She'd lost the spunk and fire I knew too well. She was tame now, eerily calm if I was being honest. She was my best friend, though. I knew she'd cave and tell me when she was ready.

"I don't think it's just sex anymore," I answered, making a left turn. "It feels real now. Almost too real...if that makes any sense."

Frankie straightened in her seat. "What do you mean by 'too real'?"

I shrugged. "I don't know. I mean, it's a little different now because when we're together, nothing interrupts it. We have so much free time on our hands and I'm learning so much about him and what he likes...it's just interesting, I suppose."

"Do you think it will last?" she inquired.

That question really got to me. Like I'd said, I had my doubts, but lately, Cane and I felt like we were growing closer together, not further apart. "I'm...just taking it day by day."

"God," she groaned. "The sneaking around must be getting exhausting, but I totally get why you're doing it." She shifted in her seat, running a hand over the screen of her phone. "You don't ever think that...maybe it's only temporary? Or like maybe it's just the thrill of it that makes you want him so much?" I looked her way when I stopped at a stoplight. Her eyes were dead serious, her lips pressed thin.

"I...always question that. But I've known Cane for too long to think of it as just a thrill anymore. Is it exciting to be with him?

Yes. But it's always been exciting to be around him. At least to me it has."

"Hmm." She lowered her gaze again.

"Frank," I said through a forced laugh. "What is going on with you?"

She snapped her gaze up. "Nothing, I swear. I'm fine, K.J.!"

"Are you sure? You know I hate pushing for answers, but I feel like there's something you aren't telling me. Is it because we don't get to hang out as much anymore?"

"No." She laughed. "Maybe you're just paranoid because you're still banging your dad's ex-best friend and thinking the whole world knows about it, when really only like five people do?"

I broke out in a laugh, pushing her with my elbow. She giggled, and then turned up the volume of the radio. She was avoiding something, but I decided to let it go until later. Not that I had much time to get deeper into it. I was pulling into Cane's neighborhood several minutes later.

I parked in front of his house and spotted a car I'd never seen before parked a few feet ahead.

"Is someone else here?" Frankie asked, unclipping her seatbelt.

"I'm not sure. Maybe his sister with a new car?" At least, that's what I hoped. A part of me was afraid it was Kelly and at the thought of it, my heart sank to the pit of my stomach. It couldn't be. He would have warned me—sent a text or something.

I pushed out of the car and headed toward the door with Frankie at my side. I rang the doorbell, too afraid to just walk inside like usual. It took a few minutes, but the door finally swung open and behind it was aqua hair and round brown glasses.

Lora! Oh, thank God.

"Hey little angel!" she chimed. "Look at you in your adorable-as-fuck dress with your even more adorable-as-fuck friend!" Lora let us inside and Frankie snorted.

"Who are you?" Frank asked.

"You mean to tell me that Kandy hasn't told you all about me?"

Lora shoved a hand on her hip, eyeing me. "I thought we were cool, kid?"

I giggled. "Frank knows all about you, Lora."

"Oh, this is Lora! Oh my gosh she really *is* pretty!"

"What, did Kandy tell you I was ugly?" Lora teased.

I laughed. "I didn't know you'd be here tonight too. Cane didn't mention it. Who's car is that out there?"

"Oh. Yeah. Cane got tired of me using the Mercedes he hardly drives and me calling up an *Uber*, so he caved and finally got me one." She shrugged, but I saw a brief look of despair run like a shadow over her face before she waved a dismissive hand and said, "My mom is cooking. Cane can't cook a meal to save his life, but my Mom makes the best stuffed ravioli. You haven't met our mom yet, have you?"

"No, I haven't." My heart sped up a notch just thinking about the woman who birthed the man I loved. When I'd visited before, his mom would be away or doing something and vice versa for me.

"Well, come on. Let's go meet her. Cane is upstairs on a quick call but he should be back down in a minute. Come on." She ushered us inside but I noticed how quickly she locked the door when we were a few steps ahead of her. I decided to ignore it, and let her walk around me to lead the way to the kitchen.

The kitchen was bright and lively, several different mouth-watering aromas floating in the air. A thin woman stood over pots and pans on the stove, most of them billowing steam, with a black apron on and her brown hair pulled up into a really long ponytail. It seemed she hadn't cut her hair in years, but somehow the untamed, simple look suited her. Her hair was the same shade of brown as Cane's, with a few gray wisps in between.

"Mom, look who's here!" Lora sang, bouncing into the kitchen. Lora moved like a little ballerina. She was petite and quick and graceful and if I hadn't admired her so much, I'm almost certain I would have envied her confidence, and how she always made her presence known. There was no way in hell any person could look over Lora Cane while in the same room with her.

Cane's mom turned her head, eyes stretching with adoration when she found us. She placed the lids on top of the pots, and then came our way, drying off her hands. "Oh my goodness," she sighed. She looked at Frankie first, her smile warm and complacent. Frankie returned the smile, and then Cane's mother shifted her eyes over to me. At first, she swept her eyes all over my face, and then the slowest, most beautiful grin swept across her lips.

"You must be Kandy," she said.

"How'd you guess?" Lora asked, popping a sliced strawberry into her mouth.

"I remember the way Cane described her eyes...the night I came home."

She kept watching me. For some reason, I didn't find it awkward or uncomfortable, but Lora and Frankie obviously did because Frankie shifted on her feet while Lora said, "Mom. Maybe you should back up? I'm sure you're freaking her out."

"She's not," I admitted with a smile. "It's really nice to meet you, Miss Cane...wait, it is Miss Cane, right?"

She let out a soft laugh. "Yes, it is, but please. Just call me Nyla." Nyla? That was an interesting name. It suited her. She extended her arm and I grabbed her hand to shake it. Even though she'd told me her real name, my father taught me manners. Anyone who was older than me—especially Cane's mom—had my respect. I wasn't going to be able to *not* call her Miss Cane now.

"Yeah, the one thing she did right was not naming us after our shithead father." I looked around Miss Cane to Lora who had hopped up on the island counter, her legs dangling.

Miss Cane rolled her eyes playfully and stepped in front of Frankie to shake her hand too. "And you are?"

"Oh, I'm Frankie—Kandy's best friend." Frankie beamed.

"It's nice to meet you, Frankie. Must be nice to have a best friend—someone to lean on."

Frankie put on an uneasy smile. "It is, actually." Before Miss Cane could get any deeper, I heard footsteps and looked to the right.

Cane was coming down the hall, his strides careful and lax. He spotted me before everyone else and put on a sexy smile. His eyes rummaged over me, burning like a heat wave, and I bit a smile when he finally pulled his heated gaze away and stepped into the kitchen.

"Hey, Frankie!" Cane greeted.

"What's up, Mr. Cane!"

"Feels like I haven't seen you in ages!" he bellowed, giving her a quick hug around the shoulders. "How's school treating you?"

"School is good! Only downfall is that my roommate is a stuck-up bitch." Frankie rolled her eyes and I laughed, just thinking about how annoyed Frankie was with her roommate. She was so fed up with Polly that she'd actually gotten a job as a barista at a coffee shop near campus to save money and get her own apartment.

Cane let out a deep laugh, and then turned toward his mother who was just about make her way back to the stove. "Dinner almost ready, Mama? Don't want to keep the girls here for too long since they have to be up early to go back to school tomorrow."

"Yep! Just have to stuff the ravioli with ricotta and bake the garlic bread and it will be done."

"Oh, God. That sounds so good," Frankie groaned, like she was already eating the food.

Lora hopped off the counter. "Cane, can I talk to you for a sec?"

Cane glanced at Lora, jaw ticking, before putting his eyes on me. His gray-green irises flashed from the bright lights in the kitchen.

"Anything I can help with while we wait for the food?" I asked, grabbing his hand.

"My mother may need some help. Don't be afraid to talk to her. She's a nice woman." He wrapped a hand around the back of my head, bringing my forehead close to his lips. He kissed my forehead before releasing me and following Lora down the hall and into the den.

"So weird," Frankie snickered, sitting on one of the stools at the counter and pulling her phone out.

"What's weird?" Miss Cane asked, looking between us as she stuffed fresh pasta shells with ricotta.

"Actually seeing them out in the open with it," Frankie laughed. "When I caught them together the last time, it was on a balcony in the dark. Now they're doing it in the light and it's super freaky."

"I swear, you are still a dork," I laughed and Miss Cane did the same. "Can I help you with anything, Miss Cane?"

"Oh, yes, please! If you could take the salad and toppings to the table, and maybe a few paper towels too?"

"Of course. Frank, wanna help me?"

"Sure." Frankie slid out of her stool and picked up a roll of paper towels while I carried the large salad bowl and toppings. I walked around the corner to get to the dining room, loving how spacious it was. There was a six-top table in the middle of the room, a beautiful chandelier hanging above it, the reflections bouncing off the walls like crystals.

While I set up the table, I heard whispering and hissing and knew Cane and Lora were discussing something important. Though I was curious, I decided not to eavesdrop this time. Not only that, but Miss Cane was making too much noise in the kitchen for me to be able to hear anything.

"Why do you think it's weird?" I looked at Frankie after fixing some of the silverware on the table. "To see me and Cane out in the open with it?"

She gave a light shrug. "I don't know. I didn't think it would get that far—especially after you told me what your dad did to

Cane. And then Kelly is still around. I guess I just don't get why you'd want to still be with him. Cane seems like a good man, but he also seems to have a lot of baggage. I had no idea he even had a sister."

"I know. He does have a lot baggage, I'm realizing."

"Yeah, and the way he's whispering with his sister makes me assume something else is going on that we don't know about."

I glanced over my shoulder and saw Cane walk past the dining room and back to the kitchen.

"I just want you to be careful, K.J. I'm certain Cane will never let anything happen to you on his watch, but there's still something else he's hiding. He knows you're young and probably won't ask, but you might want to learn more about him before things get too deep."

She had a point. A big point. Too bad I didn't have much time to discuss it. Cane's mother was finished with the ravioli and walked into the dining room to place a serving plate full of it on the middle of the table. Frankie and I smiled at her, and as she went back to the kitchen, Cane and Lora walked into the dining room.

Lora rubbed her hands together. "Gah, I'm so ready to eat!"

"Same!" Frankie chimed.

We all sat at the table. Cane took the chair beside mine and when he slid his in, his palm ran over the top of my thigh. "You good?" he asked.

"Yeah," I breathed. "I'm fine." But was I really?

We dug into the food, which was delicious by the way. Especially the ravioli.

"Wow, Miss Cane. This is so good," Frankie moaned over her food. "There's a serious orgasm happening in my mouth right now. Not even kidding."

We all laughed.

"Thank you, Frankie. I'm glad you like it." Miss Cane chewed a little, then took a sip of water. "You know, I used to read cookbooks in rehab. I would crotchet. Read and study recipes. I remember promising myself I would make my kids a nice, big meal once I got out."

"That's really nice," I said, slicing a piece of ravioli.

We mostly ate over small chatter and Lora and Frankie goofing off. I was glad they were hitting it off—that they didn't feel so out of place.

On the other hand, Miss Cane was very watchful. She watched me and Cane a lot. Whenever Cane would look at me or rub my shoulder, she'd smile at us like she admired it. Did she admire us? Or was it just him?

After dinner, Frank, Lora and I helped Miss Cane clean while Cane went up to his bedroom to check emails. Something was going on with Cane and Lora. Lora was good at pretending, but every time she looked at Cane or her mother, I saw the tension in her eyes.

"Do you ladies like strawberry cheesecake?" Miss Cane asked. "It's homemade, one of my favorite recipes."

"Oh, yes, please!" Frankie sang. "Only K.J. knows this, but I have a huge sweet tooth."

"She really does," I chimed in.

"So does Lora," Miss Cane said with a soft laugh. "Her favorite when she was a little girl was strawberry shortcake. I used to make it for her birthdays a lot."

"Yeah." Lora put on a simple smile, her gray eyes distant. "I remember."

Miss Cane served the cake and while we ate, Frankie's phone buzzed. She checked it and then rolled her eyes with a grumble.

"What is it?" I asked.

"Mom. Needs me to pick her up from work. Her car's in the shop." She sighed, finishing off her slice of cheesecake.

"Didn't you ride with Kandy?" Lora asked.

"Yeah, I did. Mind dropping me back off at home, K?"

"I can take you," Lora offered. "I have to go to the pharmacy anyway to pick up my mom's prescription. Plus, I'm sure Cane didn't bring Kandy all this way just to share a meal with her."

"Really?" Miss Cane huffed a laugh and stood from the table, collecting the empty plates. "I'll wait for you here then." She took the plates to the sink and Lora and Frankie got up from their chairs.

"See you later, K.J." Frankie rubbed the top of my head like I was a puppy and I shooed her hand away, standing.

"Later, Frank." I gave her a big hug, knowing I wouldn't see her again for a few months. I hated the distance between us too, but as my mother always said, "this is life."

When they walked out the kitchen, Miss Cane wrapped up the cheesecake while I picked up my plate and took it to the sink.

"So…it must feel really nice to be reunited with Lora and Cane after so long." I tucked a few strands of hair behind my ear.

"It is," she breathed. "Feels so good to have them as a support system. I feel like a new leaf has turned over and I have this new slate and everything is much clearer."

"That's really good. I'm glad things are better."

She put on a warm smile, resting her lower back against the edge of the counter. "Do you know that Q has never looked at a woman, the way he looks at you?"

I stood a little taller, arms folding. "Aw…yeah, Lora was telling me the same thing when I'd first met her."

"I personally have never seen him this way." She looked away, laughing a little. "When he was younger, he used to tell me that he loved me. He said he loved me so much that no girl would ever be able to take his heart." She pushed off the counter. "If I can be honest, I wasn't really sure how I felt about him being with someone so young—and being Mr. Jennings' daughter too. I thought he was selfish for it, but then he explained it to me. Told me it just happened and that what he felt was beyond his control." She shrugged a little and smiled. Rubbing my shoulder, she said, "I'm happy to see him happy."

I smiled at her. It was all I could really do. She rubbed my shoulder once more and then turned with a yawn. "I'm going to watch some TV, lay on the couch. So exhausted."

I watched her go, then I went upstairs to Cane's bedroom. Of course he was sitting at the desk, typing away on his keyboard. His shirt was unbuttoned, the sleeves rolled up to his elbows, like he had to prepare himself before diving in.

I cleared my throat at the door, resting my head on the frame. "Should I come back in a few months?"

Cane stopped typing, looking my way. "Hell no." He dropped his hands and patted his lap. "Come. Sit."

I bit a smile, shutting the door and walking his way. He spread his legs wider when I approached, placing his hands on my waist and guiding me down on the center of his lap. My back was to his chest and he reached around me to finish off an email on his laptop before closing it.

"Your mom is watching TV and Lora took Frankie home," I said when he was done.

"Really? That's a first for Lora. She's nicer now." Laughter erupted, starting deep in his chest.

"Was she mean before?" I asked, turning inward and draping an arm around the back of his neck

"Not exactly. Just really stubborn and really lazy, which made her always say no to things. I've learned since she's been back that she says yes a lot more. It's a good thing. Means progress."

I nodded, resting my head on his chest. "What were you two talking about earlier when she asked to speak to you?"

He inhaled deeply before exhaling. "She's worried."

"About what?"

When his body stiffened, I looked up, finding his eyes. "She heard Buck was released."

"Buck?"

"My biological father," he said through his teeth.

"Holy shit. So soon?"

"Right? Too fucking soon."

"When was he released?"

"A week ago." He dropped his eyes, staring down at the floor. "I knew he was out. I have eyes inside and outside the prison, people to keep me updated, but I didn't tell her I had those people. She was pissed that I kept it from her."

"Cane, you can't keep stuff like that from her. She deserves to know too."

"I know, I know." He brought a hand up, pinching the bridge of his nose. "I just didn't want her to flip out, like she just did before dinner. She overthinks everything—gets paranoid way too easily. She does stupid shit when she's scared."

I sighed, putting my cheek to his chest again. "Are you scared?"

"Scared for myself? No. Scared for my mother and Lora? Yes. He can get to them way easier than he can to me. Especially my mom. He knows what to say to get inside her head. And nine times out of ten, if my mother is around, Lora is close by. I'm tempted to hire a bodyguard, but the man I have keeping tabs on him said he's been staying in a motel. Said he doesn't do much or seem like he's leaving the area anytime soon, but I know him. He's plotting."

"Do you think everything will be okay?"

"It has no choice but to be." I peered up and his jaw was clenching. When his eyes found mine, I realized they were cloudier. Darker. "I refuse to let him tear us apart again."

"Well, do what you have to do," I murmured. "Protect them as much as you can. Hire a bodyguard if things get suspicious with Buck."

"I plan on it."

I sighed, pulling my arm away and dropping my feet. When I stood up, I tugged on his hand, forcing him to stand.

"I know you're stressed," I said, running my hands up his chest until they reached his shoulders. I pushed the arms of his dress shirt down, running my palms over his inked arms. "But it's my last night here. You probably won't see me again for a few months."

"I know. I'm sorry. Just under a lot of stress."

I smiled up at him. "Well, tell me how to relieve it."

A faint smile swept over his lips.

"Should I get on my knees?"

"I think you should," he rumbled, but I was already on my way down. I unbuttoned and unzipped his pants and he let out a sigh.

"Just let me take care of you." I tugged on his boxers and his cock sprung out, semi-hard but still so big. I found it astounding that my mouth watered at the sight of him. He was all man, pure perfection, and I wanted a taste. Badly. I wasted no time taking him into my mouth.

"Oh, yeah," he let out a raspy groan, holding the top of my head. I held his hips and pulled my mouth away, forcing him to sit back down in the chair.

"Just relax. Okay?" I looked up at him as he spread his legs apart again. His eyes were fierce and hungry as he watched me run my tongue over my lips.

I started at his shaft, licking my way up to his now swollen head, and he breathed harder. "Oh, God." His voice was breathy, heavy.

I wrapped my lips around him, just enough for him to feel me there, but didn't suck. Not yet. He groaned, still staring down at me, waiting for what was next.

I gripped his cock in my hand, lowering my face to suck on his balls. "Oh, fuck," he groaned, and this time his head fell backwards and hit the chair. He was relaxing, but his hips were pushed up, his cock eager and in need of release.

I kept going, his cock growing harder in my hand, then I came back up, resting my elbows on the tops of his thighs and taking his entire cock into my mouth. I gagged around his thick, full length, and he let out a deep moan before cursing under his breath.

"Look at me," he insisted, and I did. I focused on him, my lips wrapped around him, sucking him in the same fluid motion. My head bobbed and he wrapped a palm around the back of it, forcing my head down for several seconds, his cock deep in my throat.

I could feel him throbbing in my mouth, like he was close. When he released me, I gasped for air and then said, "Do whatever you want to do to me right now."

If his eyes weren't hot and hungry before, they were on fire now. Without warning, he held either side of my head and thrust his hips upward, fucking my mouth.

He wasn't gentle or easy. He literally fucked my mouth like he was releasing all of the stress and pent up frustrations. My vision became blurry as I gagged around him, but I didn't look away. I wanted him to know that I could handle this and that I was here for whatever he needed.

He kept pumping his hips upward, but moved one hand away and used the other to grip the top of my head. With one final thrust up, he shoved himself deep into my mouth, and then let out a ferocious groan.

"Ah, fuck, Kandy," he growled. "Just what I needed." His body tensed as he came, and as his warm cum spilled down my throat, I swallowed every drop.

He pulled his hand away and I moved back, wiping the corners of my mouth with the pad of my thumb.

"Better?" I asked, smiling up at him.

He smirked and sat forward, cupping my face in his hands and kissing me hard. "Hell yeah, baby. I'm so much better with you."

I beamed, and he released my face, pushing his laptop and some of the loose papers out of the way. "Sit on the desk," he commanded. "I need to take care of you before you go."

I blinked rapidly, heart booming. I stood quickly, and on my way up, his hands ran over the fabric of my dress. He pushed it up, lifting me with his strong hands, just enough to get me seated on the desk. In the chair, he rolled forward, staring up at me with heated, hungry eyes. I tilted my hips up, and he tucked a finger beneath the waistband of my panties and pulled them down.

My anxiousness got the best of me, so I planted my palms on the desk, spreading my legs apart. He hovered in front of my pussy, still teasing like he always did.

"I can feel how eager your pussy is," he rumbled between my thighs. "Your heat...your scent." The tip of his tongue ran over his bottom lip as he studied my pussy. I panted as he neared it, and when he pressed his mouth to my lips, I shuddered. He kissed me down there again and again, like he was making out with it, and my pussy clenched, dying for him to spread them apart and devour me.

"Cane," I panted.

He groaned, grabbing my hips and bringing me toward the edge of the desk. He kissed my pelvis and worked his way down. He kissed the area just outside my clit and a gasp shot out of me. And then, finally, when his eyes shifted up and locked on mine, his tongue plunged through and landed on my aching clit.

"Oh my God," I breathed. He squeezed my ass, burying his face deeper between my thighs, his tongue circling my clit repeatedly before sliding down and plunging inside me.

"This pussy," he rasped between my legs when he resurfaced. He drove his tongue back up to suck on my clit again and my legs shook violently, my moans heavier. "Fucking incredible." He looked up at me beneath thick lashes and I swear I lost it. His eyes alone could make a woman come—so heated and hungry, stirring up all the naughty, insatiable bits inside me.

My legs trembled and my arms became weak as I used them to keep my balance. I was so close, right on edge. Every swirl and lap of his tongue sent me spiraling into a beautiful abyss of pleasure and passion. With my eyes squeezed so tight, I saw stars, and then, when one of his guttural noises vibrated between my legs, I let go.

I cried out his name, squeezing his hair between my fingers and he groaned, finishing me off with his velvety tongue.

"Shit," I breathed, head falling backwards and eyes still shut, soaking it all in. My chest heaved up and down as Cane kissed my pussy once more. I opened my eyes and he got out of his chair to stand above me, face hovering over mine.

"You're so beautiful when you come. You know that?"

I blushed, shaking my head. "I'm not. I look and sound stupid."

"No. You look amazing and sound so damn sexy." He dropped a kiss on my cheek. I kissed him back, and then laced my arms around the back of his neck. I pressed my cheek to his chest, sighing. I didn't want this to be our last night.

"I'm going to miss you."

"I know. I'll miss you too, baby." He cupped a hand around the back of my head, kissing the top of it. "We'll see each other soon. I'll call every chance I get."

That made me smile. I picked my head up and he held my face, rubbing the skin behind my ears. "You better," I murmured, and then I leaned up to kiss him again, wishing I could stay like this with him forever.

CHAPTER THIRTY-THREE

KANDY

It was bittersweet going back to school, only because I knew I wouldn't see Cane again until spring. I thought going weeks without seeing him was bad when I was back at home, but going *months* without him felt like torture.

I'd flown back to school after kissing my parents goodbye. The good thing about our departure was that Dad didn't make it awkward. He kissed me and sent me off like any father would, and there wasn't any remorse or dread in his eyes. There was more hope than anything, but I'm certain the hope I'd given him was false.

If only he knew...

I'd settled into school again, following the same schedule of practices and conditioning. Of course, the upperclassmen gave me shit, especially Sophie. Her arm was better, so she was practicing her pitches and I couldn't lie, even with a hurt arm, she had a cannon on her. She would smirk at me as she passed by, and when it was my turn to pitch she'd make stupid coughing noises and pretend something was in her throat to try and get to my head, but it didn't work, and she knew it, which was why she probably couldn't stand me.

Poor girl had no clue that in high school, I used to ignore bitches like her on the daily. She and her clique weren't anything I couldn't handle.

A week later, I felt on top of the world. Cane was texting me at least every other day to check in. Sometimes he would call late at night and I'd have to sneak out of my dorm to get away from Morgan and Gina, just to have a little privacy on the phone with him.

Even though we were a secret, things were falling back into place again. My parents called at least once a day, and even Dad started calling and having casual conversations with me while he was in his cruiser or just at home watching sport. Yes, it could be frustrating sometimes, especially when Mom called and asked about Brody, but I dealt with it. I didn't tell her about me and Brody no longer hanging out because I knew she would ask a million questions just to get down to the bottom of why we weren't. She would have caught onto me, and at the moment, that was the last thing I wanted her to do.

Honestly, I liked the secrecy between Cane and I. I liked that only a select few who accepted us knew about us, and kept it as their treasured secret too.

But most of all, I liked that even though what we had was hidden in the dark, we understood each other enough to let our time shine bright.

On a crisp winter Friday, when the snow had dried up on campus, the leaves were still frozen, and sun was hiding behind the clouds, something terrible happened.

I was in the locker room after practice, packing my bag, when

Sophie walked in. I felt her scan me twice with her eyes before going five lockers down to get to hers.

She hummed a song by Halsey while she took out her bag and packed it. I slammed my locker shut, slinging the strap of my tote bag over my shoulder, brows narrowed as she looked at me again.

"Is there something I can help you with?" I finally asked. She was really starting to annoy me with her stupid stares.

She grinned. "Nothing at all."

She grabbed her bag and slammed her locker shut too, trotting out of the locker room. I rolled my eyes and pulled my phone out to check the time. I had some time to catch some food and grab a coffee before heading to my building to meet Morgan and Gina for a study session.

I made my way out of the locker room and down the dimly lit hallway, but as I rounded the corner, I saw two silhouettes. The sun was still out, and the silhouettes blocked the way to get out of the locker room. I rolled my eyes, realizing from the frizzy blond hair, that one of them was Sophie. The other was a guy with a baseball cap on.

I kept walking, keeping my eyes ahead. I didn't care about her little make out session. She was an idiot for doing it in the hallway anyway. Coach Carmen hated seeing her athletes doing vulgar shit, especially with guys.

"Fuck," the guy groaned, and it made me stop dead in my tracks. His voice was too familiar. So familiar that I looked over and when I did, his liquid brown eyes sparked from the sunlight, and locked right on mine, like he was waiting for me to look.

"Brody?" I narrowed my gaze, my heart catching speed.

Sophie looked over her shoulder, lacing her arms around the back of his neck. She rested her head on his chest, and Brody gave me a disgusted once-over, before saying, "What?"

"Nothing." I shook my head. I didn't give a shit that he was with Sophie. I mean, okay—maybe not on the outside, but on the inside I was pissed and I didn't know why. Why did I care? I didn't want him…but seeing him with a girl I wanted to punch in the face made it worse for some reason. I turned and started to walk off. Just as I did, my phone chimed, a text.

"Who is that? Your old-as-fuck boyfriend?"

My brows stitched then, my grip tightening around the phone as I glared at Brody. "How about you shut the hell up, Brody," I growled.

"Wait…she has a boyfriend?" Sophie asked.

"It's none of your fucking business." I glared harder at him. I had read him all wrong. I thought he was better than this, but it turns out he was no different than any other guy who hated being rejected.

Sophie ignored me and looked up at Brody. "What are you talking about? What boyfriend? I only ever saw her with you."

Brody shrugged it off and wrapped an arm around her shoulders. "It's nothing. She's just not who I thought she was."

I turned my back to him, shoulders hunched as I walked away, but I still heard Sophie say, "Because she wouldn't suck your cock? Who cares! I'll do it for you. You know that."

So that's what he'd told her? Wow. I wondered who else he might have told that lie to.

My eyes burned as I rushed away from the locker room and across the field. I made it to my building in no time, but wasn't up for the study session.

I told the girls I would catch them after I grabbed some food, but I didn't even go to do that. Instead, I showered, but while I was there, I kept fighting the tears. I wanted to blow up, I really did. I wanted to slap the shit out of Brody. He was telling people that we weren't talking because I wouldn't suck his cock? Really?

As bad as that was, it was better than him going around telling people that he caught me with Cane.

The next day, I got a text from Coach Carmen, asking me to meet her in her office. After my class, I went straight there. I knocked on her door and she called for me to come in.

Her office was quaint. The walls were a pastel blue and her desk was piled with papers. An open laptop was on the middle of the desk and she was typing rapidly, until she caught sight of me. She stopped tapping her fingers, peering up through the glasses on the bridge of her nose.

Coach Carmen was a pretty woman. Her brown hair was always in tight pin curls, her skin tan, and her eyes a stark blue. Though she was beautiful, she was also very intimidating. Not only from her height—she was a good six feet—but from the coldness of her eyes. I could tell a lot had happened to her in her life by her eyes alone. The way she stared always sent a chill through me, like she could read me like a book and knew everything I was trying hard to hide.

"Jennings," she greeted, gesturing to the chair on the opposite side of her desk. "Come in. Shut the door behind you."

I shut the door, walking to the cushioned chair and sliding my tote off my shoulder. Carmen had started typing again, looking through her spectacles. I ran a thumbnail over my cuticle, waiting for her to finish. When she finally did, she closed the laptop and then grabbed her iPhone.

"Is everything okay, Coach?" I asked, sitting up higher in my chair.

"I don't know, Jennings. You tell me." She cocked her head.

"I'm confused..." I gave her an uncertain once-over. "Did I do something wrong?"

She sighed and sat up straight, resting her elbows on the desk. She swiped left on her phone a few times, and then set it down on the desk, sliding the device toward me. "Can you tell me who he is and what that was about?"

I frowned at her a bit before picking up the phone. When I saw what was on the screen, I held back a gasp. *Holy shit.* What! *How?*

On the screen was me in Cane's rental car, the night he dropped me off after leaving his hotel. He was holding my face and kissing me. Coach Carmen swiped left again and there was another picture of us, lip-locked.

My heart galloped.

"Well?" she asked, when I jerked myself back in my chair.

"H-how did you get those?" I knew the answer, but I didn't want to believe it. How could he do that? Why would he do that?

"A teammate told me she was concerned about you. Said you might be trapped in a sticky situation…but from what I'm seeing, you seem perfectly content with this man and with what he was doing to you." She pointed at the screen again, while my mind ran in circles. The only teammate I could think of that would do this was Sophie. It had to be her and Brody.

"Who is this man?" Coach Carmen asked.

"I—no one. Just a friend."

"Oh, really? Just a friend? An older friend that you kiss in the parking lot after curfew?" She sat back in her chair. How the hell would she know it was after curfew? She wasn't there. That was proof that it was Brody. That ignorant son-of-a-bitch!

"He came to campus to visit me, Coach Carmen," I stated. "It was on a weekend. What I do during my free time shouldn't be anyone's concern."

"Well, on this team, we are like family, and I'm sorry Kandy, but this is unacceptable. Doesn't matter if it was the weekend, you are still under the care of this school. This is an older man who came onto this campus with one of my athletes and was touching her. How do you think that makes me look? I'm sorry but I have to tell your parents."

"What? Why?" I asked rapidly, sitting up higher in my chair.

"I don't know who this man is, Kandy. For all I know, he could have preyed on you, tricked you into getting off campus. Things like this have happened to young girls like you. Maybe not at this university, but all over the world."

"He's not just some stranger! I know him—I grew up with him!"

By the way she'd narrowed her eyes, I realized I had said too much. *"Grew up with him?* And he touches you that way?"

I wanted to scream. Why was this happening? Why would Brody and Sophie do this? All because I wanted Cane over him? Was he that ignorant and selfish?

"You can't tell my parents, Coach Carmen. I'm nineteen. This isn't their business."

Carmen scoffed. "You kids really blow my mind! Just because you're nineteen and considered an adult by law, it doesn't mean you know what's good for you. You may be out here on your own, but I expect better decisions to be made. Now, if you were doing this with another Notre Dame student, that would be different. But this is a fully-grown man who came onto campus and pulled a childish stunt. It's not right, Kandy. And your teammate has a right to be concerned about this."

"My *teammate* shouldn't be sharing pictures of me. That's invasion of privacy."

"She did it to protect you."

"No, she did it to humiliate me! I know who did this, Coach Carmen! I'm not an idiot! Sophie wants to see me fall! She's afraid I'm going to take her spot and be better than her!"

Carmen shook her head, and let out a heavy sigh. "Look, Kandy. I am supposed to tell your parents. It's what I am told to do by the school when something like this occurs. You are right about the activities you do during your free time being your own business, but when its brought onto campus that is a completely different story."

My leg bounced and I bit my bottom lip, tasting blood.

"*But* I also have the opportunity to hold off on this information with your parents," she went on, her eyes catching mine. Her mouth formed into straight line.

"But?"

"But I will have to discuss it with the board and they don't take these things lightly. Your scholarship will most likely be taken away and you will no longer be able to attend Notre Dame."

"Are you serious?" My voice broke into a million pieces. I couldn't believe this. The scholarship that I'd worked so hard for would vanish, just like that?

She pressed her lips.

"But I—I don't understand, Coach. I work just as hard as every other girl here. I mind my own business, attend every single class, stay out of trouble as much as possible, and all of that will be taken away from me because of what I do in *private?*"

She sighed. "I will have to tell the president and the board. I can't keep something like this a secret when it is brought to me from another student. Then there is a chance that I will lose my job if they hear about it and know that I knew but didn't speak up. I can tell them to keep this confidential, but I know for a fact that this will not sit well with them. This school is all about faith, Kandy. They will feel you are undeserving of the scholarship and will revoke it regardless. There's no difference between telling your parents now, and telling them later when they let you go. That's just how the system works here. They like to protect their students and this school's reputation."

Telling my parents that Cane had visited me on campus was going to ruin everything all over again. My family was finally on steady ground and so much happier. Dad was getting promoted soon and Mom was going to be starting her own law firm within the next year. Cane had his mom and sister back and was content. He was under a lot of stress, yes, but it wasn't because of me for once. I couldn't ruin that or disturb the peace again.

"My parents—they don't like this guy. That's why I kept it under wraps. I don't want to stop seeing him. I—I can tell him to not visit campus again, I swear. Just *please* don't tell the board, Coach. I can talk to Sophie—maybe we can work something out.

I'll tell her she can keep the number one spot. She can have it—I just don't want my parents to find out about this!"

Carmen shook her head, giving me a perplexed gaze. "Kandy, I wish I could sit on this. I really do. Trust me, if it had been me that saw you in the parking lot with him, I would have kept it to myself. You are an amazing player and I know you have a good heart, but since a teammate and another student at this campus knows, I can't keep this to myself, sweetie. I'm sorry."

My bottom lip trembled as I stared at her. I dropped my face into the palms of my hands, shaking my head and fighting a sob. This couldn't be happening. I swear there was always one thing after another and it wasn't fair. Why did my life have to be so unfair? I swear Nana cursed me!

"Maybe they'll show mercy," Carmen went on, voice softer. "Maybe they'll give you another chance since it's your first offense…" I didn't listen to whatever else she had to say. Her words were going in one ear and right back out the other.

She finally dismissed me and because of my panic, I didn't go to classes for the rest of the day. Hell, would there have been a point? One of them was a class with Brody and I didn't want to see him right now, worried I would punch him so hard he'd be left unconscious.

I camped out in my dorm room for the most part. I called Cane but his phone went straight to voicemail, so I assumed he was on a flight or very busy.

I hardly ate and my friends constantly asked if I was okay but I shrugged it off. I tossed and turned that same night. I could feel something bad getting ready to happen and it twisted me up inside. I wasn't ready.

I'd worked so hard…why was this happening to me?

CHAPTER THIRTY-FOUR

KANDY

I was on edge for three days straight. I hadn't heard anything from Carmen or the school, or even Brody and Sophie. Deep down, I had hoped that Carmen never even brought it to the board's attention. Maybe she spoke to Sophie and Brody and told them to back off...but the fourth day after, proved otherwise.

A man in a gray suit had knocked on our door. Morgan had answered it and when he asked for me, my heart dropped to my stomach.

"Kandy Jennings?" the man requested.

"That's me."

"The president of Notre Dame has given me instruction to bring this letter to you. He asks that you please read it carefully and then meet him at 1:30 for a mandatory hearing."

I nodded, taking the letter, and the man bobbed his head and walked off.

"What's going on?" Morgan hissed at me as I read over it.

"I don't know," I murmured, but I knew exactly what this was.

1:30 was in an hour. I guess they didn't want to waste any time on this one.

"What does the president need to see you for? What did you do?"

I sat on the edge of my bed, blinking hard as I read over the sentence that was printed on the paper, a dozen times.

Kandy Jennings,

This letter hereby states that you have a mandatory board hearing to discuss documents and proof of misconduct on the premises of Notre Dame University. Please report to the main building at 1:30 p.m. sharp.

The campus president himself signed the letter.

Morgan was over my shoulder, reading the letter as well. "Holy shit! Misconduct? What the hell did you do, Kandy?"

I sighed, blinking the burn out of my eyes. "Remember that older guy I was telling you about? The one I can't get over?"

"Yeah..."

"He was the man who spoke at the seminar we went to before break. Remember?"

"Wait—shit! The hot one with the tattoos?" Her eyes stretched wide. "*He's* the guy?"

"Yes."

"Well, shit! Now I see why you can't get over him! He's fucking hot!"

"I know but...Coach Carmen had pictures of me kissing him in the parking lot. The day when I skipped out on going shopping with you and Gina, it's because I was hanging out with him."

She gasped. "Shit. How did she get pictures? Was she watching you?"

"No. I'm certain it was from Brody. Brody showed up the night Cane dropped me back off. It was a little after curfew and no one else was around. Brody got all mad at me and called me a slut. I think he showed Sophie and Sophie told Coach because Carmen said it was a teammate who told her."

"Are you fucking kidding me! That bitch!"

I shrugged. "Not only that, but Coach said there's a possibility I can lose my scholarship over this."

"Wow...if you do, that is really fucked up. This team needs you! What are you going to do?"

"I don't know. Maybe the board will give me a pass or a warning?"

She nodded, but it was very unconvincing.

My shoulders sagged, my eyes dropping to the letter again. Morgan kept trying to convince me that everything was going to be okay, that I was a good student and had good grades to back me up, but deep in my heart, I knew things wouldn't be okay.

I left the room forty-five minutes later, crossing campus to get to the main building.

I walked up a tall flight of stairs and checked in with a secretary with white hair and thin-framed glasses, sitting behind a desk. When I rounded the corner after checking in, Coach Carmen was sitting in one of the chairs. She gave me a wary smile when she spotted me.

"How's it going, Jennings?" she asked.

"Could be better," I mumbled.

I was upset, but not really at Coach Carmen. She was just doing her job and I couldn't fault her for that. I was an athlete and easily replaceable. This was her livelihood.

We waited for ten minutes before they called Carmen in. She rubbed my shoulder before going inside.

My heart was clanging against my ribcage, my mouth dry, and palms slick as I waited. I kept checking my phone for the time.

I wanted to text Cane and let him know that I may or may not have been losing my scholarship in less than an hour, but I would have had to tell him why and I didn't want him to blame himself. I wanted to talk to him…just not about this. Not yet. He had enough on his plate as it was, plus I could have been jumping to conclusions.

Thirty minutes passed before the door pushed open and Coach Carmen walked back out.

The look in her eyes as she focused on me, told it all.

"I hope I convinced them enough to let you stay," she said, and then she walked off.

A minute later, my name was called.

CHAPTER THIRTY-FIVE

KANDY

The board meeting room was huge—probably too big for only five people to occupy.

A row of tables with leather rolling chairs behind them, were across from me, and there were two men and a woman occupying some of those chairs. They had folders in front of them and were murmuring amongst themselves as a man escorted me inside, asked for my cellphone, and then told me to sit at the table in the single chair in middle of the room. In front of the single chair was a microphone on the table.

When I sat, the chairmen and woman looked at me. The woman was young, with brown hair pulled up into a top bun. She gave a small, sympathetic smile, but it only pulled at my heartstrings, making this much more complicated.

"Kandy Jennings, correct?" the man in the middle, with an obvious toupee, inquired.

"That is correct."

"Nice to meet you. I am President Reverend Jones, this is Vice

President Richard Grayson, and the school psychologist and therapist, Leslie Bailey. Can you say your full name and date of birth into the microphone please?"

"Yes. It's Kandy Alexandra Jennings. I was born on September 19th, 1999."

"Okay. Thank you for that. We are going to get started. While this is happening, please direct your answers to the microphone and answer as honestly as possible."

"Okay." I glanced down at the microphone.

"Miss Jennings, we're going to get right into it. I'm sure you know why you're here." Mr. Grayson started. He was chubbier, bald with rosy cheeks, the collar of his shirt tight around his neck. "We have several images here of you with a man who is not a student or a teacher, on our campus. You were in his car, correct?"

"Yes," I answered.

"And what were you doing in his car?"

"We had hung out that day and then he dropped me off."

"Where did you go, if you don't mind us asking?"

"He had booked a hotel here."

All of their eyebrows nearly touched their foreheads. My heart sunk.

"Were you inside his hotel room, Miss Jennings?" Mrs. Bailey asked.

"I was."

She nodded, looking down at one of the papers in front of her. "Okay. And is it true that this same man is Mr. Quinton Cane? He was here as a speaker for a business seminar but saw you and took you to a hotel?"

"N-no. That's not how it happened," I answered. "We knew each other before the seminar even happened. He knew this was the school I was attending so he signed up to be a speaker, but it wasn't planned for me to go to his hotel. We agreed to do that when we spoke after the seminar."

"Okay. We spoke to one of the student athletes this morning, and he told us that Mr. Cane was very aggressive with you? That something seemed off and you seemed afraid to be alone with him. Is that true?" she went on.

"That is not true." I tried hard not to let my voice waver.

"Could it be that he forced you to go to his hotel? Made you feel as if you had no choice?" the president asked.

I shook my head. "No. What we did was a mutual understanding and consensual."

Mr. Grayson sighed, folding his fingers on top of the table. "Listen, Miss Jennings. We may be able to help you keep your scholarship here, but not if you are covering up for this man. If you felt uncomfortable in any way while he was around, you can let us know and we can report it to the authorities. We want to protect you as best as we can."

"I understand that, but Mr. Cane did not harm me, or threaten me, or make me feel like a victim, if that is what you are implying."

They all looked at each other, before dropping their gazes.

"You told Coach Carmen that you did not want us to tell your parents. Why is that?" Reverend Jones asked.

I swallowed hard, my leg bouncing as I answered. "Because my parents don't approve of him."

"Why? If you don't mind me asking?" Mrs. Bailey asked.

"Because...he used to be really good friends with them."

"I see." She wrote something down. "So you don't want your parents to know because they don't know about what you are doing with him? That you're sneaking around with him?"

"Something like that."

Both of the men stared at me.

"Miss Jennings, I am going to be completely honest with you here." Reverend Jones shut his folder. "To me, it seems you are trying to protect this man, and I can understand wanting to do that for someone you care about, but what he did is intolerable and what you did with him by leaving campus and sneaking around with him, is just as unacceptable. You are a young nineteen-year-old woman. He looks to be in his forties, perhaps? You have no business messing with a man that age. At Notre Dame, our athletes represent what we stand for. We take pride in our athletes and our students. Imagine if someone else had caught wind of this, had taken pictures and of you with him and put those pictures in an article. Imagine if that article had circulated and went into the world about an older man messing with a young student on our campus? It would make the school look bad. It would make me look bad. It could cause us to lose sponsors and have families wanting to pull their children out of our schools." His brows dipped into a frown. "Even though Coach Carmen pleaded your case and wanted you to stay, I just cannot jeopardize the image of my school for one person's actions. Furthermore, we refuse to take this to an actual court and make a spectacle out of this situation. I'm sorry, Miss Jennings, but we are going to have to have your scholarship annulled so we can give it to someone else at this time. Someone who will respect the rules and understand the faithfulness of our university."

I had no words. I knew this was coming, but even still, all forms of languages were lodged in my throat. The first thing I felt was brokenness, all over again. The next thing I felt was fear, because the words that came out of Mr. Grayson's mouth next, froze me right up.

"We have already had arrangements made for Coach Carmen to contact your parents. By Wednesday afternoon, we expect you to have your dorm room cleaned out and for you to have left the University of Notre Dame. We will send security to check that this has been followed through and then follow up with an official letter as to why this has happened. The letter will most likely be sent to your home address."

I huffed, as if it would decrease the weight on my chest, but it didn't. I pushed out of my chair as they asked if I had any questions. No, I didn't have any questions, but I was fuming.

After getting my cellphone back, I yanked the door open and

rushed down the stairs, out to the cold. The wind nipped at my cheeks and tousled my hair but I didn't give a flying fuck.

I kept going until I was across campus and in front of the familiar fraternity house. I banged on the door with a heavy fist, and Leo answered. "Yo, why the fuck are you knocking so damn hard?" he snapped.

I shoved past him and went through the living room where two girls were topless, and right for the kitchen where I heard people talking.

Standing in the kitchen was my culprit. Sitting on the countertop right beside him was Sophie, and there were a few other football players around but I didn't care to figure out who they were. My eyes pinned on Brody as he stood with his lower back pressed to the edge of the counter, a slice of pizza in one hand and a drink in a red cup in the other.

"Well, look what the cat dragged in! My balls are already blue just looking at you! Get the fuck out!"

He was trying to show off in front of his friends, and yes, he got a good laugh from them, but he wasn't going to have the last one. Not after what he did to me.

I stormed toward him and snatched the drink out of his hand, bringing it up and dumping it right over his head. All of the football players in the kitchen belted out roars of laughter and Sophie started to snicker, but I grimaced at her, snatching the wet pizza out of Brody's hand and smashing it on her face. I smeared the warm, soaked pizza all over her, including the top of her head, and then dragged it down to her white blouse.

She shrieked while Brody stood with his hands out like a fucking idiot, like he couldn't believe this had really happened.

"Thanks to you two, I just lost my scholarship," I seethed.

"Good for you," he chortled, still clinging to his pride. "You fucking deserve it. Go be a slut somewhere else."

Normally, it wasn't like me to blow up. It took a lot for me to get truly, truly angry, and Brody had struck a nerve. My hand struck his face before I could tell myself to back away and leave. His face was wet so the slap was loud and it echoed. My hand stung afterward and I knew for sure it had hurt him. The entire kitchen went silent when Brody's head turned with the hit.

He breathed hard through his nostrils, fists clenching, but I shoved him away, making him stumble backwards and hit the counter edge. "Fuck both of you!"

I stormed out of the kitchen and out of the house before any of them could stop me.

I jogged away from the fraternity house, going all the way back to where my dorm building was. When I'd made it safely, I dropped on the bench, letting the adrenaline wear off and catching my breath...but I shouldn't have. Because when it wore off, reality pummeled me like a swift train.

I was heaving hard, trying to catch my breath and cry at the same time. It was chilly outside, but the tears were flaming hot, running down my cheeks. People walked by and looked at me as if I were insane and I couldn't blame them.

In the span of four days, my life had been ruined all over again.

All for wanting Cane.

Was this how it was going to be for the rest of my life? I didn't know if I had it in me to keep going through stuff like this. Ever since I started wanting Cane—like really, *really* wanting him—my life has spiraled.

This one question ran through my mind the rest of that day. It didn't matter that my parents were blowing my phone up trying to reach me. I knew they would be angry, but their anger held no weight to this one question.

Was it even worth it to love Cane, only to lose everything I loved and cared for in the end?

CHAPTER THIRTY-SIX

CANE

I landed back in Atlanta well over six hours ago and had just wrapped up on a conference call when my cell phone buzzed on the desk. Kelly had been calling nonstop, but I ignored every single one of them. This time it was a call from Kandy.

"How's it going, Kandy Cane?" I answered.

"Not good," she said, voice thick. She sounded winded, like she was working out or something.

I walked toward the windows that overlooked the city. "What's wrong?"

"I…um…well, you're not going to believe this, but I just had my scholarship revoked."

"What?" I snapped, frowning. "How? What the hell happened?"

She sniffled. "Remember that guy you saw me with after the seminar?"

"Yeah?" My fist clenched, grip tightening around the phone just thinking about it. "What about him? Did he do something to you?"

"I didn't tell you this because I didn't want you to worry, but he saw us together the night you dropped me off. He confronted me about it and called me a slut, then the next thing I know he sends the pictures to one of my teammates and my teammate told my coach."

"What the fuck," I grumbled. "Are you fucking kidding me?"

"No, I'm not Cane. And that isn't the worst of it."

"What the hell could be worse than that? You worked hard for that scholarship, Kandy."

"I know I did, but I had a hearing a short while ago. They said they've already made arrangements to tell my parents about the pictures. My parents have been calling me nonstop and I don't want to answer because I don't know what to say!"

She was panicking now—I could hear it in the shortness of her breaths and the gasps bubbling out of her.

"Fuck, Kandy. Just calm down, all right. Calm down."

"How can I calm down, Cane? My life is fucking ruined! Softball was all I had! I actually made friends and was looking forward to starting the season, and now all of that is gone because of wanting to be with you!"

Well, shit.

I stepped away from the window and turned, pressing the phone harder to my ear. "Kandy, I didn't mean for this to happen to you. I'm sorry that it did, but we both knew the consequences! Shit, I never should have visited the school. This is all my fucking fault."

She whimpered and my heart fucking broke for her even more. I hated hearing my girl cry. "This scholarship was all I had, Cane. I didn't think I would lose it."

"No. That's where you're wrong, Kandy."

"How? What are you even talking about? Do you hear what I'm telling you? My parents know, Cane! They're calling me and I don't know how to explain it or even go back home and look them in the eye!"

"You didn't let me finish, Kandy!" I barked. "Calm down. I mean it! Find somewhere to sit right now and take a second!"

She sniffled harder, letting out an exasperated breath.

"What are you doing right now?"

"I'm packing. They want me off of campus by Wednesday."

"Damn. Not much of a notice." I sighed. "Look, you don't have to face your parents right away. If you need time or think they'll need time to digest this before talking about it, take it. I'll book you a flight, you can fly back to Georgia, and I'll pick you up from the airport myself. Just say the word."

"I—I don't know. I just feel like I'm back at square one again. I feel like I'm ruining everything," she whined. "What am I going to do without a degree? I can't afford to pay for college myself and now my parents are going to come out of pocket instead! They're going to be pissed!"

"I understand your frustrations. I do. I get them. I know it feels like you're in a glass case and the roof has shattered. I know you feel like life is fucking you over, but you need to realize that I am here for you. Whatever you go through, I'm going through it with you. And when it comes to college, I know plenty of people who would take you just from my recommendation alone and I have *plenty* of money to take care of loans and fees and whatever the hell else you'll need. Money is not a problem. Getting you into another school is not a problem. We can fix this, so suck it up, finish packing your shit, and come home. I'll take care of the rest."

"I'll have to face my parents eventually, Cane," she sobbed. "I don't want them to look at me like they did before. I don't want anything else bad to happen to you."

"You can talk to them when you're ready. You're old enough to make your own decisions. Ignoring them will only piss them off though, so be honest and tell them where you'll be if you don't want to go home right away. They'll be mad, but they'll be glad you told them and should respect your privacy enough not to push for more until you're ready to give it."

Her sobs weakened, and the sniffling died down. "I love you," she murmured.

"I love you too." I slouched down in my chair. "Come home, Kandy," I said, hoping it would sooth her. "Let's figure this out together."

CHAPTER THIRTY-SEVEN

KANDY

My parents had called twenty-one times, left six voice messages, and sent fourteen text messages combined within eight hours. I know because I'd counted.

I felt horrible for ignoring them, but at this point, I didn't know what else to do. Plus, Dad's voicemails didn't make the situation any easier. He kept threatening how he was going to go to Cane and pick a bone with him. Mom on the other hand was more concerned about me losing my scholarship and wondering what I was going to do for school in the long run.

I decided to take Cane up on the offer he'd given me, so the next morning I sent a text to Mom and told her not to come for me—that I had it handled and would see them soon. She called a million times after that one message, but I didn't answer the calls. I couldn't at the moment. I needed time to think.

I didn't have a place to put all my belongings, but luckily Gina had relatives that lived near the campus and agreed to drive me there to let me store my things at their place. I wasn't allowed to leave anything in the dorm. If I did, it was going to be thrown away. Morgan kept some of it, like the comforter and a few of my softball gloves.

I hugged Morgan and Gina goodbye for good and we all shared a few tears. Afterwards, I caught the flight Cane had booked for me and flew back to Georgia.

Like he'd promised, he was waiting for me up front. He was standing in front of the exit with his hands tucked in his pockets and a pair of sunglasses covering his eyes, like he'd just arrived. I spotted him before he could see me, and my heart sped up several notches the closer I got.

Seeing him, reminded me of when I was a little girl and was looking at him for the first time. Though I was hopeless, the sunglasses shielding his eyes and his bad boy demeanor did something to me—whirled me up inside and drove me crazy.

He looked around for a moment like he could feel someone watching him, and when he was facing my direction, he put on a warm, welcoming smile, pulling the sunglasses off. He opened his arms and I dragged my suitcase on it's wheels, rushing into them.

I hugged him hard and squeezed so tight. This hug was exactly what I needed. No questions, just outpouring love. My parents would have hounded me first, questioned me later, and maybe hug me after making the same "mistake" twice. And that was a *big* maybe.

But Cane was no mistake. He couldn't be. Why would he have been brought into my life, if we weren't meant to be something? It didn't make any sense. There had to be a reason for this. There had to be happiness at the end of our story.

"Ready to go?" he asked after kissing the top of my head.

"Yeah. Let's go."

Cane grabbed my suitcase and carried it in one hand, using his free arm to hook it around me and walk with me out of the airport. I clung to him, and though I felt low and like the world was against me, I was comforted and whole being right next to him.

He took me to lunch at a quiet restaurant. I'd ordered a chicken salad but with so much anxiety coursing through me, I only picked at it. I wasn't very hungry and he noticed, I'm sure, but didn't say anything.

After lunch, we were on the way to his house. A part of me panicked, thinking maybe my parents would know where I was and would be waiting there, but the driveway was empty.

We got out of the car and unloaded in the house. A spur of relief struck me, being back here again.

I noticed Cane didn't really say much. He would ask little questions here and there about what I wanted to do, or if I was thirsty, or if I'd talked to my parents since the hearing, to which I'd answered yes, but he wouldn't push beyond that. That was one thing I loved about him. He knew when to give me space.

After I'd taken a shower and changed into comfortable clothes, he let me stay upstairs to curl up in his bed while he worked downstairs. It was probably the wrong thing to do though, because being alone made me think too much, and all I could think about was how miserable my life was and how maybe being with Cane wasn't the right thing for me. The signs pointed to it. Everything bad that was happening to me was happening because of my attachment to Cane and my unwillingness to let go.

I wished in that moment I had answers. I wished a psychic could just come up and tell me whether I should stick it out with him for ultimate bliss and happiness, or if I was wasting my time.

When I looked into Cane's eyes, I felt safe and whole, and I didn't feel like what we had was time wasted. But when we were apart, everything was being ripped to shreds and I was drowning, and I don't think that's how I was supposed to feel.

I cried that night.

Cried over losing my scholarship.

Cried over Brody and Sophie tarnishing me.

Cried over losing my good friends Gina and Morgan. I would never see them again and even though we promised to keep in touch, it wasn't going to be the same as being there.

I cried mostly because for the first time in a long time, I couldn't rush to my parents and let them take care of my troubles. I couldn't because they would make me choose. They wouldn't understand, nor would they let me be free…and in that very moment, I needed freedom to decide what I wanted to do, not their chains of negativity.

CHAPTER THIRTY-EIGHT

KANDY

The next morning, someone nudged me awake.

"Kandy," Cane murmured on my lips. He kissed me on the mouth and I groaned, twisting over so my back was facing him. "Kandy…you've been sleeping all morning," he chuckled.

"Sleeping is the only thing I can do. I don't have a job and I don't go to school anymore. Might as well stay in bed," I muttered.

"Ha. Funny, but no." He grabbed my hand and pulled me up. I shrieked a bit and he stepped closer to the edge of the bed, tipping my chin. "I'm not going to let you sit around and mope. Get dressed. Today is going to be our day for a little fun."

"Our day? What do you mean?"

"Let's go shopping. Buy some things. Get some food to cook together."

I bit a smile. As badly as I wanted to wallow in my own pity, that did sound nice. "As long as you promise that we get to eat spaghetti. Gah—I didn't think I'd miss spaghetti so much but I do."

"We'll make it with extra sauce and extra parmesan, just the way you like it. Now come on," he insisted, grinning as he clapped his hands. "Get dressed and meet me down stairs."

"Okay, okay. Fine." I shooed him off playfully and climbed out of bed. I went for my suitcase in the corner and decided on a sky blue maxi dress. I didn't want to keep him waiting long so I freshened up and then tied my hair up, letting a few stray tendrils hang at the nape of my neck and around my face. When I was done, I met him downstairs.

Cane took me to the mall first, and there I grabbed a cinnamon pretzel and devoured it. To my surprise, he walked with me hand-in-hand in public, and it made butterflies flutter in my belly. Like he noticed my glee, he smiled down at me and squeezed my hand.

We walked through the entire mall, making stops here and there, especially when I saw a cute pair of purple Chucks. Of course he bought them, even though I insisted that he didn't have to.

Then I saw a store that caught me by total surprise.

"Oh my gosh," I gasped.

Cane stepped beside me as I gawked. "I wanted to show you instead of telling you."

"Oh my gosh, Cane! You have a store in the mall?" The store had a neon red sign above the entrance, the word Tempt in a bold, fat font. The store was playing dance music, and Cane grabbed my hand, leading the way.

When we got inside, it was somewhat darker than the rest of the stores. There was a section that had various chocolates and red boxes lined up, and on the other was a line of lingerie. A tall woman with blond hair stood behind the counter and smiled way too hard when she saw us coming in.

"Oh my goodness. How do I have the honor of serving *the* Quinton Cane?" she squealed, and Cane put on a smug smile.

"Just doing some shopping, Elizabeth."

"Well, that's always fun!" Her eyes swooped over to mine. "And are you shopping for lingerie or chocolate?"

Cane smirked then, dropping his gaze to lock it with mine. I shook my head.

No! He'd better not!

"Lingerie," he answered, and I wanted the floor to swallow me whole. I blushed way too hard when Elizabeth beamed her perfect smile at me.

"Lingerie for the young lady. Yes, let's see what we have!"

Elizabeth turned and I pulled my hand out of Cane's to give him a light slap across the arm. "Are you insane?" I whisper-hissed.

He got a kick out of that, laughing as he gestured in the direction Elizabeth had gone in. "It put a smile on your face, didn't it?"

As much as I was blushing and my face felt like it'd caught fire, I *was* smiling, and I wanted to slap him silly for embarrassing me, but wanted to hug him even more for giving a damn.

"So, do you like red or black?" Elizabeth asked, picking up two sets and weighing them up and down in her hands.

"Um…black," I said, tucking a strand of hair behind my ear.

"Black," she sang. "Good choice. Black compliments all skin tones. This is our bestselling set. The women love it, and I think it would look great on you." Elizabeth looked at Cane. "Mr. Cane, will this suit you?"

Cane slid his hands into his front pockets. "I think its perfect. Then again, she looks good in anything."

Of course he approved. And of course he was still getting a kick out of this embarrassing situation. He was such a goof.

Elizabeth took me to a dressing room to measure me, which was equally embarrassing, and then we were back out, meeting Cane at the register. He'd ordered the same set of lingerie in three different colors—red, black, and navy blue. I had no idea why he was wasting his money. I loved nice panties, especially lace ones, but G-strings were on a whole other level.

When we left the store, Cane carrying the paper *Tempt* bag proudly, I hooked my arm through his and said, "You did that on purpose."

"Of course I did. I need my Kandy back—the one who loves being teased." He grabbed my chin and pinched it lightly between his forefinger and thumb.

"I'm here, I promise. Just have to get used to it I guess. When did the store open?"

"Two weeks ago. Believe it or not, it was Lora's idea to have a store built into a local mall."

"Really?" I looked up at him. "I'm glad she's back. She's been helping you out with a lot of things."

"Yeah," he sighed. "I'm glad she's back too. Truthfully, I think she's just trying to find things to do to occupy herself, which I don't mind at all. I'd rather her be here and in my hair, than somewhere else."

"That's good."

"What do you say we head to the grocery store? Grab the ingredients for the spaghetti?"

I beamed up at him, just thinking about the yummy spaghetti. "Sounds like a plan."

At the store, we'd grabbed all the ingredients needed to make my mom's favorite spaghetti recipe. As we walked out of the store, Cane put his visors on and said, "I hope you know what you're doing with this stuff."

I laughed and started to respond, but a voice called my name from a distance. It was familiar and scared the living shit out of me.

"Kandy?" the deep voice called again and I looked to my left. I knew the voice before I saw the person it belonged to, and my heart dropped to my stomach. I stopped walking as my dad crossed the parking lot in his police uniform, brows narrowed and eyes locked right on me.

Cane stopped walking too, pulling off his sunglasses.

"Kandy, what the hell?" Dad yelled. "Your mother and I have been calling you! Why haven't you been answering the phone?"

"I—I was going to call back when I was ready—"

Dad looked at Cane and grimaced. "I am so *sick* of you manipulating her, Cane! I swear to God, every time some shit goes down you're in the fucking picture!"

"Dad, stop!" I shouted, rushing between them. "It was my choice to go with him! I knew how you would react after the school called you so I called Cane and he booked a flight for me to come back here!"

"Why?" Dad barked. "Why couldn't you just call me and ask me to schedule the flight? Why the hell did it have to be Cane? You told me you weren't talking to him anymore, but then I get a call from school saying your scholarship was revoked because you were with him? Just doesn't make any fucking sense, Kandy! Don't you see he's ruining your fucking life?"

"He is not ruining my life, so back off, Dad! I mean it!"

Dad's eyes stretched wider, like he was shocked that I'd spoken to him that way. I could understand why he was. I had never spoken to him that way. I'd shocked myself, to the point I was literally shaking.

"Kandy," Cane tried to speak, but I held my hand up at him. Cane was only helping and my dad was being a selfish asshole and letting his anger get in the way of what I wanted. Yes, he had a right to be upset, but he needed to realize that he didn't control me. I'd had it with him.

"Kandy...out of all the men—all the people in this fucking world—you decide to be with him?" Dad questioned, voice lower. "I just can't wrap my head around it. It doesn't make any sense to me."

"Well, sometimes things like this don't make sense, but that doesn't give you the right to hurt him or me because of it, or make me do things just because you want it to be your way. My life is not yours."

Dad scoffed. "Hurt you? Kandy, I am trying to *protect* you! I know Cane! I know where he came from and it's not a good place. I don't want you getting caught up in any of that!"

"I'm fine," I asserted.

Dad's head shook. "Your mother isn't going to be happy knowing you're in Georgia and didn't tell her."

"I was going to come home and talk to both of you when I was ready. I didn't want to talk to you while your head was hot. I wanted us to talk when you'd cooled down. I knew you were pissed, that's why I stayed away."

Dad ran a hand over his face. "Can't believe this shit," he grumbled, looking from Cane to me. He stared at Cane, but Cane matched his stare, not backing down this time.

"Look, D, I—"

"No—don't even fucking talk to me!" Dad snapped. "This is what's going to happen. Mindy is off work tomorrow and so am I. Kandy is coming back home tonight, where she belongs, and tomorrow you are coming over for dinner. I don't give a shit if you have meetings or flights—you better fucking cancel them because if you don't show up tomorrow, I will be sure that you *never* see my daughter again. You aren't the only person who knows people, Cane."

I stepped back, peering up at Cane. His jaw was ticking, and his grip tightened around the paper bag of groceries cradled in his arm. "She's only going home if she says she wants to. Otherwise, she's coming back with me. You don't tell her what to do anymore, D. She's not your fucking puppet."

Dad started to charge him, but I pressed a hand to his chest and forced him back. Dad was seething like a bull. He hated being challenged, but Cane had a point. My father couldn't make me do anything I didn't want to do, and he needed to realize that. I wasn't nine anymore and he couldn't ground me over choices like this.

"Dad. Back. Off." I forced him back some more and he lowered his eyes to mine.

"I want you home, Kandy. Tonight. I mean it," he snarled.

"And I'll come home, as long as you promise not to hurt Cane."

Dad's seething settled a bit. His eyes flickered over to Cane's before dropping again. "Fine. But if he's not there tomorrow, he stays away. I mean it."

"Fine."

Dad grunted, jerking himself away.

"I'm going back with him to get my suitcase and I'll have him drop me off."

"I mean it," Dad repeated, pointing a finger at Cane. "You don't show and I will fucking ruin you. She claims you love her so much? Well, tomorrow you're going to fucking prove it to me."

Dad turned his back, shoulders hunched, and trekked through the parking lot to get to the store. I let out the breath trapped in my lungs, turning toward Cane who was watching Dad go.

Without so much as a word, he trudged to his car, popping the trunk, dropping the bag of groceries in it, and then going for the passenger door, snatching it open.

"Get in," he grumbled.

"Cane, don't take what he said to heart. He's mad at me and taking it out on yo—"

"Just get in the car so I can take you home, Kandy. Please."

I clamped my mouth shut and climbed into the car, sitting back against the leather. Cane got in immediately and started the car.

He drove in silence, but I noticed how tight his grip was on the wheel. The silence was deafening. I had to say something.

"I don't have to go back tonight, Cane. We can go together tomorrow. Maybe it'll make a statement—show him that we're serious."

"No. That'll just make him angrier. You can go home tonight, settle whatever feelings need to be squashed, and I'll come for dinner. I have a flight tomorrow night, but I'll reschedule it. It's fine."

"You shouldn't have to do that for me."

"I want to. I want him to know that what we have isn't just meaningless sex, like I'm sure he assumes it is."

I sighed and focused on the road ahead. When we got to his house, I packed up my suitcase—there wasn't much to put back inside it—and met Cane back downstairs. He was raking his fingers through his hair, like he was annoyed about the entire situation.

I held the handle of my suitcase tighter and met him at the door. He opened it, letting me walk out first, but stopped me before I could get completely out. "Are you sure you want to put yourself through this to be with me?"

I shrugged. "I'm positive. They'll have to understand eventually, right?"

He looked me in the eyes carefully before nodding. "Right."

He shut and locked the door behind him, then followed me to the car, popping the trunk and grabbing my suitcase to put it in. We were in the car again, riding in silence, but this time our fingers were entwined.

We made it to my parents' house, where Cane shut off the lights before pulling into the driveway. Dad's truck was parked there, and I was sure Mom was home by now too.

Warily, I got out of the car and Cane followed suit. He carried my suitcase to the porch and I was glad the lights weren't on. When he placed it down, he brought a hand up to cup one side of my face. "Let me know if you want me to come back. I will."

"I'll be fine," I assured him.

"Okay." He dropped a kiss on my lips. "I'll be back tomorrow."

"Kay." He pressed his forehead to mine, leaving one more kiss on my lips before pulling away. "Go, before he catches you," I said, trying to smile for him, but it came off crooked.

"Call or text me if you need anything."

I nodded and grabbed the handle of my suitcase, but Cane came in for one more kiss, wrapping a hand around the nape of my neck. He dug his fingers into the back of my neck just enough for me to feel it—most likely to let me know that this changed nothing. That he was still mine and I was still his.

When he pulled back and walked off, I ran my tongue over my bottom lip, heat blooming in the pit of my belly. I watched him get inside his car and start it and his headlights flashed on me and across the house.

As he pulled out of the driveway, the lock on the door clinked and then swung open. Mom was there, and when she spotted me, she let out a loud gasp and rushed toward me, reeling me in for a hug around the neck.

I hugged her back. "Oh, Kandy. God, you had me so worried!" She sighed when releasing me. I walked into the house and she closed the door behind us.

Holding my face in hand, she looked me all over. "Tell me what happened, sweetheart. Was Cane really on campus?"

I dropped my eyes. "Yes. He came for a business seminar."

"So he took initiative to come out and see you? All the way in Indiana?"

"Mom, please. It wasn't like that." I pulled away from her.

"Well, tell me what it was like, Kandy, because right now, his behavior doesn't make any sense."

"Doesn't have to," a deep voice said behind Mom. She turned around, and both of us looked at Dad. He was standing by the opening of the kitchen, arms folded. "He'll be over tomorrow. He'll have no choice but to explain himself. Explain all of this."

Mom let out a breath. She looked at me like she had so many questions, but didn't want to overwhelm me with them right now. Not yet anyway.

Truthfully, with Dad lingering in the background brooding, I wasn't up for talking about Cane anyway.

"Well, go up to your room, get settled in, then meet me back down stairs." She rubbed my shoulders. "We can talk—just you and me. Okay?" She whispered the last part.

"Sure," I muttered.

She walked to Dad. They both went into the kitchen, Dad's eyes staying back a little longer than Mom's. It seemed he had a lot to say too, but was saving it for dinner the next night.

I went up to my room and showered, but I didn't have it in me to go back down and talk to Mom. If she came up to my room and wanted to talk, sure, but I didn't know what to tell her that I hadn't already said.

I think it was pretty obvious why I'd gotten back with Cane again. I wanted him. I loved him. Plain and simple...they just refused to understand it.

To my luck, Mom didn't come back upstairs. I curled up in my bed, which was freshly made by the way. Apparently, they were looking forward to my arrival. That was good to know, at least. They loved me enough to want me there.

Cane sent me a text around midnight. Thankfully I was still awake.

Cane: It won't be easy, Kandy Cane.

Me: I know.

Cane: Hopefully things will be okay tomorrow.

Me: I hope so too...my dad is looking at me weird again.

Cane: Try not to let it get to you...

Me: I'm just ready to see you tomorrow. Prove to them that it's real.

Cane: We will.

I shut my phone off, eyelids getting heavier.
    I hoped everything would go back to the way it was before.
    I hoped Cane was right. Everything needed to be okay. Not just for my parents' sake, but for ours too.

CHAPTER THIRTY-NINE

KANDY

I'd spent the morning helping Mom prepare food for dinner. She and I had gone grocery shopping, cleaned potatoes, meat, chopped broccoli, and seasoned it all throughout the day.

Of course she asked about school, and wanted to know what they'd told me at the hearing. Mom believed there was a way I could take it to court, seeing as it was such short notice that they revoked my scholarship, and refused to take it to court and give me a fair chance to talk to an attorney, but that was her lawyer side speaking. It was better to just let it go. Plus, I had a feeling Coach Carmen wouldn't have wanted me around anyway. Imagine if I'd won the case and still had my scholarship, the school would have grown a disdain for me. I would have been the talk of the campus. It was better to start fresh somewhere else.

I told her all I could remember about the hearing, and even told her and Dad about Brody and Sophie, and how I dumped my drink on him and smeared a slice of pizza in Sophie's face. Mom found it humorous. Dad didn't. Of course he was still upset. Definitely on edge, probably ready to confront Cane and try to squash it all. Or worse, tell Cane to leave me alone out of respect for him. Ugh.

To be fair, my parents didn't speak much of Cane, and even though Dad walked around with a bit of an attitude, it felt like home again somehow. Not a complete and happy home, but home nonetheless.

Before I knew it, dinner was getting started.

I had gone through the same routine, almost like I was a teenager again, meeting Cane for our usual weekend dinners. I styled my hair and wore a more conservative black dress that stopped at the knees just so I wouldn't piss my dad off anymore than he already was. When I heard a car door shut, my heart skipped a beat.

He's here.

I finished up rapidly, hoping to answer the door before my parents could. They were out back, by the grill. When I made it down, my parents were nowhere in sight. I could hear things rattling in the kitchen and the patio door sliding open and closed. I glanced over my shoulder once before focusing on the door, gripping the knob and twisting it.

When I pulled it open all of my worries seemed to subside, because there he stood, and when his eyes found mine, I smiled.

"Hey," I breathed.

"Hey, Kandy Cane," he murmured, scanning me with his eyes. "You look great."

I gave him a small laugh. "You're lying. This is one of my modest dresses. Wore it because I don't want to piss my dad off."

When I said that, Cane looked over my shoulder, his smile slowly fading. "Where is he anyway?"

"He's probably out back. He's grilling steak tonight."

"Steak?" His brows shifted, nearly touching his hairline. "Wow. He must really mean business. I don't think we've had steak since the very first time I had dinner here."

"Wow. How can you remember that?"

"Because it was the best steak I'd ever had. Homemade. Fresh." He put on a lazy, lopsided smile.

I had the urge to hug him, kiss him even, but instead I let him come inside. When he made it into the foyer, I shut the door behind him and looked up to meet his eyes. "Are you sure you want to do this? We don't have to, you know? He can't tell me what to do anymore."

"I know he can't, but out of respect for the friendship I had with him before, and for you, I have to."

I sighed. He was right, but I didn't want to see him being hounded.

I heard the patio door slide open. "Kandy! You almost ready?" Mom called. Not even two seconds ticked by before she was trotting around the corner from the kitchen and into plain view. "Oh!" she exclaimed, like she was surprised to see Cane standing there. "Wow, you're here early!"

Cane smiled. "Hope you don't mind."

"Of course not!" She walked closer. "I'm glad to see you made it."

Cane smiled, eyes softening, then he lifted his hand, holding up the bottle of wine that I didn't even realize he had. "I brought your favorite again."

Her laughter chimed, bouncing off the walls. "Aw! That will go great with dinner. Thank you."

The patio door slid open again, and Dad stepped around the corner too. He looked up as he dusted his hands off on his jeans. When he saw all of us standing there, he froze a little, looking between the three of us.

When he looked at Cane, I saw a spark of fury light his eyes, but it quickly subsided when they fell down to Mom's. She smiled for him in a way only he would be able to understand. Dad's face softened and he drew in a breath, exhaling slowly.

"Cane," he acknowledged.

"How are you, D?" Cane put on a wary smile.

"Fine. Could be better, you know..." Dad ran a hand over top of his head, focusing on me. "Food should be ready in twenty. Just waiting for the steak to finish grilling."

"Okay, Dad."

"Cane, let me grab that from you," Mom insisted, reaching for the bottle of wine. "I'll pop it open, grab us some glasses."

"Sure." He handed it to her. "Sounds great."

Mom forced a smile at him then dropped her eyes to me. She smiled at me but it didn't touch her eyes. Turning on the spike of her black heels, she headed back to the kitchen.

The tension was at an all-time high. I knew Cane was uncomfortable. I remember when he used to come over for dinner, before we got too serious, he would make himself right at home. Now, he was walking around, completely unsure of what to do with himself.

"Help me set the table." I grabbed his hand and led the way to the dining room.

He drew in a deep breath, going straight for the silverware on the middle of the table. Silently, we placed the utensils outside of each plate. My heart drummed, and I couldn't help peering up at Cane every few seconds, hoping he would say something to make things less awkward.

His shoulders were tense, and he avoided my eyes for the most part, but when our eyes would latch, he would give me small smiles to ensure he was okay.

After setting the table, we walked into the kitchen, Cane trailing closely behind me. We stood there, not touching, and not really looking at each other. Just standing.

It felt strange not touching him after being alone with him so many times before. I wondered what was going through his head. There were plenty of other places he could have been, yet he was there with me—*for me*—and knowing that he would put himself through something like this and lower his pride for my sake, when he truly didn't have to, made me admire him even more.

Mom came back into the house, grinning at us both. That was Mom, always smiling through awkward situations. She reached into a cabinet and pulled down some wine glasses.

"So, how have things been, Cane?" she asked, uncorking the bottle he'd brought and pouring some into a glass. She handed him a glass and he accepted it with a gracious nod.

"Things have been great. Work is picking back up. Also have some really great opportunities happening in North Carolina. I may be relocating there actually."

"Really?" Mom seemed surprised to hear that. I was too. He never told me that.

"Yes. We'll be opening a building for Tempt there with bigger offices, more work space—much more accommodating than the one here."

I figured he must have been doing this because of Buck being out. Still, I wondered why he hadn't said anything to me about it. He had to have been planning this for a while.

"Wow. That sounds amazing. I'm glad to know the company is doing better after...well, you know." She sipped her wine, letting him fill in the blanks.

Cane waved a dismissive hand. "Water under the bridge."

Mom forced a smile. She took a small sip from her glass. "Let me check on the asparagus," she said, then excused herself, walking to the patio again.

"I didn't know you were thinking about going to North Carolina."

"I was going to tell you after all of this blew over. I just settled on the idea yesterday."

"Is this because of Buck?"

He nodded, then shrugged. "Better to be safe than sorry."

"He can still find the company building, can't he?"

"He can, but security will be better there. It's not as open as the office here."

"Hmm."

"I'll still have my house here," he assured me. "Don't worry."

I still wasn't sure how I felt about that. He would be away a lot more with an office in another state, but right now wasn't the time to get into that. Instead, I blew a breath, almost tempted to pour a glass of wine for myself.

Mom came back into the kitchen with Dad following behind her. Dad had a tray of steaks in hand, and walked past us to take them to the dining room. Mom started grabbing the salad and pasta and even the beer that dad had bought just for tonight's occasion.

"Well!" Mom clasped her hands together. "Lets eat!"

Dinner was very quiet at first. We ate, Mom mumbled to Dad here and there, mostly about a new coworker who was a margarita lover. Cane and I ate silently, listening, but mostly observing.

I noticed that Dad's hand was clutched tightly around his fork almost like he was holding a knife. He sawed into his steak with the knife, on the verge of cutting his plate in half. Mom placed a hand on top of his as he sawed at his steak, and when he looked up and met her eyes, he released a deep, trapped breath. "Sorry," he mumbled.

"It's fine, honey," she whispered.

Silence swept over the table again. We finished dinner and were lucky Mom had so much to say about work and new clothes and new recipes, and how much fun she had making the pasta salad when Cane complemented the flavors.

When she rose from the table and went to the kitchen I went with her to help get forks and plates for the chocolate cake. I knew not to leave Cane and Dad alone for too long. When I came back Cane was focused on the table, while Dad was giving him a death stare.

I placed the plates and utensils on the middle of the table and Mom came in with the cake, cutting into it right away.

God. I wanted this dinner to be over with as soon as possible. Dad hadn't talked about anything yet, which made be curious as to why he even bothered inviting Cane to dinner. Did he want him to come, just to try and intimidate him? It obviously wasn't working.

After the cake was cut, I sat and looked up, realizing Dad's brown eyes were boring into mine. He then looked over, putting his full attention on Cane. "So, I'm sure you're wondering why I wanted you here."

Cane looked up. "I know why I'm here."

Dad's eyes shifted over to me and he looked me over thoroughly before putting his eyes on Cane again. "Why did you choose my daughter?"

"I didn't make a choice out of it, D. It just happened."

"Yeah, but how?"

"I don't know. It just did. Just like you and Mindy happened. Spur of the moment that led to more."

Dad's jaw ticked. "When did it start?"

Cane gave me a sideways glance before focusing on him again. "She was eighteen."

I thought that would give my father some sort of relief but I was wrong. Instead, it seemed to make him angrier. "I just…I don't get it. I mean, a look at the two of you sitting there and it doesn't make any sense. I don't understand why she wants *you* so badly. What is it about you that has her so attached?"

"Perhaps you should ask her that, D."

Dad met my eyes. "What is it, Kandy? Tell me so I can better understand."

"I told you this before. On my first day of college I told you it just happened. That I wanted him."

"I mean—shit. Is he really that good in the sack?" Dad asked snidely.

I frowned while Mom cleared her throat and scowled at him. "Derek," she warned.

His head shook. Instead of continuing the conversation, he finished his slice of cake in seconds, picked up his plate, and stormed into the kitchen. Mom watched him go, and when she could no longer see him, she looked at me and Cane and exhaled.

I remember her constantly telling me to give it time, to let him think, and to let him breathe, but deep down in my heart and in my mind I knew that time wasn't going to heal this.

He was at odds with it—had been for months. He was a stubborn man and I knew that. I don't know why I was expecting him to be the bigger person.

"Look, maybe I should go. I don't want to cause too much trouble tonight," Cane murmured, starting to push up from his chair.

"No." I grabbed his wrist and he looked down at it before focusing on me. "Stay. Finish your cake."

He looked from me to Mom, then back down at me again. He sat and dug into his cake again.

"Let me go talk to him," Mom said, then left the table.

When she was out of earshot, Cane said, "Agreeing to this was stupid."

"Its fine. Just…stay here. Let me talk to them." I gave him a kiss on the cheek before standing up and walking around the table to get to the kitchen.

Mom was pouring another glass of wine, like she needed it before going out to face him. She guzzled most of it down, her eyes bouncing over to me as she finished it off.

"What is he doing?" I asked.

"Patio. Sulking."

"I'm going to go talk to him."

I grabbed the handle of the door, stepping out in the cold. It was chilly outside, but the sun was beaming, providing a comforting warmth.

Dad sat on the bench with a bottle of beer in hand, his elbows resting on top of his thighs. When he heard me come out, he looked sideways and sighed. I could still smell the meat from the grill, the asparagus too.

I took the spot beside my father, wrapping my fingers around the edge of the bench.

I waited for him to speak, but when two minutes passed and he didn't utter a word, I knew he wasn't going to bother starting. He was never the one to start a conversation.

"Why can't you just accept what we have?" I finally asked.

"Why did you hide it from me? And did you ever stop talking to him like you said?" he demanded.

"We stopped talking for two months, right after I went to college, actually. We started talking again when he visited campus, and this time we promised not to let anything get in the way of it."

He turned his head to stare at me. "So, you're telling me I'm in your way? In the way of you and a man who's almost twice your age? A man who can pretty much be your father?"

I dropped my gaze. "Is that how you see it?"

"How am I supposed see it? To me, you're just young and naïve and gullible and he knows that and is taking advantage of it."

"If he is really taking advantage of me, do you think he would be here right now?" I looked up to meet his eyes to see his reaction. He didn't falter. He was still angry, probably livid.

He scoffed, dropping his head. "You know what? I always knew you were different. You weren't like the other kids or like the girls your age. I used to worry because you were never good at making friends or staying at sleepovers, and you hated birthday parties."

I looked away.

"Seeing you with him at that store shocked me, Kandy. All this time, I thought we were making progress, but it turned out that you had backtracked."

"Dad, I never backtracked. Cane and I have moved forward. This is what we want—what I want. I don't understand why you don't get that?"

"Because it doesn't make any goddamn sense!" he growled, slamming his bottle down on the bench beside him. "It doesn't make sense that this almost forty-year-old man had his hands on my teenage daughter! It's fucked up, and it makes me feel fucking stupid for not seeing it. All that time he was around when you were younger—was he looking at your butt? Your breasts? Your legs?"

I narrowed my eyes, sliding back from him. "That is a very dumb thing to say, Dad. When I was younger, I *never* saw Cane look at me that way until I came onto him. Before that, he was genuine and good friend. He never advanced, never touched me in the wrong way, never gave me signs of interest. Not until I told him that I wanted him. Like any man, I'm sure he noticed the differences and the changes in me, but that's normal. You've noticed them too."

Dad stood, pacing the deck. "You don't know what the hell you want, Kandy. You're nineteen. What could you possible know?"

"I know that I love him," I declared, standing too. "I know that it's not just in my head and that there is a reason I think about him so much. It's because we are a good match, Dad. You don't see it, but when we're together, I feel unstoppable and like I can take on the world. I feel elated and exuberant and good about myself. But then there's reality, and coming back home to *this*—to you being so damn hostile about the fact that I fell in love with someone like him!"

"He was my best friend, Kandy! What the hell did you expect? For me to accept it and be all willy-nilly about it? No! Fuck that!" he barked, and I flinched as he towered over me. Dad had never spoken to me this way, but apparently something had snapped inside him too. The patio door slid open, and I heard Mom's pleading voice begging Dad to back off. But he didn't.

And just as my father was stubborn, so was I. I matched his stare, though I gave him a dose of sympathy too. I had hurt him. I truly did.

"I'm sorry if I hurt you, Dad," I said lowly. "I'm sorry if this has broken you or ruined things and has made you look at me as this foreign object that you don't understand. I'm sorry for that," I whispered. "But...*I love him*, Dad. I really do. I know you think I'm being ridiculous and that I'm young and dumb—and maybe I am! Who knows! Like you said, I'm too young to know what I want—but if so, I will learn from it!" I laughed dryly, the rims of my eyes hot, burning with too much emotion. "Maybe I don't know what I want! Maybe I am stupid for wanting him more than I want to breathe, but you know what...it feels right! Being with Cane feels right. I have been pushing that feeling aside to make you happy. I hid him and my love for him, all to keep a smile on your face, but...I'm tired of it, Daddy. I'm so, so tired of it." Dad's face softened, his huffing slowing down too. His eyebrows strung together and his lips parted. "I want to be with him. I. Want. Him. Can you at least try to accept that and stop making things so hard for everyone? Mom's trying! Why can't you?"

He looked me all over, his eyes lined with tears. His bottom lip trembled, and when he shut his eyes, one tear fell. He lifted a hand and cupped the back of my neck. A warm, deep kiss was dropped onto my forehead before he pulled back and stared into my eyes. His were both sincere and stern.

"I love you with all of my heart, Kandy. I love you more than anything in this world. I raised you. I clothed you. I bathed you. I watched you grow into this wonderful woman who deserves the world...but your world does not stop at him. You have so much more ahead of you. So much," he insisted, and my heart slowly sank. "You haven't even lived yet—traveled. You haven't done much of anything to settle for him. So no, I can't accept it. I won't.

Not when I know there's more out there for you. Someone better than Cane. I know Cane. I know what he came from. He is not what you need, and if wanting the best for my daughter makes me the bad guy, then so be it. I've been the bad guy all my life. It's nothing new."

Those words.

They weren't what I wanted to hear. Dad dropped his hands to his sides and I looked down at the tips of my toes. My vision blurred because it hit me then, what I had to do. It hit me that he was never, ever going to accept what I wanted.

I picked my head back up and threw my arms around his neck. I kissed him on the cheek, and felt him let his guard down, his shoulders relaxing as I held him for nearly twenty seconds. When I let go, I gave him a soft smile before turning.

Cane and Mom were standing by the door, watching.

"Kandy," Mom cooed, reaching for me, but I walked past both her and Cane without saying a word and went upstairs. When I made it into my bedroom, I set my gaze on the duffle bag and suitcase in the corner. I had packed it the night before, just in case things didn't go as I'd planned.

Choking on a sob, I grabbed the bags, tossing the duffle over my shoulder before marching back down the stairs. Cane heard me coming and looked up the stairs. When he noticed the bags, he cocked his head and frowned.

"Kandy, what are you doing?" he asked in a loud whisper, eyes wide and serious. "Take those back upstairs."

I ignored him, and Mom obviously overheard his whisper because she came barreling around the corner. Her eyes stretched wide as she looked at the bags in my hands and then at me. "Kandy, honey." She pushed past Cane, meeting up to me, gripping my shoulders. "What are you doing, sweetie? Why do you have these bags? Where are you going?"

"I'm leaving, Mom."

"Leaving? Where, baby?"

I lowered my line of sight. "I'm leaving…with Cane." My voice broke, betraying the strength I was tying to hold onto.

She sucked in a sharp breath, like she'd already known the answer, but had hoped it would be something else. "Honey, please think about this," she pleaded, grabbing my face and trying to put my eyes on hers. But I didn't. Couldn't. If I looked at my mom, I would have caved, and that was the last thing I wanted to do, so instead I lightly brushed her off and walked around her, handing Cane my suitcase and then the duffle bag.

"Kandy," he mumbled, and I looked up, wiping my face. "Don't let it happen like this…"

"I don't think I have much of a choice, Cane. He's never going to accept it, and I know what I want. I've thought about this all morning. My mind has been made up."

He made a noise, like he wanted to say something to make me reconsider, but held back, because even he knew there was no other way around it. My dad was stubborn and could be very selfish when he wanted to be. He'd been around Cane for so long that I knew he was never going to accept the fact that his ex-best friend was the man who had his daughter. He expected Cane to look over me, protect me, and treat me like his daughter. Well, two of those had happened, but treating me like his daughter wasn't one of them. He treated me like his other half when it finally came to it, and I'd accepted that because I felt like I was his other half. We belonged together, our hearts like magnets, always holding on, hard to pull apart.

Cane finally gave me a simple nod and walked around me to get to the door. He didn't walk out though. He stood there, probably hoping I would change my mind.

Mom grabbed my hands. "Kandy, please think about this! Please! Derek!" she yelled. Dad finally stepped around the corner. His shoulders were slumped, and he looked over Mom and I, at Cane, who had my bags.

"What are you doing?" he growled, taking a step forward.

Cane's eyes softened.

"I'm leaving," I answered, and Dad's eyes flickered down to mine.

"Leaving to go where? Frankie's?"

"No. Leaving to be with Cane…for good."

Dad's eyebrows drew together. "Why the hell would you do something so stupid?"

"Jesus Christ, Derek! Shut up and let her be! Let her have him—she isn't asking you for anything but to accept what she wants! How hard is that to do!" Mom screamed, tears streaming down her cheeks.

Hearing the raw emotion in her voice was doing me in. Seeing Dad's walls crumble, his pride slowly but surely chipping way but not nearly enough, was killing me.

I thought he would say something—make amends and tell me he would at least try to accept it. Instead, he turned his head and stared down at the floor. My heart shattered right to pieces and as if Mom felt the same wave of hurt, she gasped and wailed, "Oh, God!"

I looked over my shoulder. Cane was already walking out of the door. Mom turned away from me, dropping her face into her hands. I reached for her, pulling her hands down and staring up into her eyes. It took every single fiber of courage and strength in me to say what I had to say.

"Mom, I love you and Dad. This changes nothing about that, I promise. I will still visit. Still call. Still see you…but, I can't stay here. I can't live like this. I don't want my life to be a lie anymore. I just want to be happy." A tear slid over my lips, the saltiness of it landing on the tip of my tongue. "I'm happy with him," I pleaded. "He makes me so happy."

She bobbed her head, but her face was stained, her mascara running. She reeled me in and hugged me tight. So tight that I felt the power of her love, her acceptance, her booming heart. As she hugged me, I looked over her shoulder at Dad. He was watching us now, but still not saying anything. His eyes glistened, but the tears refused to fall.

I let go of her and walked to him.

"Kandy," he said, but even his voice broke. "We can talk. There's no need for you to leave like this. You're breaking your mother's heart and mine."

"Dad," I whispered. "You have broken my heart every day since you found out about Cane. If I stay here, there will be nothing left of me."

As if I'd shot him in the heart, his eyes stretched wide. A stray tear rolled down his right cheek. I reached up to wipe it away. "I'm going with him," I murmured. "I choose *him*."

Pulling my hand down, I wrapped my arms around his thick torso and hugged him. He held the back of my head, hugging me just as tight. My damp face was buried in his gray shirt. I could hear his heartbeat, and remembered those moments when I was a little girl and would rest my head on his chest, just to hear the soothing thud of his heartbeat. It was still the same boom, only much more rapid now. I was going to miss this a lot. So much.

My chest felt tight and raw when I pulled back. His shirt was wet with my tears. When I looked back, Cane was standing at the door with his head hung low, waiting for me. Dad looked at Cane and his fists clenched. I could tell he wanted to blame him for this, beat him into a pulp.

"It's not his fault," I said, catching Dad's eyes. "None of this was ever his fault."

Dad scoffed, another tear falling, and turned away, storming into the kitchen. I hugged Mom one last time, but it only made her break down even more. She pressed a fist to her upper lip and shut her eyes like she couldn't watch me go. I hated seeing her like this. I hated that I was even doing this, but it was too late to back out now. She was just as torn as I was, and I hated that.

"Love you, Mom," I whispered, wrapping an arm around her.

I pulled away, but she caught my hand before I could get too far. "Kandy, honey, please. You know how your father is. You know he needs time."

I lifted her hand and clutched it tight. "Mom, please?"

Her eyes widened, and with that one simple request, she let me go. Her tears slowed, her mouth no longer trembling. She stared at Cane, but didn't frown. Just stared. Then she took a step back, and dropped her head.

I met Cane at the door. He escorted me out, but before he could close it, I took one look back. Mom was sitting on the bench in the hall sobbing. Dad had rounded the corner and was watching us go. The last thing I saw him do was pinch the bridge of his nose and break down in a sob too, before Cane shut the door behind us.

CHAPTER FORTY

KANDY

"You okay?" Cane asked when we were inside his car.
 I didn't answer. I couldn't, honestly. I stared back at the house knowing that I wouldn't see it again for a while, if ever again. I knew in that house that my parents were broken and it was all because of me.
 Cane put the car in gear and pulled out of the driveway. When he drove away, my heart dropped to my stomach. I took one last look back at the home where I was raised. The home where I learned how to flip my first pancake, and had my first sleepover, and big birthday party with a bouncy castle at the age of seven.
 Was it selfish of me to leave them like that? Should I have stayed a little longer, tried to convince Dad to accept who I loved?
 I knew it was hard for him to understand. He was a man with voluptuous pride and Cane had been his best friend. But at the end of the day, I was his daughter, and he was supposed to love me more than anything—more than what he thought was wrong or right. More than his disdain for Cane and even his stubborn-

ness. He was supposed to show me that no matter what I wanted, or how I wanted it, or who I wanted, that he would be there. But he didn't.

Instead, he looked away. He pleaded, but it wasn't enough because I knew if I'd stayed he would have tried to convince me to look the other direction and pretend that my heart didn't beat for his former friend. But it did.

When I looked up at Cane, my vision was blurry. He felt me looking at him and met my stare. Grabbing my hand, he held the tips of my fingers, bringing the back of my hand to his lips and kissing it. I don't know what it was about that one kiss that gave me a spark of hope. I could feel his emotion too. He was breaking as well, and knew that the decision I made was going to hurt me more than anything. It would hurt my parents too, but they weren't the ones living this life.

We rode in silence for the most part, a melodic song by John Legend pouring from the speakers. Cane pulled into his neighborhood and up to his house and when he got out of the car, I sat there for a moment, staring at the house—this large beautiful house—and realizing that I was going to spend more time here than I would anywhere else.

I realized that my life had changed so much from what it was before. I'd lost my scholarship and probably my family too. I was no longer the little girl who was afraid of this man. I was the little girl who had blossomed into a woman and fell in love with this man. I felt my love for him deep in my soul, right down to the core. I cared for him more than I thought I ever could care for anyone. I never thought a time would come where I actually had to choose between my parents and Cane. Not like this.

Maybe it was dumb to think that Cane and I were going to be together forever. Maybe I was in over my head and maybe Cane would only want me for a couple years or even a few months, and then toss me aside, like the women he used to be with. Like Kelly.

What would I do then? I would be helpless and hopeless and have to beg my parents for forgiveness because they were right.

But when the passenger door opened and he revealed his face, stretching his arm to offer his hand, I grasped the idea that maybe he would never leave. In his eyes, I saw hope and passion and love. In his eyes, I found comfort and peace. He looked at me like he would be there for me every step of the way, that he wouldn't leave me stranded ever again.

"Coming inside?" he asked, eyes swimming with sympathy. I drew in a breath and took his hand, climbing out of the car and walking with him to the door.

He unlocked it and I thought he would take me to the kitchen or the den or even the living room but he didn't. He took me upstairs to his bedroom. We walked past his king sized bed, by the dresser, and past the armoire until we reached the bathroom. He started the shower right away and then turned to me, undressing me slowly. I wanted to ask him what he was doing. Why was he doing this right now? I wasn't in the mood for a shower or sex or whatever he may have wanted at the time. I just wanted to think, sulk really.

"Cane," I murmured. But he merely ignored my plea. He continued undressing me and undressed himself. He watched my eyes the entire time, and when we were bare, he grabbed my hand, turning toward the shower and letting me in first.

He watched me, eyes intent, serious, then he cupped my face in his wet hands, still staring down at me in the loving, heated way only he could.

"I know what you're thinking," he said. "I know how you feel." His thumbs stroked the apples of my cheeks. "You're hoping you're doing the right thing..."

I blinked my tears away, the stream of water beating on my back. "Am I?"

He sighed, and even he wasn't sure if this was the right thing to do. Being together was both a risk and a challenge. So many things set us apart. He exhaled, studying my eyes, still holding my face.

"Do you love me?" he asked, voice lower.

"Yes," I answered.

"Do you trust me?"

I shut my eyes but nodded. "Yes."

"Are you certain that I am the man you want, Kandy? Because I'll tell you now, I am not a saint. Though you think I'm this perfect man, I'm far from it. I have flaws—many of them. There are moments when you will not be able to stand the sight of me." I opened my eyes and water spilled over his lips as they pressed together.

"I don't care about any of that. I know who you are. I know what you are capable of. I know you have many flaws, but I can accept them because I love you."

The skin around his eyes softened a bit, and his eyes seemed warmer. Deeper. He lowered his head and pressed his lips to mine. I moaned, wrapping my hands around his forearms and melting into the kiss. My heart boomed and my knees buckled and I held his arms tight, never wanting to let go.

"Then it's settled," he breathed on my lips. "Because everything you have said, I feel too. It hurts to be selfish—to take what you want and also hurt the ones you love in the process—but when it feels right, nothing should stop that. Nothing should get in the way of a person's happiness. So, yes...I think you are doing the right thing. Just...give it time." He kissed the tip of my nose and then reeled me into him. "He'll understand eventually."

I really hoped so.

Even though his words were encouraging and deep, they also moved me in a way that made my heart jump and my belly clench tight with anguish. I buried my face in his chest and held him close to me. The hot stream of water poured down my back, but the warmth couldn't be matched to his.

"My Kandy," he sighed, and a sob that had been brewing inside me finally broke out.

Just like Mom, I broke down, crying into his chest so hard I could barely breathe. But he didn't say anything. He just held me tight and let me weep. He stroked my hair and kissed the top of my head. He didn't tell me to stop or to calm down, because he knew this was necessary. I was glad.

When my sobs became soft whimpers, Cane picked my head up and looked down into my eyes. He cradled my face in his hands, eyes sincere. I'd never seen him so gentle. So open.

"I will take care of you. I will be with you. I will not sway or leave you. I am here. I am yours." His damp lips meshed with mine. "I am yours," he repeated, breaking the kiss, his mouth feathery light as it brushed across mine.

"You...are mine," I whispered brokenly. "And...I am yours."

He shut his eyes for a brief moment, water trickling from his hair to his thick lashes. The corners of his mouth tipped up, and he breathed slowly through his nostrils.

"That's my girl." He placed a kiss on my forehead. My cheek. My lips. "My sweet, sweet Kandy."

CHAPTER FORTY-ONE

CANE

The last thing Kandy needed was to be reminded of what had happened the night before, so while she slept in my bed, the left half of her face buried in the pillows and curly, dark-brown wisps of hair on the right, I went downstairs and called one of my favorite local chefs who owned a nice brunch restaurant. He told me he'd send someone within an hour to cater a nice breakfast for us.

Luckily when they arrived, Kandy was still asleep. After what had happened the night before, I was sure she was sulking more than anything. The caterers set the counters up with food and fresh-cut fruit while I sat at the kitchen table, working on my laptop.

About fifteen minutes after they left, Kandy walked into the kitchen with one of my white button down shirts on, her hair pulled up into a messy bun, several loose strands hanging around her face.

She spotted the counter covered with food and her eyes expanded. "Holy shit," she gasped. "What is all of this?"

"For you." I stood and walked toward her, dropping a kiss on top of her head. She peered up at me with big brown eyes. "Want us to start fresh."

She beamed and instead of speaking, she nodded. That one nod was proof that she understood what I was getting at. I'd promised her that we would make this work, that I would be here, and I was ready for it to begin.

She trotted past me and picked up a strawberry, biting into it. Her lips were full and supple around it, and if I weren't so mesmerized by the simplicity of the act, her natural beauty and how she grinned after chewing, I'm almost certain I would have gotten hard. Who knew a woman could look so damn gorgeous while eating a strawberry?

"You mind if I turn on the TV?" she asked after filling up her plate.

"Not at all." I looked toward the TV on the counter. "Thing hasn't been turned on in ages. Hopefully it still works." I laughed.

She giggled. "Yeah, I forgot you aren't a TV person. Why did you even bother getting one in the kitchen then?"

"Good question." I shrugged, picking up my mug of coffee from the table and then pressing my lower back to the edge of the counter. "I guess to use when the house is too quiet, but with you around, it should be okay."

She pressed her lips to smile, taking a stool at the bar counter after picking up the remote control for the TV. She flipped through the channels while nibbling on apple slices, but then I heard a name while she stalled and my blood ran cold. I pushed off the counter, almost certain my ears had deceived me.

"Wait." I slammed my mug down on the counter a little too roughly and Kandy flinched.

She frowned, looking at me. "What? What's wrong?"

I walked around the counter, taking the remote from her and flipping back a channel.

"Oh...*shit*."

"Cane? What?" she demanded, looking between the TV and me.

I wanted to answer. Honestly, I did, but I was fucking speechless. I turned up the volume.

"*...it's been three weeks now and not one sign of Draco 'El Jefe' Molina,*" the anchor said. "*Following the massive explosion during the raid of his mansion that left seven officials injured and nine killed, it has been reported that Draco Molina had plenty of time to escape and could be anywhere by now. One injured officer who was lucky to make it out of the explosion, reported that he'd seen Molina getting away on a speedboat, and on the boat, he spotted a young Caucasian male, a Caucasian female, a younger Hispanic male, and two Hispanic females.*"

Kandy turned toward me. "Cane?" Her voice trembled. "Do you know him?" she asked.

I nodded. It was all I could do.

"*Officials are calling Draco Molina the most wanted man in the world. He has been accused of over eighty reported murders and is known for running one of the largest cocaine and assault rifle cartels in Mexico. The FBI has pushed their two-million dollar reward up to four-million today, so if you have seen this man or know where he could be hiding...*" The screen flashed to the infamous Draco Molina himself. It was a picture of him in a suit, standing in front of a building, his hair slicked back and his jaw flexed.

I'd always known a time would come when he would get caught up. I just didn't think it would be so soon. Lora had told me Draco kidnapped a woman named Gianna, who was the daughter of Lion, a well-known Italian mobster, but murdered her husband on their wedding day before taking her. Was she the Caucasian woman who'd escaped with him after the explosion? My head was spinning. What the fuck was he doing?

A hand wrapped around my wrist and I didn't even realize

Kandy had gotten off her stool and was standing in front of me now. "Cane, you're scaring the shit out of me right now. You look like you've seen a ghost."

"It's fine. Promise. Just…need to check something."

"Wait, wha—" I walked past her and out of the kitchen before she could ask anymore questions.

This was fucking insane. How hadn't I heard about this before now? I took the stairs two at a time to get to my bedroom, heading into the closet and opening the bottom drawer of the dresser inside it. I shuffled through it, snatching out underwear and ties and leather belts, until I came across the little black flip phone.

I powered it on, every second filling me with dread.

When it was on, it took a while for the messages to pop up, but I knew they were coming.

One by one, they flooded in, until finally it stopped. Twenty missed messages.

Shit. I hadn't checked the phone in weeks. I was supposed to check it once a week, but got so caught up with work and my family…

"Cane?"

I pushed to a stand, heart thundering as I focused on Kandy standing between the frames of the closet door. "Sorry, Kandy it's um…just a bunch of shit." I scrolled through the messages. It was from a new number, but some of the code words were very clear.

Trouble with lead.

He's out now.

Funds needed.

State reunion.

The messages went on and on until I came across one that truly had my blood running cold.

ATL landing in a few weeks. Be ready.

That particular message was sent two days ago.

I snapped the phone shut. "Kandy, I need you to go home."

"What? Why? What's going on?"

"That man you saw on TV? The one wanted for four million? I know him."

"You know him? How?"

I snatched a T-shirt out of the closet then walked out, tugging it over my head. "Used to work for him. And he might be in the state right now. He's not safe for you to be around."

"Seriously?" Her voice was shrill, her eyes so wide they were nearly bulging out of her head.

"I can't explain this right now. I think he has people who are coming to meet me, or he's coming himself. I don't want you around when that happens. You can crash at Lora's until this blows over."

"Are they bad people?"

"Anyone who works for him is a bad person. Not all of them can be trusted."

"But you worked for him," she pegged, giving me a thorough, uncertain glare.

"I know…and luckily I got out, and that's only because we made a deal."

"I—I don't get it. Should I be worried? Should I call the cops?"

"No." I rushed her way, gripping her shoulders. "You call the cops and I am a dead man walking. You hear me?"

She breathed raggedly, face paling. "It's that bad?"

"It'll be fine. But I need to call Lora. Let her know what's going on."

"Shouldn't she stay away too?" She shuffled through her suitcase, snatching out a pair jeans and sliding her legs through them.

"I may need her."

"God. I can't believe this." Her voice shook as she started to unbutton the shirt she was wearing.

I cupped the back of her neck. "Kandy, I told you there were things about me that would be unpleasant. I don't want you to be—"

"WHAT THE HELL IS SHE DOING HERE?" A voice thundered, cutting me off mid-sentence, and if I thought my heart was racing before, it was about to burst out of my chest at this point because standing between the frames of my bedroom door was Kelly.

She wore a black T-shirt and black leggings, her face makeup free, and her eyes broiling with rage. She looked like she hadn't slept in days, dark circles beneath her eyes and her hair slightly frizzy. I'd never seen her this way. So...unhinged. She always kept herself neat.

A gasp spilled from Kandy's lips, and when I dropped my eyes, I realized why.

In Kelly's hand was a knife. A long, sharp knife.

And before I could say anything or get her to stop and wait and listen, she was screaming so loudly her face turned red. She rushed toward me, eyes pinned right on mine. I knew what was going to happen. The sharp blade was coming toward us, glimmering from the sun pouring through the window, ready to pierce me. Even more so, I'd prepared for it, because I knew I wasn't going to be able to stop it in time.

Kelly's screech made my ears ring. "I hate you!" she screamed. "I fucking hate you!"

She had swung the knife in my direction, but I felt nothing. Perhaps with all of the adrenaline rushing through my body, it was impossible to feel anything.

But I looked down and saw blood.

It slowly seeped through the white shirt and then in an instant, spread like a red flood.

"Cane," Kandy croaked, clutching her lower belly. She collapsed instantly, knees dropping on the floor, and that's when it hit me.

Kelly wasn't trying to kill me.

She was trying to kill Kandy.

CHAPTER FORTY-TWO

CANE

Rage had blinded me.

I didn't think, just acted, and charged Kelly, tackling her to the ground. She screamed as I snatched the knife out of her hands and tossed it aside.

"What the fuck is wrong with you!" I roared. "You stupid bitch!"

As badly as I wanted to strangle her, I shoved myself off of her, going for Kandy who lay feebly on the floor.

I rubbed her face and then grabbed one of my shirts that was on the floor, pressing it on the wound. "Kandy, baby! Stay with me, okay!"

She hardly responded. She moaned, head rolling. Her face had paled even more, her lips parting like she wanted to speak but didn't have the strength to.

"Shit! Shit shit shit!" I snatched my phone out of my back pocket, running wet, red fingers over the screen as I dialed 911 and hit speakerphone. "Kandy, baby. It's okay. Stay with me."

I glared back at Kelly. "Get the fuck out of my house! Now!"

"Quinton, just let her go! We were fine before you did anything with her! She doesn't belong with you! I do and you know it!"

"GET THE FUCK OUT OF MY HOUSE YOU CRAZY FUCKING BITCH!" My call had been answered but the woman on the phone was asking too many damn questions. There wasn't any time for this. If I didn't get her to the hospital soon, she was going to bleed out. I tucked my phone in my back pocket rapidly, picking Kandy up in my arms and storming out of the room.

On the way down, it hit me that this had happened to someone I knew. This was probably how Derek felt while trying to save one life, while another person threatened his. It was a tough situation to manage, but I refused to let what happened to the girl D couldn't save, happen to me.

I grabbed my keys off the hook on the way to the door and went outside, putting Kandy in the passenger seat of my car. I heard Kelly talking, her footsteps quick, but I didn't give a fuck what she was saying. I would take care of that bitch later, but for now, it was do or die and my Kandy wasn't about to die on me.

Kelly was beating on my back as I rushed to the driver side of the car, but I couldn't feel any of it. I shoved her away and got behind the wheel, starting the car up. The tires screeched as I pulled out of the driveway and away from my house, Kelly's loud voice following me. Through the mirror, I saw her standing in the driveway, smiling as I left. Her smile was too complacent, like she hadn't just attempted murder. It sent a chill over me, but I kept driving.

I knew I had one call to make. One call that would piss everyone off. I dialed a number I hadn't used in months, and pressed the phone to my ear. After three rings, he answered.

"You've fucked up my life enough, Cane. What the hell are you calling me for?" Derek grumbled.

"Look, I'm not calling to argue with you. Something bad just happened."

"What the hell are you talking about?"

"Kelly showed up at my house and stabbed Kandy. I'm on the way to the hospital with her but she's bleeding a lot."

"WHAT?" he shouted. "STABBED HER? WHAT THE FUCK HAPPENED?"

"I'll explain later! Just please. Get to the hospital uptown! She needs you!"

He didn't respond. He'd hung up and I knew he was on his way.

I looked at Kandy, dropping my phone and pressing down on the wound. She groaned, lips turning a dark shade of blue.

"No, baby. Stay with me. Please. Stay with me. Fuck!" A rage I'd never felt before consumed me. I drove like a madman and didn't give a damn if I was breaking the law.

When I finally got to the hospital, I pushed out of the car to get to Kandy's side, took her out as she moaned, and charged into the emergency room, demanding the first nurse I saw to take her.

The nurse panicked, but she moved swiftly, calling for back up. They had me place her on a flat bed and then rushed her down a hallway. I started running with them, asking if she was going to be okay but when they got close to double silver doors, one of the male nurses told me to stay back, that I couldn't come past that point.

"I need to be in there with her!" I bellowed, but the nurse shook his head and pointed back to the waiting area. He was talking but I wasn't listening. I didn't give a damn what he had to say. Before it could sink in, a security guard was escorting me back to the waiting area.

My heart hurt so fucking much, my eyes tight as I fought tears. This was my fault. If I'd gotten rid of Kelly the right way, this never would have happened. If only I'd taken a step in front of Kandy instead of standing there like a fucking idiot.

"Fuck!"

Everyone in the waiting area stared at me as I turned swiftly to punch the nearest wall. I didn't give one single fuck. Not even five minutes later, as I paced the area, Derek rushed into the building. He panted like a wild bull when he spotted me. "Where the fuck is my daughter?"

"She's with the doctors now."

He seethed, glaring at me. "Why would Kelly do this? Why would she hurt my little girl?"

"Because she's fucking crazy!"

Derek started to charge me, but a security guard came toward us, stopping him in his tracks. "I'm going to have to ask you both to leave," he ordered. "Right now. You're making the guests feel uncomfortable."

Derek eyed me for a long time before snatching away and storming out of the hospital. I followed after him, but made sure to keep my distance this time. The last thing I needed was another black eye and a blackout.

Derek walked until he'd reached a shaded area. He marched back and forth in front of a tall tree, fists clenched, eyes focused on the ground.

"As if I didn't want to kill you already! Then this shit happens! Why the fuck would Kelly just flat out stab her?"

"I broke it off with Kelly several weeks ago. I told her she couldn't show up at my house anymore. Told her to pretty much leave me the fuck alone after finding out some shit about her. She disappeared for those few weeks but then she showed up in my house today and saw Kandy. She already had a knife in her hand, like she was coming for me, but saw Kandy, and changed her mind."

"Fuck!" Derek's voice broke and he stopped his pacing to run his hands over his head. "I knew I should have kept my family away from you! I knew it! All you've done is tear us apart! My wife won't even look at me and my only child distanced herself from me to be with you, and not even a day fucking later, she's hurt! She could be dying because of you!"

"She's not going to die!" I snapped. "She won't!"

"Cane...man." Derek shook his head, dropping his arms and letting them sag at his sides. "There's blood all over you, man. All over you. That's her blood. Too much blood."

"She is not going to die," I growled.

"You know what—fuck off, alright? Stop pretending you love her and just let her go. All you're doing is ruining her fucking life."

"Oh, I'm ruining her life? Really, D? Instead of being like Mindy and accepting the fact that your daughter loves me just as much as I love her, you had to be a stubborn asshole and watch her leave? I never held her back from you! Not once! Kandy made all of those decisions on her own and I never influenced them! You think I don't know she deserves better? Trust me, I fucking know! I've told her repeatedly that I'm not a good man. She knows it, but she loves me anyway and your head is too stuck up your ass to accept what she wants! I'm sorry to fucking tell you, man, but it's not up to you anymore. She's grown now, and if she pulls through this, I am still going to be here for her, whether you like it or not."

He grimaced at me, jaw clenching repeatedly. I didn't give a fuck if he hit me this time. At least he knew the truth, and if he felt the need to hurt me for giving him facts, then so be it.

Fortunately, the sound of a car door shutting behind me made him look away and Mindy rushed toward us in nude heels, her blond hair bouncing and her eyes stretched.

"Where is she?" she demanded.

"They've taken her back. We can't do anything but wait right now," Derek grumbled.

"Oh my God!" she cried, fixing her eyes on me. "What the hell happened Cane?" She rushed my way, getting in my face. "You said Kelly did this? Why would she stab my daughter? We're friends! She wouldn't do that to me! What did you do?" Mindy shoved a hand into my chest. They were both angry and they had every right to be, but Mindy's fury shocked me. I suppose that day, she was unleashing all of her pent up frustrations on me and that was fine. Perhaps she needed the outlet.

Like I'd said, I deserved whatever came my way. "I'm sorry, Mindy. She came so fucking fast. She showed up at my house with a knife and I...fuck. I froze, Mindy. I should have stopped it or—"

I'd let this happen. I could have stopped it—moved or thought faster, but I was too slow. Too late.

Mindy scoffed, shoving me one last time before pointing a finger in my face. "I swear to God if anything goes wrong, I will come after you and Tempt. You'd better pray she pulls through and can tell me the truth!" She rushed away, toward the entrance of the emergency room. Derek followed her lead, looking me over with his upper lip curled up and his nostrils flared, before turning his head.

My phone rang in my back pocket and I snatched it out. "What?" I snapped.

"Q, where the hell are you?" Lora said, voice rushed. "Why is there blood on the floor? What the fuck is going on?"

"I'm at the hospital."

"What? Why? Are you hurt?"

"No, but Kandy is."

"What?" she gasped. "What the hell happened?"

"Kelly is what happened. She stabbed Kandy. She bled a lot on the way. When it happened, I fucking froze, like a goddamn idiot! If she dies, I'll..." My voice broke. What was I going to do if she died? That was a guilt I didn't want to have to live with. It was one I wouldn't have been able to get through.

"It's okay. She'll be okay. Stop. Breathe. Just breathe, okay?" Lora said, her voice calm. It helped a little. "Where the fuck is Kelly?"

"I had no choice but to leave with Kandy. Kelly was still there when I left. Is she not there anymore?" I panicked then, looking around the parking lot. For all I knew, she could have followed us.

"I don't see anyone here. Just blood, and a knife."

"She left the knife? What kind of shit is she playing at?" I shook my head. "Look, don't call the cops right now. I'm sure they'll be here for a report and when they show, I'll give it to them. For now, will you do me a favor?"

"What?"

"There's a black flip phone I left in the room."

"This burner phone on the floor?" she asked, like she'd already spotted it.

"Yes. That one. Write down the number from the text messages and then get rid of it."

"Fuck, Q. You can't be serious right now. This isn't who I think it is, is it?"

"I'm afraid it is."

"Shit."

"They're coming soon," I said. "Probably already close. I don't know if it's him or some of his crew. Text that number and tell them my place will be too hot for them to just show up. Ask for more time."

"Fine, but you will have to explain to me why you still have this fucking phone. I thought you were done working with him."

"I am done, Lora. We settled on a deal a while ago but I don't get to choose when shit happens or make him wait. Just do what I said and make it quick."

"Okay, fine. But keep me updated on Kandy. Can't believe that bitch did that to her!"

"Yeah. Apparently a few other people don't believe she's capable of something so crazy either." I looked to the left and spotted Mindy and Derek standing by the entrance with a cop.

Derek was talking to the cop, still edgy and fuming. He pointed a finger in my direction and they all looked my way, the cop included. "I gotta go," I said hurriedly as the cop came my way with his hand on his cuffs.

CHAPTER FORTY-THREE

KELLY

AFTER CANE LEFT...

"You need to get out of there right now!" my mother screamed into the phone. "Now, Kelly! I'm not kidding! Leave the house!"

See, that was the thing about my mother. She was a runner. I wasn't. What I did wasn't a mistake or a crime. It had to happen. Kandy needed to leave in order for Cane to be with me. The only way she would be gone for good was if she didn't exist.

Simple.

"Kelly, please!" my mother pleaded.

"I'm not leaving. Cane will come to me and we will talk."

"You attempted *murder, Kelly*! You just admitted it to me! Jesus, I knew you weren't well! I'm calling our lawyer!"

"I'm fine and I haven't touched any drugs! I've finished my meds—I'm fine!"

"Wait—what do you mean you've finished your meds? There is no finish line! You're supposed to take them every single day! When exactly did you *finish* them?"

"Months ago, Mom."

"Oh my goodness. I can't believe this! Kelly, you may not be doing drugs, but you are venting in other ways. Trying to kill someone is unjustifiable! If you don't leave, I can't help you or save you this time!"

My eyes fell to the puddle of blood on the floor. Cane had left several minutes ago. I came back upstairs and spotted the knife, the blood, utterly satisfied with what I'd accomplished.

At first, I came to make amends, tell him that we should start from scratch and forget about the past and the things we knew about each other, but then I heard Kandy's voice, and something snapped inside me.

"Your disorder hasn't gotten better. You said you were doing good! I trusted you enough to stay in that city and out of trouble! Goodness!"

Goodness!" my mother went on. "This behavior is wrong and the fact that you're being so—so *calm* about what you just did frightens me! I have no doubt the cops will arrest you once they're informed. Look, I'm catching a flight there and calling Chase. Hopefully, he will be able to plead another mental case for you. Can't believe you would do something like this again! Go to your apartment and stay put, do you hear me? Do not leave. Don't look for Quinton. Go home and wait for me to get there!"

I hung up, not bothering to answer. I looked from the blood to the knife again. The nicer side of me begged me to pick it up and ditch it. But the dark side of me—the side that didn't give a damn and wanted to make a statement for Kandy to never fuck with me again—cackled and pushed me just enough to walk out of the bedroom.

Just like everything else, I would get out of this. I'd probably be threatened by a judge again to go psych or, with my lawyer at my defense *and* since I laid off the drugs this time, I'd get lucky and only have to do mandatory therapy for a few months, but if Kandy died, all of it would be worth it.

I left Quinton's house with a big smile on my face because this was my small victory.

He wanted to try and get rid of me? Choose her over me? Fine. But if I couldn't have him, no woman could.

Especially not some teen slut.

I know. I know. Don't hate me! LOL!
Book 3 of the Cane series, *Loving Mr. Cane* will be releasing on September 13th, 2018.

Sign Up For the live alert by visiting
www.shanorawilliams.com/mailing-list

After *Loving Mr. Cane* releases, there will be a 4th book coming out in November, but it will be a novella. There will be more answered questions and some closure in book 3, for sure. ;-)

(Keep going to read the prologue of book 3!)

FEEL FREE TO FOLLOW ME!
Facebook | Instagram | Twitter
Join My Reader Group |Add Me As A Friend
Visit www.shanorawilliams.com for more info and details.

psssttt... by the way, I'm most active on Instagram, my reader group, and Twitter. ;-)

LOVING MR. CANE PROLOGUE

CANE

When I was younger, I heard tales about a man that the whole world was afraid of. Men who I thought could never be spooked by anything, were afraid of him. Men who shot back at police officers, served lengthy prison sentences, and faced the barrel of smoking guns daily, were afraid of him.

It astounded me that when they spoke of him, they never spoke ill. It was always proper, never any dirty talk. They never made fun of him—never called him names. Never disregarded him. They only called him by *one* name, and had even told me several times that if he were called by anything else, there was a 99% chance that you'd be dead within a week. The 1% meant you'd live the rest of your life looking over your shoulder, cowering in fear, and that was worse than being dead. It was a name that, at the time, made no sense to me...

But then I met him, and I understood why he was so intimidating.

He wasn't your typical dealer. He wore expensive suits and shiny watches and kept up with his appearance. Like most, he didn't use his supplies. He was 100% clean, and that's what kept him on top of his game.

He was smart and dedicated.

Persistent and precise. He played the drug world like a game of chess, always making the right move that would keep him one step up, never swaying or deterring. He'd never slipped up—not once—and it was insane of me to want to work with someone like him…but when it came down to it, I had no other choice.

His name was Draco Molina. Many knew him by *El Jefe. The Boss*. And a boss he was, because when he made a statement, it was abundantly clear. When he ran jobs and scheduled deliveries, they were always on time, and when he needed his money, he came for it, whether you were ready to pay up or not.

If you haven't already met the vicious Draco "El Jefe" Molina, you can meet him in the first book of the Venom trilogy, Passion & Venom for <u>FREE</u> right now!

Grab your copy to see how Draco's story will tie in with the rest of the Cane series! :-)

MORE BOOKS BY SHANORA

CANE SERIES
WANTING MR. CANE
BREAKING MR. CANE
LOVING MR. CANE (Sept 2018)
TITLE TBA (Nov 2018)

NORA HEAT COLLECTION
CARESS
CRAVE
DIRTY LITTLE SECRET

STANDALONES
TEMPORARY BOYFRIEND
100 PROOF
DOOMSDAY LOVE
DEAR MR BLACK
FOREVER MR. BLACK
INFINITY

SERIES

<u>FIRENINE SERIES</u>
<u>THE BEWARE DUET</u>
<u>VENOM TRILOGY</u>
<u>SWEET PROMISE SERIES</u>

Most of these titles are available in Kindle Unlimited.
Visit www.shanorawilliams.com for more information.

Feel free to follow me on Instagram! I am always active and always eager to speak with my readers there:

Follow Me:
Facebook | Instagram | Twitter
Join My Fan Group | Add Me As A Friend
Visit www.shanorawilliams.com for more book information and details.

Printed in Great Britain
by Amazon